Daughter of the Dawn
A Pilgrim Romance
By
Elizabeth N. Shaffer

To my husband,
Dr. H. Lawrence Shaffer,
for his warm and loving support and
encouragement

Son-Rise Publications & Distribution Company
143 Greenfield Road
New Wilmington, PA 16142

About the Author and the Artist

Elizabeth (Betty) N. Shaffer has had one book, *Lisa*, a story of a crisis pregnancy, published by Bethany House. She is a graduate of Westminster College in New Wilmington, PA, where she currently resides with her husband, Howard Lawrence Shaffer, a retired physician. Betty grew up in Wildwood Crest, NJ, and traces her ancestry back to the Mayflower. She is descended from Elizabeth Tilley, whose granddaughter moved to Cape May County, NJ, in the latter part of the sixteen hundreds.

To give authenticity to her story, Betty visited all the ports that the Mayflower touched from London through Southampton, Dartmouth and Plymouth. She also did research in Plymouth, MA, visiting Pilgrim Hall, the Jabez Howland House, and the Living Museums of Plymouth Plantation, and the Mayflower. All the pictures used in the book were taken by Betty on her research trips.

J. G. McGill of New Wilmington, PA, did the cover, using Julianna Shaffer, one of Betty's eight granddaughters, for his model. McGill is a nationally known artist, acclaimed for capturing authentic scenes from Amish life. The family Bible Julianna holds belonged to her great-great-great-grandfather, through whom Elizbeth Tilley's line is traced.

Mayflower II — Replica of the original — built in London then sailed to Plymouth, Massachusetts

Chapter 1

Elizabeth Tilley shivered with excitement. "Mayflower." In awe she read the name on the towering stern and gazed up at the three mist-shrouded masts. This was the ship that was to carry them from England to a new world!

"Look out!" someone shouted. A boy, chased by an older lad, was catapulting along the wharf. Almost colliding with Elizabeth, he suddenly changed course by grabbing her cape and circling her. As his pursuer lunged for him, he ran into Elizabeth and sent her staggering toward the dock's edge.

Ugh! I'm going in that stinking river, flashed through her mind.

Teetering over the murky Thames, she felt a strong hand grab her and whirl her back from the brink. She looked up at a broad-shouldered man who continued to hold onto her until she regained her footing.

Just as she was finding her voice to thank him, her attention was diverted by one of the two boys howling, "It's all his fault!"

A grizzled man had him by the ear and was dragging him along as he went after the other. Catching the second boy, he banged their heads together with a crack that resounded off the ship's hull.

Elizabeth winced for them and agreed with the woman who bustled up remonstrating, "Tut, Goodman Billington, easy on our sons. You'll mince their brains."

"Fat chance. They got no brains," Billington growled.

Watching the man march them back to the cluster of colonists waiting to board the Mayflower this damp July morning of 1620, Elizabeth couldn't help but feel sorry for the children. She thought of the little ones that had been entrusted to the care of her parents just a short time ago. They looked so pathetic huddled together beside her mother at a safe distance from the dock's edge. She experienced a pang of guilt about wandering off to satisfy her own desire to get a better look at the vessel.

Then she remembered her rescuer. Where was he? She should thank him. He must be the man striding toward Christopher Martin who was only now puffing onto the dock trailed by his wife, son, and a servant. *How like Master Martin to be late*, Elizabeth thought. How many times had they waited for church to begin until he arrived, especially when it was his turn to lead the service?

What business did her rescuer have with this peacock of a man in his pretentious plumed hat and bright blue waistcoat? Why would anybody bother with this pudgy soul?

"Boarding time!" A cry rang out above Elizabeth, and she looked up at a man in a master seaman's peaked hat standing at the taffrail. This would be the Master Jones. *What will he be like?* she wondered, realizing that their lives would soon be in his hands.

"Just a minute," Christopher Martin boomed, elbowing his way through the crowd pressing toward the loading ramp. "I'm in charge."

That figures, Elizabeth sighed inwardly. *He always has the most say of anyone in the church, and now he is taking charge of our voyage.*

Then she spotted her rescuer making his way among the waiting passengers to join several children and some young men. Who is he, she wondered, appreciating his adroitness.

Suddenly it dawned on her that she had better rejoin her family. She began to wriggle against the human tide pushing toward the ship.

"Everything will be done in its proper order. You'll board as I call your name." At Master Martin's words the crush eased as everyone fell back, everyone except the family with the two boys who had almost landed her in the river.

"Families first. Mistress Martin, Samuel, and servant," Martin boomed, fishing a paper from his wide pocket and unfolding it officiously.

As Martin's family boarded, Elizabeth made it back to her parents, just in time.

"Tilleys," Martin called.

"Where did you get to?" her mother's tension was released on her. "Hurry or Master Martin will be furious with us."

"We'll help the children get their things on board. Come as soon as you collect yours," her father said. "And don't forget the Bible box."

In snatching up her feather tick, the rope that held it gave way, spilling her extra clothing that had been rolled up inside. She felt her face flame as she bent to collect them.

Behind her an amused voice said, "Here, let me help you." It was the same voice that had shouted, "Look out!"

Partly angry and partly embarrassed, she refused to look up as she went on gathering up her nightgowns, drawers, and extra petticoat. But as she plunked them onto the recalcitrant ticking, the man knelt, rerolled, and retied it over her feeble protests.

Just as he finished she became aware of angry voices from the gangplank.

"I paid for my passage meself, and I got a right to board with the best of ye." It was the man with the two boys.

"You'll board when I say!" Master Martin blasted. "Where is Elizabeth Tilley?"

In consternation she snatched up her bedroll and dashed to the gangplank. Her confusion was compounded as she realized everyone was watching, and the ship's master shouted, "Time and tide wait for no man. Get your people on board."

With that Master Martin's order broke down into confusion again as she scurried onto the ship with the grizzled man and his family close behind.

Her parents had disappeared, apparently taking the children and their belongings below. But anxious to see everything that was going on, Elizabeth positioned herself by the railing.

Suddenly she remembered the Bible box. She had to get it. It contained their few precious sheets of paper and the quill for writing, the *Fox's Book of Martyrs* with its inspiring stories, and their most cherished possession, the Bible.

She must get back to shore. Once more she wriggled against the oncoming passengers and was ready to rush to the dock when there was a break.

As a child straggled up behind its mother, she chanced it, weaving around him, keeping an eye on the river, and hoping Master Martin wouldn't notice her. But as she made it to the shore he looked up from his paper.

"Elizabeth Tilley, where do you think you're going?" he blustered.

"I left the Bible box..."

He wasn't listening. "Get back on the ship this minute," he ordered.

"I have to get our Bible! I'm not going until I do," she burst out.

"You'll do as I say!" His face was turning red.

Defying him, she dashed back to where she thought her folks had been standing. No Bible box! She looked around distraught. The dock was empty now except for the few people who had come to see some of the passengers off.

"Take up the gangplank," she heard the ship's master call.

How could she face her parents without their beloved Bible? Yet she dare not search any longer. Would they ever forgive her? Defeated, she turned back to the ship.

Master Martin was standing now on deck yelling, "You're going to be left. Serves you right!"

She made a wild dash up the gangplank to face the glares of the sailors standing with ropes in hand ready to pull it up. Master Martin promptly screamed at her, "Young lady, your parents will hear about this."

"Cast off," the ship's master's call rang out from the poop deck. "All passengers below."

A smooth-cheeked young man who had been watching her turned and hauled his baggage toward the hatch opening. Even though she was reluctant to leave the deck Elizabeth found her ticking, and obediently lugged it along behind him. Disturbed as she was over the loss of the Bible, she was also curious about the things the sailors were doing on deck.

Before the young man could reach the opening Master

Martin was beside him blasting, "Hurry up!"

Obviously flustered, he stumbled down the steep steps and lay sprawled at the bottom.

Realizing how embarrassed he must be, if not really hurt, Elizabeth paused when she climbed down. "Are you all right?" she asked.

Master Martin was breathing fire down the back of her neck, but she didn't care.

With a grateful look the young man scrambled to his feet. "I'm fine," he said and hurried away to lose himself among the people who milled about in the common area at the end of a narrow passageway.

Elizabeth blinked as she tried to assess the cavernous 'tween deck lit only by the light filtering from above. She sniffed. There was an odd smell, sort of a mixture of fermentation and green lumber. Her father had commented that the Mayflower was a so-called sweet ship because it had carried wine from the Mediterranean.

Tiny cabins built of new wood with canvas flaps for doors lined the hull. Anxious not to block the passageway, she shoved her tick under the first canvas and joined the rest of the passengers.

Master Martin had already brushed past her and was taking charge. "Before I assign quarters, we need to ask the Lord's blessing on our voyage," Master Martin puffed, pulling out a lace-edged handkerchief and wiping his red face.

There wasn't time then to locate her parents. Amidst the swish of women's skirts being arranged and men's broad-brimmed hats being removed, she knelt on the rough boards with her fellow voyagers. Such a momentous undertaking certainly needed prayer, but she wondered if Master Martin's prayers wouldn't bounce off the low beams and fall back on his head after the way he had been acting.

Just before closing her eyes, she realized that she was kneeling in front of a rough ladder. She grasped the second rung with both hands and leaned her forehead against the one above.

"Dear Lord, Maker of heaven and earth, Ruler of land and sea, Creator of all that lives and breathes, Deliverer of thy children, Israel....." Master Martin began his familiar recital of

Old Testament history. But Elizabeth had her own praying to do. "Dear Lord, what am I going to do about the lost Bible?"

Then it came to her. Of course, it wasn't on the dock because someone had brought it on board. It would certainly turn up. "Thank you, Lord," she breathed.

With that settled, her attention was drawn to noises overhead. Orders were being shouted and many creaking, squeaking and slapping sounds were coming from the ship.

On an irresistible impulse she opened her eyes. There rose the ladder like a mountain trail demanding to be explored. Everyone else appeared intent upon the prayer and with the noises above no one would notice if she....for shame, she scolded herself and closed her eyes again.

Master Martin droned on, "...brought them safely through the Red Sea, and fed them with manna..."

Elizabeth blinked her eyes open again and the ladder lured. How many times over the years had she dreamed of escaping Master Martin's endless prayers? Her hands were already on the rails. How easily her feet could follow. Almost without willing it, the deed followed the thought.

Carefully she set her foot on the first rung and lifted herself to the next. With a groan, the ship began to move, further covering her escape. "...and they sinned against Thee..." were the last words she heard as she climbed the ladder.

At the top Elizabeth found herself in a three-sided cabin facing a high box that held a compass. Behind her she heard someone mutter, "Blimey, a woman!" and turned to face a man firmly grasping the tiller rod.

Elizabeth tried to smile, but he scowled at her and growled, "No women allowed. Master Jones will settle you."

"I only wanted to see what's happening up here," she said.

"Out there and up over top 'a here," he indicated that she move forward and climb to the deck over his head.

What would the ship's master do to her? She had heard seamen were flogged. Whatever it was, she hoped fervently that he would handle it himself and not turn her over to Master Martin.

With wobbling knees she passed the capstan with its coil of anchor rope thick as a chair leg. Her palms were sweating as she paused in the shadows to look out on the main deck. One sailor on each side was winding ropes around wooden pins stuck in a board mounted the length of the inside railing. She heard a flapping like a flight of pigeons high above her head and looked up to see sails being dropped by men dangling out of the working top on each mast. They flapped like sheets hung from a line. One by one they caught the light breeze that had sprung up on the widening Thames. The vessel tilted, seeming to rush toward the opposite bank. Soon it steadied and she remembered she was on her way to see the captain.

Pausing at the bottom of the ladder that led to the poop, she looked up at the man who was to guide their ship across the ocean wastes. The captain, standing on sturdy legs braced apart was too absorbed in navigating to notice Elizabeth. While she waited, she studied the lines etched around eyes that lay deep in ruddy cheeks, weather-beaten as old boards.

"Steady now," he called down to the helmsman and to the men on the deck, "Brace topgallants." They began winding ropes around another set of pins.

His broad chest lifted his brass-buttoned jacket. He was exhaling strongly when suddenly he stiffened.

"Hard to the larboard," he shouted to the helmsman.

Elizabeth glanced out over the river in time to see a bark on collision course with the Mayflower.

"Look sharp you filthy swine, pull the royals!" he screamed at the sailors on deck.

Elizabeth reached out and grabbed the rail to hold herself up. The hair on the back of her neck prickled. They would surely crash.

"Bloody curs," one of the sailors shouted back. "Let 'em look out for them own selves."

As the Mayflower fell off sharply, the bark skimmed by a hairbreadth away.

The second the danger was over Master Jones leaped onto the main deck, grabbed the impudent sailor by the shoulder and whirled him about to face him. Without a word he slammed his fist into the man's jaw and laid him flat on the deck. Then he stared down the crew who had descended from the rigging.

"Anyone else have something to say?" he said quietly.

There was a shuffling of feet and some mumbling, but no one spoke.

Elizabeth's knuckles were white on the railing. She had never seen a man strike another man and it left her shaking. There was no question about who was in charge, no doubt a good thing. How much more she dreaded facing him now.

Just then he saw her. "And what are you doing up here young lady?" he demanded.

"Sir, I climbed the ladder in the back of the 'tween deck because I wanted to see what was happening." Her voice quavered as she spoke.

"Wasn't everyone ordered off deck?"

"Yes, sir."

"Have you figured out why?"

"So we wouldn't get in the way?" Her voice sounded small in her ears.

"Right, and when a master gives an order on a ship he must have obedience for the good of everyone. I'll forgive you this time since it's all right now for the passengers to come topside." With that he called down, "All clear."

Sighing in relief, Elizabeth slipped to the hatchway opening and mingled with the people who came swarming up to wave farewell to family and friends.

Elizabeth watched as the mists swirled like a veil curtaining off the ship from the shore. Even as she heard the sobs of women around her, she lifted her eyes heavenward and caught the first glimpse of the sun, silver white as a shilling tossed into the sky. Her spirits soared. Surely, they were on their way to a land of sunshine, a land beyond the fear of a knock on the door which meant King's soldiers had come to arrest them.

Once shortly after they had arrived in London she had begged her mother to take her on her weekly trip to deliver food to a Separatist friend in the Clink. She shuddered. How vivid remained the dank smell of huge grey stones, the clanking of iron bars, and the penetrating cold of the prison. How angry she had been to think this person was imprisoned because he refused to worship God in the King's church.

"There's Greenwich," Elizabeth heard someone say.

"That was a favorite retreat of Queen Elizabeth," someone else in the crowd added, and everyone craned their necks for a view of the cluster of classic white buildings set back from the river on wide sloping lawns. Elizabeth sighed with relief. That meant they were free of the city, really on their way.

Several years ago when her uncle, Edward Tilley, and his wife Ann, had fled to Leyden to join Pastor Robinson's congregation of English Separatists, her father had considered leaving too, but finally decided that it was God's will that he stay. Anyway, the King's power reached across the North Sea.

Elder William Brewster of the Leyden congregation was in hiding now. The king had persuaded the Dutch to try to arrest him on charges of having printed material critical of the Church of England.

The ship had passed the palace when her father found her. "What happened to you? We've been wondering where you were."

Elizabeth couldn't deceive him, but neither did she want him to worry about the Bible. "I stayed as long as I could on the deck to see what was happening," she said.

"Come now," Goodman Tilley said, "Your mother wants to get settled in our cabin."

"Can't I wait a little longer? I want to see as much of England as I can." Elizabeth pleaded.

Her father smiled and relented. "I suppose there is lots of time to get settled. We'll probably be on the ship for a month, but your mother has taken the children below, so come down soon."

Other passengers, too, began drifting back to the 'tween deck. But Elizabeth stayed topside trying to figure out how to retrieve the Bible box and its valuable contents.

She was scarcely conscious of someone moving to the railing beside her until he spoke, "I've been looking for you, I wanted to meet the young lady that I've had the privilege of helping."

Startled, Elizabeth turned to face her rescuer.

Chapter 2

Elizabeth looked up at a man a head taller than she. His hazel eyes flecked with green looked into hers. There was a twitch of laughter in the corner of his strong mouth that made her look away, partly embarrassed, partly angry. She studied her long fingers grasping the high railing until her instinctive good manners won out.

Finding her voice, she said, "Oh, I'm glad you found me because I wanted to thank you." She glanced at him.

"No need. I just happened to be in the right place at the right time. Let's call it Providence," he said with a grin and then went on to introduce himself, "I'm John Howland, Master Carter's servant, at your service any time. Are you John Tilley's daughter?"

"You know my father?"

"Yes, only casually, and I don't know your name."

When she told him, he seemed to savor it. "Elizabeth, the name of a queen," he said and then added, "But I did know that! Your Uncle Edward has spoken of you. Edward Tilley is your uncle, isn't he?"

Elizabeth nodded assent, and he added, "I sometimes stayed at Edward Tilley's when I was in Leyden and the Carver's had a house full. He spoke often of his brother's little girl."

Elizabeth's eyebrow arched, "So now you know he was wrong. I'm not a *little* girl."

Chuckling, he answered, "Big or little, you pulled a good

trick in getting away from Martin's long-winded prayer."

Elizabeth's mouth dropped open, and her eyes grew round. "You saw me? I suppose you're going to tell Master Martin." Her defenses were up.

"Not on your life. My lips are sealed" He put his finger across his mouth.

He's laughing at me, Elizabeth thought. "You don't have to. I can take my punishment," she said. Turning her back on him, she lurched to the hatchway and climbed down, embarrassed by the awkward gait imposed by the unaccustomed motion of the ship. She had intended to be so dignified.

Below she found Master Martin ranting about the number of children in the party of settlers. "Where did they all come from?" he was demanding to know.

"I guess you were buying supplies in Kent when we agreed to take my sister-in-law's two young cousins. This is Humility Cooper, and Henry Samson," her father said drawing each child to his side in turn. "They will be turned over to Mistress Tilley when they meet us in Southampton."

"And these are the More children that Thomas Weston arranged for us to take. Since you weren't here when he brought them to the dock, he entrusted them to me," John Howland, who had followed her, spoke up.

"I want no part of them. I only hope they know how to behave themselves, and appreciate what we are doing for them." Master Martin stomped off to examine the cabins.

Coming to the first, he lifted the canvas and saw Elizabeth's baggage. "Whose is this?' he bellowed. "No one was to put anything in any cabin until I told you to." Grabbing her bed roll and clothing bag, he hurled them into the aisle.

Anger overcoming her fear, Elizabeth stepped forward. "It's mine. I was only trying to clear the passageway."

"You again! You do as I tell you, do you hear?" His black eyes burned into her. "John Tilley, you've raised an impudent one."

She caught a twinkle in her father's eye. Before he could speak, a little boy, who was standing nearby with a girl about Elizabeth's age, began to cry, obviously frightened by Master Martin's outburst.

The belligerent man turned to him, "Children! That's what I mean. They are to be seen and not heard. We can't put up with a bunch of howling brats in these cramped quarters."

The child cried harder.

"Quiet!" Master Martin ordered.

At that point an obviously pregnant woman swept the child into her arms and carried him to the far end of the 'tween deck where he could still be heard sobbing.

"That does it! My family is NOT staying down here. The captain must have something better to offer." Master Martin lumbered to the hatchway and labored up the steep steps.

Elizabeth heard someone beside her sigh with relief, and turned to meet a pert-faced girl about her own age.

"I'm Constance Hopkins," she said with a crooked smile.

As they talked Elizabeth learned that she was traveling with her father, stepmother and the young child, her half brother, Damarius.

"My father is also taking two servants with us, both good-looking fellows," she said, arching an eyebrow, and leaving Elizabeth a bit surprised by her comment.

Before they finished getting acquainted, Master Martin reappeared, and assigned families to cabins, letting it be known that *he* would be housed on the main deck.

By supper time Humility and Henry had made friends with John Howland's charges, and Goodwife Tilley offered to prepare the meal for all of them. Elizabeth wasn't happy about having John Howland eat with them, but she could easily avoid him, since everyone was eating in the common area set aside for cooking and general gathering anyway.

In all the excitement of meeting new people and settling in, she had almost forgotten the missing Bible box. Fortunately her mother had, too. How would she ever find it? Then it occurred to her, much as she hated the idea, she would have to ask Master Martin to make an announcement.

As the men sat on chests for supper, balancing plates of boiled beef, biscuit and salad greens, they began discussing the problems the Leydeners had had getting the expedition together. Even in the dimly filtered evening light, Elizabeth was aware that John kept glancing at her with a twinkle in his eye.

It was apparent that this man wouldn't report her act of irreverence, but she was upset with him for laughing at her. Still she didn't withdraw as she had planned, because she was anxious to know everything about the colony.

She remembered the fateful day her father had come home enthused about meeting with John Carver. He had been sent by the English Separatists, who had taken refuge in Holland, to seek a charter and obtain funding for a plantation in the New World.

"They are going to ask the king for religious freedom for our plantation," her father had said, and she had gotten goose bumps. "Our plantation?" Was he thinking that they, too, might cross the wild Western Sea? No woman had ventured there since Sir Walter Raliegh's colony had disappeared! Fear and excitement had struggled for control of her.

But it had taken several years of negotiations, and the king had only tacitly agreed not to bother them on the other side of the ocean. After many letters back and forth to Leyden, her father had determined that it was God's will that they join the Planters.

"Underway at last! I can scarcely believe it," John Howland was saying to her father, echoing her own thoughts.

"Two long years, the Lord has really been testing our patience and commitment," Master Tilley said.

"I hope Thomas Weston didn't misrepresent our case to the backers he got for us," John Howland said, spearing a morsel of beef with his knife and popping it into his mouth.

"Those who put up venture capital certainly expect to make money," John Tilley replied. "It's too bad we couldn't have sailed in May as we had hoped. I'm afraid they won't realize much this year."

Elizabeth thought of the russet fields of ripening wheat they had seen from the bay this afternoon. It occurred to her for the first time that they wouldn't be able to grow any of their own food this year, and she had a sudden premonition of starvation. Nonsense, she told herself, our leaders have surely prepared to feed us. She looked at the barrels lashed nearby and felt better.

"The Leydeners can be trusted to pay off the loan if it takes years." John Howland devoured half a biscuit with one bite.

"But we haven't signed the agreement yet. I wonder if the Leydeners will sign," her father's brow furrowed.

"They aren't happy with the revisions," John Howland said. This was news to Elizabeth. *What revisions*, she wondered, but before she could learn her mother drew Elizabeth aside, "We are to use sea water from a barrel on deck for dishes. You can do it." Her mother had already collected the empty plates and handed the pile to her.

As she reluctantly left, she thought she heard her father say, "I can always go back to my job in London if they can't get it settled." He couldn't back out now, she told herself as she emerged topside.

She was dipping plates into the barrel when the smooth-faced youth who had fallen down the hatchway appeared at her elbow and dunked his plate too. He smiled at her broadly.

"I'm Richard Gardiner," he said. "It was really nice of you to ask if I was hurt when I fell. Isn't Old Man Martin a pistol?"

Elizabeth smiled back at him and nodded.

"You know," Richard said looking appreciatively at Elizabeth, "I don't think anyone has ever cared what happened to me since I left home."

Elizabeth couldn't help feeling sorry for him as she asked, "Where was home?"

"A farm in Essex. I always wanted to be a farmer, but my older brother will inherit the land. My father apprenticed me to a cobbler in London. I haven't seen any of my family since. They don't even know I'm leaving." There was a wistful note in his voice.

"Why didn't you tell them?" Elizabeth asked.

"I can't write," he said.

"I can write," Elizabeth said, glad that she had been taught to read and write so that she could study the Bible. "I'll write a letter for you that you can post in Southampton."

"Would you? I'd feel so much better if they knew."

When she assured him she would be glad to, he asked, "What did your father do?"

"He's been a silk worker since we moved to London, but I was born in the country," she replied.

"You're father belonged on the land, too. Don't you miss it?" Richard asked.

Elizabeth nodded and edged away from the barrel, eager to go back to the discussion she had left, but Richard wanted to talk.

"I hated London," he said. "I can't wait to work outdoors

again. Just think, in the New World I'll be able to have a farm of my own. As soon as I do, I'll need a wife to help me."

He looked at Elizabeth meaningfully and waited for her comment. When she didn't say anything he went on, "You going with your parents? You'll be wanting to get married and have your own place too, won't you?"

For the first time Elizabeth really looked at him, noting the strong arm muscles under his shirt, and taking in his round almost baby-like face. He seemed like a pleasant enough person, but she wasn't ready to talk marriage with anyone, least of all with someone who sounded as though he was hiring a servant.

"You'll have to excuse me now. Mother will be waiting to put the dishes back in the chest," she said.

Richard followed her below where more men had joined the discussion, and it had almost become an argument. Little Damarius Hopkins, being carried around by Constance, was crying again, and Elizabeth became aware of the round frightened eyes of the older children.

"Let's take the children down into the tiller flat," she said to Constance. It was the area in the stern that was lowered to allow the tiller rod to move freely, "I'll tell them a story."

Constance agreed, and soon they were settled in a cozy spot beside some of the well-lashed barrels. Elizabeth chose the story of Daniel in the lions den.

"If God could protect Daniel from wild lions, he can take care of us on the wild ocean too." As she finished she realized that John Howland was looking down at them.

"Do you know any nursery rhymes," he called. "How about, 'Hey diddle diddle, the cat and the fiddle, the cow jumped over the moon?'" At that point John leaped over the railing and came down with a thud that shook the deck around him and set the children to laughing for the first time in Elizabeth's experience with them.

"Tell it again," Henry begged as the other children crowded around John.

He began the rhyme once more and when he came to "the dish ran away with the spoon," he grabbed Elizabeth's hand, pulled her to her feet and dragged her along as he snaked around the barrels. Soon all the children, squealing with delight, followed them until they were all breathless. By this time many of the adults were leaning over the railing laughing with them, and Elizabeth was glad Master Martin wasn't there.

When she caught her breath she scolded, "John Howland, you've got the children wide awake. How will they settle down to sleep?"

"They'll sleep the better for it, won't you?" he challenged them.

"Oh yes," they chorused.

Elizabeth wasn't so sure.

John arranged them back into a circle, and launched into the story of Jesus and the little children. As he talked she put her arms around Humility and Henry, and Constance took Damarius in her lap.

John concluded the story saying, "Jesus loves each of you, too, and will take care of you tonight if we ask Him. Close your eyes tight. You pray inside while I pray out loud."

He prayed a long time. Elizabeth heard Humility's breathing grow shallow and regular, and soon her head dropped into Elizabeth's lap. When Elizabeth looked up after the prayer, Damarius was asleep, too.

Both girls, bracing themselves against the swaying of the ship, carefully carried their sleeping charges to their cabins while John led the bigger children back to their guardians.

Just as Elizabeth rejoined the passengers in the main cabin, Christopher Martin came tramping down from his quarters and called everyone to evening prayers.

Prayers! That meant her father would be looking for their Bible. Evening prayers always included Bible reading, and he liked to follow along. She would have to tell him and face Master Martin. For a minute she felt as though the ship was sinking from under her.

Just then John Howland strode toward her carrying a Bible box which he extended toward her.

"Are you looking for this?" he said with a twinkle in his eye. "You left this on the wharf in your hurry to board."

Relief flooded through her, then anger. Why hadn't he given it to her sooner? She snatched it from him and hurried off to the cabin before her parents could realize what had happened. She placed it on the bunk above Humility, opened it, and quietly lifted out the precious book.

Then it hit her how ungracious she had been to John Howland and she was ashamed of herself. She wanted to crawl in with the sleeping child. How peaceful she looked. For now all her problems seemed to be lost in pleasant dreams. But just then her father lifted the curtain. Elizabeth put her fingers to her pursed lips, handed him the Bible and followed him back to the main cabin.

Constance was already there giving her whimpering brother to his weary-looking mother who began patting and shushing him.

Elizabeth had no intention of rousing Humility, but Master Martin was examining the gathering as if taking roll. His eyes came back to her and he boomed, "Where's the girl? No one can miss evening prayers, especially the orphans. If the little heathens are going with us they need to be instructed in the holy disciplines. We're responsible to God for their souls."

"But she's already had a Bible story and prayers. She's asleep." Elizabeth was too provoked to realize that she was being disrespectful.

Master Martin turned on her father. "John Tilley, if we were on land, I'd have that girl put in stocks."

Elizabeth's cheeks burned. She was immediately sorry for having disgraced her family in front of all these people, most of whom were strangers.

"Elizabeth Tilley, bring that child here. Now!" Martin ordered.

Not wanting to embarrass her father further, Elizabeth, choking back an angry sob, started out the passageway. Before she had taken many steps someone caught her elbow and turned her around. In the faint light there were sparks in John Howland's eyes.

"There's no sense in this," he whispered. "We're not going to waken that child. You stay here."

Chapter 3

Elizabeth wove through the silent crowd trying to get close enough to hear what John was saying to Master Martin. She couldn't make it out, but there was no mistaking Martin's reply.

"Why you upstart! How dare you, a mere servant that can be bought and sold at his master's will, tell me, the governor, how I should conduct prayers. For such insolence the devil take the lot of you. You're no better than Sodom." He wheeled around and stomped out the passageway shaking each foot as he went. To make sure they understood his action he shouted back before he climbed the hatchway, "Jesus said to shake off the dust of people like you."

A collective gasp rent the air followed by a short silence before everyone began talking at once.

Elizabeth fled down into the tiller flat and tried to hide behind some barrels. She was sobbing with rage and shame when she felt comforting hands on her shoulders, and was turned about to face John Howland.

"Please don't cry," he said.

"It's all my fault," she gulped back her sobs. "I should have wakened her, but..."

"No, it's not your fault," John said.

"But Master Martin was hateful to you because of me. I'm so sorry. Can you forgive me?" Her lower lip trembled.

"Of course I forgive you." John lifted her chin so that she could look directly into his eyes, dark now, but shining in the faint light from the lantern swinging on the 'tween deck. His look made her feel as if she were falling from a cliff.

Suddenly the ship swayed throwing her against him. His arms closed around her, and she clung to him until her whole body tingled. Almost afraid, she drew away.

"Come," he said, abruptly turning from Elizabeth, "We must join the others. Someone else will lead devotions tonight."

Elizabeth woke early after a restless night in the tiller flat. Was it the strangeness of trying to sleep in a moving ship, or was she plagued with guilt because she had defied Master Martin, or was it John's arms that disturbed her? Perhaps the sea breezes would clear her mind. Wriggling from her bunk barefooted, she tiptoed from the cabin and climbed to the main deck.

She reached the railing in time to see the sun rise, a huge fireball rolling a red carpet across the flat white ocean. The ship was rocking gently with water lapping its sides and its sails flapping feebly. A lone sailor clambered down the rope ladder from the mainmast, and lighted on the deck nearby.

He leered at her, "Been feeding the fishes early, eh?" It was the brazen fellow the captain had sent sprawling yesterday.

For a second she was puzzled, then realized what he meant. "I'm not seasick," she declared.

"Just wait 'til we hits the 'Lantic. The lot of ye'll wind up fish food." His laugh was evil.

Suddenly the sailor ducked into his quarters in the forecastle, and Elizabeth turned to see Master Jones standing on the poop deck smiling down at her. At the same time John Howland's head appeared in the hatchway and he came on deck. Elizabeth felt a sudden flutter in her stomach followed by a strong urge to hide.

Before John could join her at the rail, the captain invited her up to the poop deck.

Elizabeth was surprised and concerned by the captain's invitation. Had he changed his mind about forgiving her yesterday? But when she reached his side, he asked if the women and children were comfortable.

When she had assured them they were, he said, "The sailors aren't too happy about having women on shipboard. Bad luck, you know."

Shocked by his trusting in luck rather than in God, and not knowing what to say, she made the excuse that she must help her mother with breakfast. She escaped below, attempting to ignore John Howland as she brushed by him.

"Let me know if there is anything I can do for you," Master Jones called after her.

Later that morning, Elizabeth and Constance took the children up for exercise. They inadvertently climbed into a scene between Master Martin and Captain Miles Standish, the professional soldier who was to organize the defense of the colony.

"What's going on here?" Master Martin appeared from the shadows behind the helmsman.

"It's time to begin turning these artisans and yeomen into soldiers," Standish said, red beard bristling.

"I'm the one who gives orders." Martin's voice could be heard all over the ship as he clumped out to face the man who was shorter than he.

"Not in military matters," Capt. Standish shot back. "I'm in charge. Fall in line."

A look of disbelief spread over Master Martin's face. As he opened his mouth to protest, Capt. Standish's hand moved to the hilt of his sword and he drew himself up to his full, though abbreviated, height.

Just then a gust of wind caught the sails, throwing everyone to the larboard and piling men onto each other with Capt. Standish on top of Master Martin. When they had all recovered their balance, Master Martin took the place at the front of the line without another word.

Elizabeth, Constance and the children had been thrown against the rail by the forecastle where they had clustered at the top of the hatchway. Realizing they were in the way, Elizabeth was about to take them below when Master Jones motioned them all up to the poop deck.

"Where do you think you're going?" Master Martin yelled, "No one is allowed up there."

Elizabeth's stomach churned. She knew the Bible taught to obey rulers, but every inch of her stiffened against Martin's unjust attack.

The ship's master quickly intervened. "They're my guests," he said.

Christopher Martin glared at Elizabeth, but Capt. Standish gave the order to march, and he obeyed.

The ship's master met her at the top of the stairs. "You're welcome up here any time," he said. "You're not as apt to be harried by the sailors, and you'll be less in the way of the activities on the main deck."

She thanked him and joined Constance and the children who were watching the men try to keep step on the swaying deck below. It amused her to see that every time the column turned Master Martin wound up in the rear.

Soon she overheard a conversation that she hoped the children missed. The same sailor who had derided her earlier snorted to another, "Ah, don't that captain think 'e's somethin', strutting back and forth. The runt of the litter, he is."

"Yea, some captain. Capt. Shrimp, I'd say," his buddy took up the sport. The two of them howled as the first one slapped his knee in glee.

"Boiled shrimp at that," he guffawed.

The children had heard and were laughing too, but Elizabeth quickly drew them aside and scolded them for their disrespect, "You'll be glad enough for Capt. Standish when the Indians come to get you." She thought a good scare was justified to sober them.

As the men stumbled back and forth trying to learn the military commands that the little captain was issuing rapid fire, Elizabeth picked out the marchers she already knew. There was Master Hopkins, Constance's father. His hair had obviously once been a sandy red, faded now though there was still fire in his beard. There were two other young men with the Hopkins. She turned now to ask Constance to point them out.

"The one with the curly brown hair is Edward Dotey, and the other with the pointed black beard is Edward Leister. Don't you think he's handsome?" Constance said.

Elizabeth studied them briefly. Neither one could compare in looks to John Howland. Her eyes kept going back to his tall well-built frame, wavy dark hair, and high-bridged nose that made her think he must have been descended from one of the Roman officers who had conquered England long ago.

"Who is the man who was talking to you over the water barrel last night?" Constance directed her attention to Richard Gardiner. The tone of her question alerted Elizabeth that she thought his interest in her was significant.

"He's the one who fell down the hatchway when we were boarding," Elizabeth said evenly.

"He's kind of cute," Constance said with an arched eyebrow.

Elizabeth chose to ignore her, and asked instead why Constance's family was going to the New World.

"My father visited the Jamestown plantation once, and he's wanted to go back ever since," Constance answered.

Elizabeth found it reassuring that a man who had been there wanted to return. She would like to ask him more about it, but at that point the drill was over, and Richard Gardiner was calling to her.

"Can you write my letter now?"

In light of Constance's innuendo and Richard's own re-marks about marriage she wasn't anxious for close contact with him, but she had given her word and she must keep it.

When Elizabeth had rounded up paper, quill and ink, she appropriated a top of a barrel in the tiller flat as a table. Richard, leaning on his elbows, watched every mark she made on the paper as he told his family very simply what he was doing. His conclusion left her in confusion again. "It won't be long before I'll have a wife and family of my own," she scratched as he dictated. Then he asked, "Could you guide the pen in my hand, so I could sign my name?"

She couldn't refuse. She moved around behind him and placed her right hand over his keeping as great a distance from him as she could. As they finished, he dropped the quill and turning his hand up caught hers in his, and drew her against him. She twisted herself away as fast as she could, but not before he kissed the back of her hand. His breath came quickly, as he muttered, "Until later."

There won't be any "later" if I can help it, she thought. Then as the memory of John Howland's arms flooded over her, she realized that she had been avoiding him, too. Being a young lady was suddenly more complicated than she had imagined.

Sometime during the second night Elizabeth awoke trying to figure out what was different. The boat was no longer moving!

They must have docked at Southampton. Was the Speedwell waiting? Would they be on the Western Sea by tomorrow night? She couldn't sleep another wink. At the first hint of dawn, she scrambled topside.

Finding herself facing the broad stretch of Southampton Water, she looked for the Dutch emblem among the many vessels already loading and unloading. Spain, Normandy, Venice, ah, the flag of Holland! But the ship was much too large to be the Speedwell.

Disappointed, she turned to the dockside where a walled city stood well back from the wooden wharves lining the water's edge. Above the walls a steeple pointed heavenward, and together with a round castle-fortress bulging out of the wall on the land side, it made Elizabeth think of a verse from the Psalms, "God is our refuge and strength." "I must learn to trust Him more and be patient," she sighed.

Almost a week later her patience had been stretched to the breaking point. She needed exercise. The July day had been hot, and with the coming of the long northern evening Elizabeth suggested taking the children for a stroll along the harbor before putting them to bed in the stuffy hold. John Howland offered to accompany her. "After all I'm responsible for the More children until I turn them over to Mistress Carver," he said.

Elizabeth knew that John's embrace had been only accidental and had meant nothing to either of them. Yet she still found it impossible to meet his gaze.

When the children ran on ahead, she sensed that John had something he wanted to say. He paused and turned to her. "Can you forgive me for taking the liberty I did the other night? I hope we can be friends."

Suddenly she felt empty inside. Was she hoping it meant something after all? Did she dare say so? While she was groping for an answer little Henry came running back.

"There's a ship coming pulling a boat behind it, and flying a Dutch flag." He waved in its direction.

Elizabeth shaded her eyes against the low sun and studied the vessel he had pointed out. The sails swelling in the light evening breeze seemed too big for the size of the ship, and she commented on it to John.

"All the better to keep up with the Mayflower," he answered. "I think that's it. That's a shallop they're towing. John Carver said it came with the Speedwell. Oh, I better let him know."

Elizabeth nodded. She knew that the white-haired man with the kind blue eyes was waiting anxiously for his wife's arrival.

As John hurried off with his promising news, and John's children ran back to the Mayflower to spread the word, Humility and Henry crowded close to Elizabeth, clutching her long woolen skirt. Elizabeth put her hand on Humility's shoulder and felt her trembling. Suddenly she understood. Having lost their parents, and then being torn from their aging grandfather, these poor waifs were facing more strangers, their unknown distant cousins.

"Don't worry. You'll love Aunt Anne," Elizabeth sought to reassure them. "Uncle Edward seems stern, but he really isn't. You'll love him, too, when you get to know him."

Elizabeth took their hands and led them back to the ship. The deck was filling with people watching the incoming vessel whose rail was lined with eager faces. Elizabeth scanned the crowd for her aunt and uncle. As it maneuvered to a pier, she was able to pick out her aunt's round crinkly face and her uncle's ragged beard.

When the arriving colonists debarked Elizabeth flew into her aunt's arms, as her father grasped his brother's hand. When her mother had greeted her in-laws, Elizabeth introduced the waiting children. Aunt Anne bent and kissed each in turn. "I'm so glad to have a family at last," she said. "We've waited a long time for you both."

A shy smile brought light to Humility's hazel eyes, and a big grin suffused Henry's freckled face, giving Elizabeth a warm feeling inside. Then her aunt turned to a petite young woman beside her, and taking her by the hand introduced her to Elizabeth, "This is Desire Minter. She's coming with us to help Mistress Carver. I know you two are going to become good friends."

But there was little time to become acquainted with Desire just then, for there were others to meet. Elizabeth counted it a great privilege to be introduced to Mistress Carver as well as Elder Brewster's wife, and their two young sons, Love and

Wrestling. All greeted her graciously, but Mistress Brewster's face seemed frozen in a frown. Mine might be too, Elizabeth thought, if I were as uncertain of my husband's whereabouts as this woman must be. The elder was to be their spiritual leader until Pastor Robinson could bring another group of settlers from Leyden, but no one had seen him yet.

A short time later the Leydeners crowded onto the May- flower to meet the rest of the colonists. After introductions, William Bradford from the Speedwell, a man about the same age as John Howland, raised his leather mug in a toast. "Congratulations, men of the Mayflower, for your wisdom and courage in undertaking this venture with us," he said.

Shortly before Aunt Anne had introduced Elizabeth to William's wife, Dorothy. Elizabeth had had the feeling as their eyes met that Dorothy was a very sad person who smiled only with her mouth. Even as everyone else took part in the festivities, she appeared downcast. Elizabeth was wondering if there was anything she could do to cheer her, when she was distracted by Desire Minter, the young woman to whom her aunt had introduced her earlier.

"Isn't that John Howland?" whispered the girl, her heart- shaped face turned up to Elizabeth. She indicated the man who had been pouring toddy from a jug into each man's jack.

Elizabeth confirmed that it was John.

"Do you know him?" Desire buzzed in her ear again.

Elizabeth nodded.

"You'll have to introduce me to him. I met him once before, but I don't know if he'll remember me."

After the formal greetings, as the young people collected on the deck in the fading light, Elizabeth complied with her request.

Blond curls escaped from Desire's prim cap and framed her pretty face as she smiled and offered her hand. "John Howland. We meet again. Our last visit was so short you've likely forgotten me."

"I didn't forget you," John answered smiling back at her and taking her hand. "Master Carver told me you were coming."

Desire laid her other hand on top of his and tilting her head looked up at him, "I'm so glad we'll have a chance to get to know each other. I've so looked forward to seeing you again."

Why couldn't I have thought of something like that to say when John said he wanted to be my friend, Elizabeth thought.

"We'll all be seeing a great deal of each other for sure," John said looking over Desire's head at Elizabeth.

"We'll be part of the same household. I've come along to help Mistress Carver." Desire chatted on. "John, I admire you so much for risking everything to go to the New World."

"It's you women who deserve the most credit," John said, pulling gently away from her. "You're all very brave."

Elizabeth who was watching Desire with admiration thought she saw a shadow fall over her face as he spoke of bravery. *Is Desire afraid or is it my imagination?* she wondered.

"You're so kind to say that. Do you really think we're brave? I was so ready for something new that I never thought about it." Desire's dark lashes fluttered, and looking appreciatively at John, her face lighted again. She moved close to him and took his arm. "Why don't you walk me back to the Speedwell and tell me all about yourself? I've thought of you so often since that night at Carver's."

John turned briefly to Elizabeth to ask if she would put the children to bed, and gently removing Desire's hand from his arm, led the way to the gangplank. As they started down, he turned and offered his hand to help her to shore. As Elizabeth watched them leave, Desire took his arm again. She shivered in the damp air as night closed in.

Chapter 4

Later that night as Elizabeth tossed in her tick, she told herself ruefully, "I guess I don't have to worry about John Howland ever being more than a friend to me." *How did Desire capture him so quickly,* she wondered, trying to replay the scene in her mind. *She's so pretty, and petite, compared to me.* Suddenly she wasn't proud anymore of having grown tall and strong for a girl. *I'm so big and awkward. No wonder he's attracted to her. Besides, she's nearer John's age.*

She thought, too, about Constance. She had believed she was attracted most to Edward Leister, and yet on deck this evening she had been talking and laughing with Edward Dotey, only giving the other Edward an occasional sidelong glance. Elizabeth didn't understand it.

Then there was Richard who seemed to be everywhere Elizabeth turned. It was Richard who had helped her get the children settled tonight. His attention pleased and annoyed her at the same time. *Once we sail, things will sort themselves out,* she decided.

Surely they would be leaving tomorrow or the next day at the latest. The men from the two ships were talking right now in the great cabin over her head. Suddenly sounds of angry voices reached her from above, making her recall the unpleasant scene she had witnessed yesterday.

Several wagonloads of supplies were being trundled onto the Mayflower under Master Martin's direction, when John

Carver had arrived on the dock with a wagon piled high with barrels exuding the good smells of butter and salt pork.

"Why did *you* get all this?" Master Martin had demanded.

Master Carver's pale skin grew pink, but he answered evenly, "The Leydeners authorized me to lay in supplies for our venture."

"Our backers put me in charge, and you're usurping my prerogative!" Master Martin's face turned purple.

"The Merchant Adventurers were to make the money available to the Separatists, and they will receive the bill," Master Carver said, turned abruptly and walked away.

The implications of the argument had left Elizabeth shaking. She was lying tense in her bunk now wondering what was going on up there, when she heard Master Martin's harsh voice rise above the others and caught the words "cast doubt on my honor." What a mess things seem to be in! "God help us," she breathed. "Will we ever sail?"

Elizabeth was up early the next morning still hoping that they would be casting off, but there was no sign of sailing preparations when she came on deck. Seeing Master Jones, she asked him about it.

"I think it will be awhile yet until your people are ready," he said without elaboration. "No one is more anxious than I am to get started. I want to get off the North Atlantic before the winter storms set in. They are said to be the most ferocious in the world."

While Elizabeth was digesting this thought Desire Minter came along the dock and waved to her. "Come, walk with me," Desire called.

"I'm so glad to see you. I've been hoping for the chance to get to know you better," Desire said when Elizabeth joined her.

Elizabeth couldn't help liking the young woman who was soon drawing her out about her family and church. Before Elizabeth knew it she was telling her about the captain's comments, the voices she had heard last night, and the argument between Master Carver and Master Martin. "What do you suppose is still keeping us from sailing?" Elizabeth concluded.

Desire shook her head. "It's the men's business, and there is nothing we can do about it," she said, then changed the subject.

As Elizabeth chatted with her, she determined to ask her father why they weren't sailing today.

Elizabeth got back to the 'tween deck in time to hear her mother complaining to her father, as she measured out their morning ration of rolled oats, "If we don't sail soon, we'll eat up all our victuals before we ever reach the New World."

"Thomas Weston is due from London this morning, and we should get things settled," her father said, but the deep lines between his eyes betrayed his doubts. When Elizabeth tried to ask him what had to be settled, he didn't answer. In fact he seemed so preoccupied, as he spooned porridge into his mouth, that she wasn't sure he heard her.

He had barely finished eating, when John Howland strode into the common area and motioned for her father, Master Hopkins and several other of the men to follow him. They evidently were having another meeting.

When he had gone Elizabeth turned to her mother. "What's wrong?" she asked, banging her spoon into her porringer. "Why are we sitting here on this smelly old boat going nowhere?"

"Elizabeth!" her mother admonished.

"Well, it is a smelly boat, and we aren't going anywhere. I wouldn't care if we were on our way." Elizabeth was surprised to hear herself talking back to her mother, and was sure she was in for a scolding.

Instead her mother sighed, "I know how you feel, but perhaps the Lord is trying to teach us patience. Now why don't you take care of these dishes?"

Grey clouds hung low over Southampton Water when Elizabeth emerged on deck, dutifully carrying the porringers and spoons. As she went to the wash water barrel, a carriage came clattering through the city gates and onto the dock area. She watched it pull up by the Mayflower and discharge a small wizened man in a blue satin waistcoat and maroon velvet jacket. He was accompanied by Master Carter.

As they passed her on the way to the great cabin, she heard Master Weston saying, "...can't give you any more money until you sign..."

What were they to sign, she wondered. Why was there a problem? They had already made an agreement with their backers promising to work five days a week for them. She lingered on deck, hoping to learn more, until it began to rain, forcing her to take refuge below.

She found her mother and Mistress Hopkins seated on a chest with their knitting. Constance was tossing a ball of yarn back and forth to the children.

"It's an outrage," her mother was saying.

"How can we ever call our souls our own if we have to work for the company every day of the week?" Mistress Hopkins clicked her needles furiously.

"And they won't even let us own our houses. It's no wonder the men won't sign," Elizabeth's mother went on.

So that's it, Elizabeth thought. It sounded outrageous to her too, but at the same time, she wished they would sign and get on with their voyage. It wouldn't matter anyway when they had an ocean between them.

When she said this to her mother in private later, she was gently reprimanded. "When we give our word, we keep it, even if there is an ocean between us. The Bible teaches us how important a vow is. You should know that by now."

But when Elizabeth's mother noticed her listening she sent her off to the Farm Market for salad greens. "We won't get any for many a month, I fear," she said. "We better get our fill of them now."

"Constance, I'd like some, too," Mistress Hopkins said. "Why not take the children? The walk will be good for all of you."

"We'll need our cloaks," Elizabeth said. The heavy wool garment with its hood would protect them from the rain.

They came up on deck at the moment Thomas Weston burst from the door of the great cabin. They watched, open mouthed, as he flounced off the ship, climbed into his waiting carriage and took off with mud splattering from the flying wheels.

"I'm glad we weren't down there just now, " Constance said, but Elizabeth was too concerned about the obvious failure of the talks to reply.

Happily, the rain had turned to a fine mist, and going ashore, they kept busy trying to steer the children around puddles as they picked their way to the gate nearest the market. When they began climbing the steps inside the wall, they met Desire coming down.

"I'm going to bring the rest of Mistress Carver's things to the Inn," she replied in answer to Constance's invitation to join them.

"It doesn't look as though she expects to be sailing soon, if she wants everything ashore," Elizabeth observed to Constance as they entered the town near the half-timbered inn that overhung the narrow street.

Humility and Henry ran ahead and disappeared into the walled market area. Elizabeth could understand why they were anxious to get there. She, too, loved its sights and smells. Early apples, faintly rouged, purple plums, the bright greens of leafy lettuce and shiny peas waiting to be shelled, piles of orange carrots and red radishes, and bunches of fragrant flowers colored the stalls to rival any stained glass window.

When they had caught up with the children and filled their baskets with crisp dripping lettuce, they reluctantly started back to the ship. The color and bustle of the market had made Elizabeth forget their worries for a little while.

As they approached the ship, John Howland, carrying a thick envelope sealed with red wax, almost passed them without speaking.

"Where are you going?" Elizabeth stopped him.

He paused long enough to answer, "To post this letter to the Merchant Adventurers."

"What's it all about, John? Are we ever going to sail?" Elizabeth was desperate to know.

"If the company fails to make a profit in the seven years we had agreed to work for them, we're offering to extend our contract until they do. It's a fair and reasonable offer, but I'm afraid it will cause more delay," John burst out before he rushed off.

She feared John was right, but several days later, when everyone was summoned to a meeting on the Mayflower, Elizabeth jumped to the conclusion that Master Carver would be announcing that they were sailing at last.

Instead he wanted everyone to hear a letter that had arrived from Lyden from Pastor Robinson. *Just what we need, another sermon*, Elizabeth fumed inwardly.

Looking around the deck as Master Carver began reading, Elizabeth realized that everyone was listening intently, except for the Billington boys, those two rascals who almost landed her in the Thames. They were sticking their tongues out at each other. Briefly she wondered if there would be another scuffle, but just then their father jerked the older one to his side. With a twinge of guilt, Elizabeth turned her attention to the letter.

"And first," Master Carver read steadily, "we are daily to renew our repentance with our God...lest He leave us to be swallowed up in danger."

Is he trying to tell us that we aren't sailing because we have unconfessed sin, Elizabeth wondered. "Lord, forgive me my impatience," she prayed silently, and remembering her mother's admonition added, "Help me to realize I must always keep my word."

She determined to listen more closely and heard Master Carver's soothing voice continuing, "Next after this heavenly peace with God and our own consciences, we are to make peace with all men, especially with our associates, that we neither give nor easily take offense."

I hope Master Martin hears that. She looked up to where he was standing just as he stared down at her. She had a great urge to follow the Billington boys' example and stick out her tongue at him, but in time she remembered she wasn't to give offense either.

Oh dear, she had missed part of the letter again.

"....also in yielding to them all due honor and obedience, in spite of the fact they are only ordinary men like the rest of you," Master Carver droned on.

Who are we to give honor and obedience to? she wondered.

".... you are to have governors yourselves shall choose."

Her thoughts raced. We get to choose our own governors? Who ever heard of such a thing? Always governors are appointed by the king or his representatives.

She caught a few more phrases... "daily incessant prayers unto the Lord...guard your ways...by his Spirit," and the letter was finished, but no one moved. Then there was a stir as the impact of the closing sentences seemed to dawn. A little shiver of anticipation ran up Elizabeth's spine. Her thoughts danced. *This is really freedom...to choose our own governor, to make our own rules for our lives! Why maybe we don't have to put up with Master Martin after all!*

The next day Elizabeth waited with the women gathered on the deck under a blue sky while the leaders met in the great cabin to choose a governor for each ship. Twisting the tie of her wide collar, she said to her mother, "I wish we could be in there, too."

"That will never happen. It's against God's law," Goodwife Tilley said. "It's our place to be subject to our husbands. You must guard against a rebellious spirit, my dear."

Was such a thought rebellion, she wondered, giving her tie such a tug that it came undone.

When the men finally emerged from the cabin, she was unprepared for Christopher Martin's announcement that he would continue to be governor of the Mayflower.

Elizabeth wrinkled up her nose. "And John Carver will be in charge of the Speedwell," he concluded.

"I wish we were on the Speedwell," she whispered to her mother. Then she caught the disapproving line of her mother's mouth and choked back any more comment.

But there was good news too. They did plan to sail on the morrow. The Speedwell was provisioned, and all was ready. It was evident they would be getting no more funds from their backers for they had reached an impasse, and it was useless to delay any longer.

That evening, after the children were bedded down, Elizabeth felt the need for a long walk. Was it because it would be her last ever on her native soil of England, or was it to escape the turmoil the conflict with the backers had created among all of them?

She had hoped to get off alone to try to analyze her feelings, but she was joined by Richard followed by Constance and the two Edwards (as she had begun to think of them). They shadowed Constance as Richard shadowed Elizabeth. John Howland also joined them, and as they passed the Speedwell, Desire called from its deck and came tripping down the gangplank to take John's arm.

In the lingering evening light, the young people strolled the shoreline of the wide tidal river past the end of the quay and on along the edge of a field that had already been harvested. Not interested in talking, Elizabeth was distracted by the conversation going on behind her.

"Pastor Robinson says we're to choose our own leader, but they didn't ask us who we wanted," Edward Dotey complained.

"Seems like only the freemen had anything to say," the other Edward took up the complaint.

"The pastor said we were all ordinary men. Nobody's any better than anybody else, even if we are bondsmen. I think we should've had a vote," Dotey said.

The little group had stopped now on a rise overlooking the water, and everyone turned to the two dissatisfied men.

"Maybe we will have a voice someday," John Howland interposed. "But in the meantime we better remember Pastor Robinson's advice about getting along with each other."

"They can get along with us as well as we can get along with them," Dotey snorted.

"Don't you think my father will treat you right?" Constance turned on him.

"He'll treat us well enough. We heard what happened when he was shipwrecked in Bermuda," Edward Leister said.

"What do you mean?" Constance was as puzzled as Elizabeth. "I only know that he was very blessed to be alive."

"What happened?" Elizabeth was giving them her full attention now.

"A whole fleet started out to found a new colony in Virginia. My father's ship was one of the few that wasn't lost in a terrible storm."

Elizabeth found a storm hard to imagine on such a lovely evening.

"You never heard about the mutiny?" Dotey said.

"Never mind," Edward Leister broke in, apparently concerned for Constance's feelings.

"You've got to tell us now," Richard insisted.

"Yes, I want to know what you're talking about. I'm sure my father had nothing to do with it," Constance said.

"Maybe he did, maybe he didn't, but somebody declared that, after the wreck, they were free from the rule of any man. I kind of like that idea," Dotey laughed.

"We're taking law and order with us," John said. "If we don't we'll have anarchy."

"Law and order, sure, but someday we'll have paid for our passage and be freemen with as much right to vote as anyone else, why not now? We're risking our lives too," Leister said, bending to pick up a stone that he hurled toward the water. Plopping into the quiet bay, it spread widening circles from the spot where it hit.

Desire broke in, "Can't we just have a nice pleasant walk on our last evening here?"

Elizabeth was deeply disturbed by what she was hearing, but she agreed with Desire. She had started out to be alone for a little while, and had ended up with this.

Richard picked up a stone and hurled it far out into the water, challenging the others to surpass him.

With everyone caught up in the contest, Elizabeth slipped away, heading for a nearby copse. If she could reach the thicket before anyone noticed, perhaps she could have a few minutes to herself.

She had scarcely reached the sheltering trees, where the late sun slanted through the slender branches, when Richard was at her elbow, slipping his arm about her waist.

"Elizabeth, will you marry me?" his voice was husky as he turned her face to his.

She pulled away, "I'm not ready to talk about marriage. Please, I need some time alone to think before we sail."

"I'll leave only if you promise to think about marrying me," he insisted.

Since agreeing seemed to be the only way to get rid of him, Elizabeth said she'd consider it. Instead of leaving, he grabbed her again and pulled her tight against him. Bringing his mouth down hard upon hers, he forced her head back, jolting her hat from her head. Elizabeth was struggling vainly to free herself when John Howland's authoritative voice cut the air. "Let go of her!"

Richard whirled around defensively, "She's going to marry me," he said.

"I never said that," Elizabeth declared.

"Get going," John ordered.

Crestfallen, Richard looked at Elizabeth and slunk away.

"When I saw Richard follow you into the woods I thought I'd better check," John's voice softened as he spoke to her.

Elizabeth was shaking now. "I'm glad you did," she said weakly.

"Are you all right?" John came up to her, studying her

closely.

Suddenly her knees gave way, and she swayed toward him.

John caught her and drew her trembling body gently into his arms. As her quivering ceased, she felt something brush across the top of her head, light as a breeze. She could see her own dark locks falling free across her cheeks catching the gold from the slanting rays of the sun. Had John kissed her hair?

"Elizabeth, I..." he began as she drew away and looked up at him.

"John, Elizabeth," Desire's voice cut John off. "Where are you? Everyone's waiting for you."

"Right here," John called back, picking up Elizabeth's hat.

Elizabeth had just settled it on her head, and was tucking her hair back when Desire found them. Coming up, she linked an arm in each of theirs saying, "My dearest friends. I don't want to lose you."

By the time the group made their way back to the ships a cold fog had rolled in obliterating the sunset that Elizabeth had hoped to enjoy. She was anxious for the warmth of her bed, but Desire led her aside. In the darkening mist Desire's face was barely discernible, but there was no mistaking her words, "Elizabeth, in these few days you've become the best friend I've looked for all my life, and now I've found you, I don't think we should keep any secrets from each other, do you?"

Elizabeth felt warm all over at the confidence Desire proposed to place in her, "I've never had a friend to share secrets with before," she replied.

"Do you want to know my greatest secret?" Desire almost whispered.

"Oh, yes!"

"I came with Carvers to become John Howland's wife." Desire reached out for her hand and squeezed it. "Isn't it exciting? Master and Mistress Carver picked me out for him. They have no children, and John is to be their heir. They are hoping we will have the family they never did. Mistress Carver told me that way she could at least feel like a grandmother."

Chapter 5

Finally on their way! Elizabeth jostled to the rail for a last glimpse of England. She had struggled far into the night to accept what Desire had told her, even though in some ways it was no surprise. This morning the fog had lifted and the day was sparkling bright. Who could be upset about anything?

Richard moved to the railing beside her, and turning to him, she exclaimed, "Isn't it exciting to be young, on our way to a young land?"

Richard didn't answer. He was looking past her, and she turned to see John Howland behind her. "Indeed, it is," John replied, smiling at her.

Not entirely ready to face John, she looked back to Richard, but he had wandered off to the other side of the deck.

"It's too bad you had to be separated from your aunt and uncle again," John said.

And you from Desire, Elizabeth thought. She turned now to let the sea breeze blow full in her face. How good it felt! She licked her lips. They tasted of salt already.

As other passengers went below John lingered with her on deck. "I think I could sail forever," she bubbled, her spirits dancing with the diamonds sparkling on the crest of the waves. She lifted her arms, threw back her head and whirled about laughing. "The sails are so white and the sky so blue, and look, John," she pointed to the red, white and blue flag flying from the highest mast. "Isn't it beautiful?"

"No question about it," John said. "Absolutely beautiful!"

Elizabeth, who had been looking up, glanced back at John, and for a second had the feeling he had been looking at her rather than the flag.

"But it is the flag of King James," he pointed out quickly. "He put the blue cross of Scotland over the red cross of England."

"It doesn't matter. That's all behind us now." It seemed nothing could dampen her spirits this morning. "Do you suppose someday the New World will have a flag of its own? I hope they use red, white and blue."

She fell silent for a moment, but then laughed again saying, "I'm so glad to be alive."

"You don't have any reservations about going, do you?" he asked.

"Yes, I do," Elizabeth spoke in measured tones, "But I made up my mind to turn them over to God, and enjoy each moment as much as I can."

As John's eyes met hers, Elizabeth excused herself to help her mother with the housekeeping chores. She must not let herself get too close ever again to this man who was to marry someone else.

By early afternoon Elizabeth was back on deck. The ship's master invited her up to the poop, and she watched as two seamen struggled up the rope ladder with a roll of canvas between them.

"What are they doing?" she asked.

"We have three sets of sails," he explained. "It depends on how strong the wind is, how heavy a canvas we need. The freshening afternoon breezes require a heavier sail than the lighter morning air."

Just then she found herself staggering across the deck.

Master Jones laughed at her, "You're finding out about the English channel. Hang on! She bucks out here."

Indeed the ship was jumping up and down like a young horse. Elizabeth clung to the railing and looked back just in time to see the little Speedwell, tilting precipitously, plunge down a wave. The sail almost touched the water and half of its dark bottom turned up.

Her own stomach seemed to flip with the ship, and an involuntary scream escaped her lips. Master Jones wheeled around to look at her. "The Speedwell," she gasped. "It almost went over."

As the master was studying their predicament, a small flag was run up the foremast. "They're in trouble," he exclaimed, and quickly gave orders for an answering signal to be raised.

"We'll have to find a port fast," he said firing off orders for the crew to change course.

"They're sinking!" Elizabeth voiced her fear. The boat was lower in the water than it had been.

"They'll make it," Master Jones tried to reassure her.

Elizabeth's every muscle strained with the little ship laboring along behind them.

Watching apprehensively as they took off one of the Speedwell's sails, her fingers groped for the strings of her cap. By the time the Mayflower shortened her sails, too, the strings were twisted into a tight spiral. When the master ordered the jolly boat to be unlashed and fitted with oars, she knew he was making ready to pick up the Speedwell's people.

As the sun sunk lower over the Western Sea, it seemed to Elizabeth that the Mayflower was heading straight into a wall of solid rock. Suddenly a dark shadow became a crack in the cliffs that grew wider with each tack. That must be the mouth of a river. If only the disabled vessel could hang on a little longer! She looked back. It was still wallowing along behind them.

At last they were riding the tide into a narrow inlet guarded on either side by two round forts. Her aunt and uncle and Desire were safe! Elizabeth suddenly became aware that her shoulder muscles were tight as dulcimer strings. She inhaled deeply, pushed her shoulders back and felt them relax.

The wind seemed to die away as they rode the rising tide between high bluffs that squeezed the Dart River.

As they approached the village clinging to the steep hillside, Elizabeth felt the dejection of the colonists gathering at the rail. In the dusk lamplight shown invitingly from windows stacked up the hillside.

When she sought out her family, Elizabeth's mother said wistfully, "Do you suppose we could find lodging in town while the Speedwell's being repaired?"

Elizabeth had to agree that it would be good to sleep in a real bed again after the weeks they had already spent on the

Mayflower.

Mistress Hopkins, Constance's mother, who seemed to grow larger ever day with her child, seized on the idea. "It would be so good to have solid ground under us again."

At the same time Edward Dotey began to grumble that they were never going to make this crossing anyhow and maybe he would just go back to London.

At that point Master Martin, who must have overheard called for attention. "No one is going ashore here," he announced. "It won't take long to repair the Speedwell, and we'll have no white-livered deserters."

A sigh passed over the assembled company, but for once Elizabeth found herself in agreement with Master Martin's orders, if not his way of delivering them. She didn't want to see their plantation end here, because half the party pulled out. She would try to contain herself on the Mayflower while the repairs were made.

When Elizabeth came on deck the next morning with Henry and Humility she was appalled to find a gawking crowd gathered on the narrow stone quay. She had come up to escape her mother's complaints to her father about the crowded conditions on the ship, and her fears that they would exhaust their supplies before they ever left England.

Just then the two Billington boys came tumbling onto the deck followed by John Howland's charges, whom the Carver's had left with him on the larger ship. Young John Billington promptly stuck his tongue out at the spectators while his brother pushed his thumbs in his ears, wagging his fingers at them. One of John Howland's boys immediately did the same thing.

"Jasper," Elizabeth admonished, "That's no way for a good Christian to act. We're supposed to love each other."

"That's a nice idea," Richard Gardiner spoke up. She had realized that he had followed her onto the deck again. "But I don't see many good Christians around here. I might feel more like being one if I did."

Elizabeth spun toward him, "You mean you don't consider yourself a Christian?" she asked.

His face flushed under her scrutiny. "I suppose I'm a Christian. I was baptized, but never confirmed. My mother used to take me to church, but it was a lot of hocus-pocus going on behind the screen as far as I was concerned."

"But you don't have to depend on understanding a priest to be a Christian. You can read the Bible for yourself, and — Oh! If you don't write, you don't read," it suddenly dawned on her.

"Maybe you could teach me," Richard suggested. "Do you think I could learn before we get to Virginia?"

"It looks like we're going to have lots of time. I'll be willing to try. Jasper, would you like to learn too? And how about the rest of you?" She looked at his two brothers and his sister. They all agreed, but when she turned back to Richard, he had walked away.

I suppose he doesn't want to study with children, she thought, *but after the way he's been acting when we are alone, I don't want to spend time exclusively with him.*

Bringing out her paddle book, and introducing the children to the ABC's and the Lord's prayer helped the trying days pass more quickly. Richard sometimes seemed to be listening, but he would never join in the recitation. John Howland was always nearby encouraging the children.

At the end of a fortnight Master Martin announced that they believed the Speedwell was seaworthy as last, and they would sail with the tide.

Glancing about at the now familiar faces gathered on the deck again for departure, Elizabeth heard one of the men mutter, "We'll never make it." Was that how Dorothy Bradford felt? Was that why, when she waved to her and Desire across the water, she never waved back? Dorothy was usually alone by the railing, and when Desire went to her side, Dorothy would move away.

When the ship reached the open sea once more, favorable winds bore them swiftly past Land's End and out into the Atlantic. *Free of England at last!* Elizabeth told herself.

She hung on the rail by the hour often watching the Speedwell as the ships raced westward. She couldn't help feeling uneasy about the smaller vessel. It seemed to ride lower in the water each time she looked back. Could it make the long voyage safely? She had heard Master Jones comment that sometimes ships disappeared out here, and offered a prayer for those on board.

Her fears were realized when, shortly after Master Jones announced that they were one hundred leagues into the Western Sea, the distress signal went up again on the Speedwell. It would have to turn back, but would the Mayflower? Her father and Stephen Hopkins had been arguing last night about this very thing. Master Hopkins felt the Mayflower should go on regardless, and her father insisted that they would have to return, if only because all the Separatist leaders were on the other ship.

As the word spread of the Speedwell's plight many of the passengers gathered on the deck while several of the men met with Master Martin in the great cabin. Master Martin soon appeared on the poop deck and called for attention. "The Speedwell is leaking badly and we're turning back to Plymouth," he announced.

Murmurs of disapproval greeted his message, and Elizabeth was wondering why they were going back to Plymouth instead of to a closer port, when suddenly the murmuring ceased. She looked up to see a dignified man, in a brown serge coat over lincoln green drawers, standing beside Master Martin. With a rush of relief she recognized the kindly features and the grey streaked beard of Elder Brewster, who had attended their house church several times before being forced into hiding.

How good it was to see this godly man at this crucial hour! She hadn't known whether he had been safely smuggled aboard or not.

"We can't abandon our brethren on the Speedwell," he said in his characteristically gentle manner. "We know we'll be welcome and receive any help they can give us in Plymouth, because the town is ruled by Puritans who are sympathetic to our cause."

And Elder Brewster should be safe there from the king's soldiers, Elizabeth realized.

"Let us pray for a safe return to England for them, and a speedy new beginning for all of us." The elder was in control.

As he took off his hat and bowed his head everyone followed his example, though later in the day Elizabeth heard Edward Dotey complaining.

It wasn't until they were sailing into the wide Plymouth Sound, bounded by bracken-covered bluffs on either side, that

Elizabeth breathed easily again. When she spotted the two forts that flanked the entrance to the harbor on the right of the headland, she whispered a prayer of thanksgiving that those on the Speedwell had been delivered from the sea.

When they dropped anchor in the cove beside the village of Plymouth, Master Martin again announced that no one could leave the ship.

Suddenly, Elizabeth felt as though she could stand these cramped quarters no longer. She had hoped that this time they could stretch their legs on shore, and she might find some time to be by herself. It was one thing to be on a ship bounding across the waves, and another to be sitting here going nowhere. Plymouth, snuggling behind the escarpment that sheltered it from the sound, was an inviting village. If the townspeople were as sympathetic as Elder Brewster had said, why shouldn't they be allowed ashore?

When she expressed her feelings to her father, he had comforting words for her, "Perhaps we can debark after Master Carver and Elder Brewster consult with the town leaders."

Later in the day, as Elizabeth paced the deck, a small boat rowed up. Soon the word was spread that they would be welcome in the town.

Desire, who was already on the dock when Elizabeth stepped ashore, ran up to her. "I don't ever want to get back on that boat. It was awful. I was sure we were all going to drown," she gasped.

Then Desire turned to John Howland who had just come across the gangplank. "John, I can't go on if I have to sail on the Speedwell!"

"Why not ask the Carvers if you can move to the Mayflower?" he suggested. "You must come with us. I know Mistress Carver is counting on you."

And so are you, Elizabeth thought to herself.

"I can't ask that when the Carvers are still on the Speedwell," Desire looked stricken. "John, couldn't you say you'd like for me to be on the Mayflower, so..." she paused groping for words, "so we could get to know each other better." She tilted her head and looked up at him from under arched brows.

Did John's color change or did Elizabeth imagine it? She

watched him closely for his answer. He studied the top of his bedroll briefly and then looking directly at Desire, said, "I don't think it's my place to ask."

She caught a hurt look in Desire's eyes as she turned back to her. "Maybe you could ask the Carver's if I could come with you, since we're best friends," Desire pleaded.

Elizabeth swallowed hard. John was right. Desire should talk to the Carvers herself, but Elizabeth heard herself saying, "I suppose I could." She understood how Desire felt after watching the Speedwell fight the sea.

"Good, let's find them," Desire exclaimed.

"I want to talk it over with my parents first," Elizabeth put her off. She knew how limited space and supplies already were on the Mayflower.

As she was looking for her parents, a man in a red robe, accompanied by Master Carver and several others in official dress, paraded down the cobblestone street.

"Mayor Thomas Townes has come to greet us. Some of the townspeople have graciously offered to take the women into their homes, and the men may stay in the town hall," Master Carver announced.

It wasn't until after she and her mother were shown to a tiny room overhanging a narrow street that she had a chance to discuss Desire's request. "Do you think there is room for her?" Elizabeth concluded.

"It might be better if we offered to change places with the Carvers," her mother suggested. "Then we could be with Uncle Edward and Aunt Ann, and no one would be more crowded than we already are."

Elizabeth, remembering the Speedwell almost capsizing, wasn't sure she wanted to cross the Atlantic in it either, but she hated to admit it.

"I'm sure they won't let the Speedwell leave until they have figured out what's wrong." Her mother seemed to read her thoughts.

"It would be good to be with the rest of the family," she agreed.

"I think the Carvers might like to have Desire on the same vessel as John Howland. Mistress Carver told me she hopes John and Desire will be attracted to each other," Goodwife Tilley confided.

Everyone has heard about John and Desire. It's not much of a secret, Elizabeth thought to herself. What did it matter anyway? She should be glad for her friends.

As soon as possible Elizabeth escaped from the walled town to climb the steep hill that overlooked the sound. Her hostess had told her that the level grassy area on top was the Hoe from which Sir Francis Drake had seen the Spanish Armada approaching.

When she reached it and looked south over a mist-shrouded sound, she could almost see the cumbersome galleons and Drake's faster ships sallying forth to meet them. She took heart as she realized that it was into this same sound that he sailed on his return from his voyage around the world. If he could make it across two oceans, surely they, with God's help, could make it across one.

Descending the hill by the fort, and looking across the cove that sheltered the Mayflower and Speedwell, her eyes were drawn to a distant white cliff that seemed to float like a cloud against the dark hills. As the days dragged on she came to think of that white cliff as a symbol of hope, a farflung banner raised for her encouragement. The dear Lord knew she needed it.

Her mother worried continually over the delay, and even her usually cheerful father had a long face. Their proposal to trade places with the Carvers was accepted, and she tried to hide her concern about sailing on the Speedwell. Moreover, no cause for the opening of the seams could be found, and at last the fateful day came when her father broke the news that the Speedwell would have to be left behind.

We're committed to the Speedwell! Does that mean we'll be left behind with it? Has the Lord brought us this far to leave us here? Questions raced through her mind.

"We'll be doubling up on the Mayflower." Her father continued pacing about the small living-dining room of their host's home. "But not everyone will be able to go," he added.

"We'll be going!" Her voice sounded high pitched to her.

He paused by the tiny leaded window and said slowly, "I haven't decided.

"There's surely room for us. You were one of the first to sign up. They couldn't leave us behind. You'll insist on a place for us." She realized she was talking faster than usual, but she couldn't help it. She had to persuade her father that they must continue.

"Master Carver wants to know tomorrow morning so they can begin loading what they can from the Speedwell onto the Mayflower. The personal goods will have to be sorted in the process," he said.

"That means we'll be even more cramped than we have been," her mother said, two lines forming between her brows.

"I'm afraid it won't be a pleasant trip," Goodman Tilley agreed.

"But it's only for a few weeks, certainly not much longer than we've already been on the ship. We can manage," Elizabeth argued.

Her mother looked at her with her lips set in a thin line and eyebrows raised. Elizabeth decided it was time to leave. The first time they had all agreed to go, but now he must decide between her wishes and her mother's.

"Be back in time for supper," her mother called after her as she started down the steps.

Outside in the shop-lined street she wound her way down to the Barbican hoping to find a friend to talk to. How was she going to persuade her parents to continue when they wouldn't listen to her?

The first person she met was Richard who was stroking the velvet muzzle of a pony waiting with his loaded cart outside a cheese shop.

"Richard, have you heard the news?" she asked, running up to him.

Stroking the docile animal's soft nose once more, he turned to her, "What news?" he asked.

Her words spilled forth like a torrent as she shared her fears. "I want to go to the New World so badly. I feel God is going to do great things over there, and I want to be part of it," she ended.

"Your father will go," Richard tried to reassure her.

"I hope you're right," Elizabeth said. "What will you do?"

"I'm going." Richard sounded positive.

Just then John Howland came out of an alley close by. When he saw them he came over. "I suppose you've heard that the Speedwell isn't going," he said. "I'm on my way to begin loading John Carver's things onto the Mayflower."

"Then you will be going," Elizabeth said, and shared her fears about her father's decision and her own wishes. It dawned on her that if they didn't go she would never see John Howland again. She felt as if a rock had been dropped on her chest. John had become such a good friend in the month she had known him. How sad it would be to lose him....and Desire, she added to herself.

"You're really counting on being a part of the plantation, aren't you?" John reinforced her thinking.

"Oh yes," she said looking at him, half expecting a plan.

"There'll be a way." She felt he spoke with a forced confidence.

As he made a move to go, Elizabeth suggested to Richard that he might help John. She was afraid he would want to spend the rest of the afternoon with her. She needed time to think and pray.

When they had gone Elizabeth cut through the alley from which John had come and made her way alongside the castle whose ramparts formed part of the city wall. When she came to a gate, she left the town, and circling around the moat, climbed between the castle and the fort to the park-like Hoe. Several young noblemen were bowling on the green much as Sir Francis Drake was reported to have been doing when the news of the Armada came. One of the young men raised his eyebrows as if to say, what are you doing here?

She felt like telling him that in God's eyes she had as much right there as he did. Instead, she hurried across the lawn and found a path cutting down through the bracken on the far side of the hill. Part way down to the water she stopped and looked around. Below her lay another harbor narrower than the cove on the other side where the Mayflower was berthed. Beyond that another hill blocked her view, but her mind soared on to the great ocean that she had already experienced. How could she go back to London's filthy crowded streets after such freedom? And those vain men up on the green thinking they were better than she, how could she live around the likes of them? She had been counting on a country where they would be choosing their own leaders.

To her right a narrow path wound off along the side of the bank. Following it into the growth of chest high ferns, at a distance from the main path, she fell to her knees. She prayed with an earnestness that she had never felt before. Recognizing, even as she prayed, that her prayer might be selfish, she ended by asking that God's will be done.

As·she got up from her knees, God's words to Abraham came to her. "Get thee out of thy country, and from thy father's house, unto a land that I will show you." Did the Lord mean for her to go even if her father and mother didn't? Would it be possible for a lone woman?

Her step was firmer as she threaded her way back to the main path. She had just begun her climb to the Hoe when she saw Richard starting down. At first she had an urge to run, fearing what he might do now that they were alone, but then she remembered that he wanted to marry her. Surely he wouldn't do anything to hurt her.

I've never given him an answer, she suddenly realized. *Can I marry Richard?* For the first time she began to consider his offer seriously. *If I'm betrothed, won't my parents have to let me go to be with my intended husband?*

Standing very still, she studied the young man coming toward her. *How does he feel about me,* she wondered. Does *he want me for myself, or only as someone to work for him?* John Howland's strong face flashed before her. How good it would be to work beside him. Scolding herself for such a thought, she thrust his face from her mind. *Desire is the one who will be working beside John Howland, and....sharing his bed.*

Sharing a bed! She felt half nauseated. *Could I sleep with Richard?* She was thinking of John Howland again, and became angry with herself. *To marry anyone is to share a bed. Obviously, I can't share John's bed. Perhaps Richard is the answer to my prayer. If only he loved me.....*

She tried to smile as he came closer, but said nothing, waiting for him to speak.

"Elizabeth," he burst out, "You've got to marry me. I can't imagine going on to the New World without you. I think of you all the time. I love you so much. You will marry me, won't you?"

If her parents backed out she could go as Richard's intended wife. Perhaps either way, she would marry him....someday. After all he said he loved her, what more could she ask? "I'll give you my answer in the morning," she said, and brushing past him, led the way up the hill. He let her go without making a move to touch her.

The next morning, when tight-lipped, silent men and women gathered in the main hall of the municipal building, it felt to Elizabeth as if a thunderstorm were brewing. Like lightning discharging, before John Howland could begin reading the list he was holding, one man cracked the silence. "I'm not going," he said.

In rapid fire order about a dozen others declared their intentions of staying in England. None were Elizabeth's friends. As John finally got to call off the names she found that the Hopkins, the Brewsters, the Carvers were all going.

"Edward Tilley?" John Howland queried.

"We want to continue if there will be room for us on the Mayflower," Uncle Edward answered.

"We will to do our very best to make room for all who want to go," John Carver assured him.

Elizabeth's hopes rose. If her uncle was going, and they would make room for everyone, surely her father would go too.

Then John Tilley spoke up, "He can have our place. Our family is dropping out."

Chapter 6

At her father's words Elizabeth felt as though a trap door had opened under her. She was shaking as hard as if she had actually dropped through. Before her head cleared Richard was at her side whispering in her ear, "You will marry me, won't you?"

She nodded her head numbly and stared at the worn floor boards, surprised they were still under her feet. The taste of blood was on her tongue. Only then she realized she had bitten her lip.

When the polling was over about twenty had resigned besides the Tilleys.

Richard turned immediately to Elizabeth's father. "I'd like to marry your daughter," he said, "And she has agreed. I want to take her with me."

"Marry my daughter?" John Tilley was taken aback, and had no ready answer, but her mother did.

"Oh, Elizabeth, I think Richard is a fine young man. I almost expected this. But how can we let her go without us?" her eyes turned pleadingly to her husband.

"She can't go," John Tilley made a quick decision that was very unlike him.

Elizabeth wasn't about to give up yet. "Father, I'm a grown woman. I'm old enough to marry. Richard will take care of me, and make me a good husband, I know he will."

John Howland, who was close by, spoke up, "Elizabeth will

be well cared for. The Carvers and I will see to that."

At that point John Carver joined the group, "John Tilley," he said, "I'm very disappointed that you aren't continuing. I never thought you would back out on us. We need mature men like you to set an example for our many young people. Remember that Jesus says anyone setting his hand to the plow and looking back isn't worthy of the Kingdom of Heaven."

Uncle Edward, who also crowded around spoke up as well, "John, I had counted on being reunited after all these years of separation. If you don't go, I may never see you again in this life."

Elizabeth's father, shaking his head in bewilderment, looked slowly from one to the other in the group. Finally, he addressed his wife. "My dear, I was leaving for yours and Elizabeth's sakes. I couldn't get a clear word from the Lord, but I felt it must be His will for us to stay in England or He wouldn't have given us this last chance. We could pick up our life in London more easily than some of the others."

Then he turned to Elizabeth, "If you have really decided to marry Richard Gardiner then you shan't be separated, but we won't let you go without us. You and Richard can't marry until we get settled. He must build you a cottage of your own. You're both young and, if you love each other, you can wait."

The cold fluttery feeling that Elizabeth had inside gave way to a surge of warmth. They were all going! As she looked around, the faces were wreathed in smiles reflecting her own.

All but one. Desire had slipped up and taken John Howland's arm, and she wasn't smiling. Suddenly Elizabeth's smile vanished too. What had she done? She had given her word to become Richard's wife, and a pledge made must be kept.

When Elizabeth and her mother went down to the ship that afternoon to rearrange their things, her father and uncle were just coming from the Mayflower. Leaving Uncle Edward, her father came over to them with a complaint. "Edward has a cloth screw that I'm trying to discourage him from taking." He addressed his wife. "It's big and unwieldy. Surely he can take his packets of cloth without it. Speak to Anne, and see if she can dissuade him."

"John Tilley, you know very well that if he's going to keep that cloth half decent it has to be under that screw. If it should get wet or unfolded, wouldn't that be a mess?" she said.

Shrugging his shoulders, he followed his brother to the warehouse, and Elizabeth and her mother stepped out of the way as the two men went past lugging a trunk between them. Soon her father and her uncle emerged and struggled across the pier under the weight of the great iron screw mounted in rough hewn beams. Richard was following, loaded down with piles of accordion folded cloth. Just as the two men started up the gangplank, John Tilley tripped and the screw teetered between them. *They're going to lose it*, was flashing through Elizabeth's mind. Suddenly John Howland was there helping to steady it and giving her father a hand. *Now it's my father he's rescuing*, she laughed to herself as they carried aboard the device that looked like an instrument of torture.

Next the two Edwards came staggering by, weighted down with a big wooden box.

"What's in that?" Christopher Martin called from his self-assigned post at the top of the gangplank. "We can't take just anything you happen to feel like dragging along."

"I don't know," Edward Dotey growled back. "We're just hauling what they tell us to."

"Be glad to drop it in the drink," Edward Leister added.

"I hope they find out what it is first," Goodwife Tilley mumbled.

Elizabeth, encouraged by her mother's comment, stepped forward and spoke up, "Don't do that. I'm sure its something we'll need or they wouldn't have given it to you."

"How dare you interfere in men's business," Christopher Martin stomped down the gangplank glowering at Elizabeth. Turning to the Edwards, he ordered, "Leave that on the wharf, and get on with loading the barrels."

Just then Richard reappeared on his way for another load. Coming onto the quay he spotted the big box and stopped beside it, "That's my shoes," he said, and, seeing Master Martin, asked him to help carry it aboard.

"Shoes!" Martin exploded. "There's no room for shoes. Everybody's brought their own. We'll be carrying no such extra cargo."

"But they represent my life's savings." Richard's usually rosy cheeks paled.

Elizabeth suddenly realized that their hopes of owning a farm might lay in that box. "Our shoes are going to wear out, and nobody's got that many extra pairs. We're going to need them," she argued.

"Well, Goodwife Tilley, I see your daughter's impudent as usual. With the likes of her its no wonder we're having so much trouble." Master Martin lashed out at her mother, then told Richard. "We're leaving them behind."

Richard's smooth face wrinkled and for a second Elizabeth thought he might cry, but he turned away without a sound.

"It's not your decision. The people from Leyden have the final say, and I'm going to ask Master Carver," Elizabeth flared.

She heard her mother gasp and saw Master Martin's face turn scarlet, but she didn't care. She was going to fight for those shoes.

"I'm still governor of the Mayflower, and you'll do as I say," she heard Martin scold, but she was on her way to the warehouse door to look for Master Carver

She found him checking barrels in the dim recesses of the long building, and spilled out her story, "It's Richard's property, but we're all going to need them," she concluded, her tone almost pleading now.

John Carver rubbed his forehead as Master Martin appeared in the doorway. "If there is room we'll take them," he promised Elizabeth. "We'll have to see."

"We'll do no such thing, and furthermore I demand an apology from this upstart girl for her sassiness," Martin bawled across the long building.

Now that Elizabeth had accomplished her purpose and felt sure Master Carver would do everything possible to take Richard's merchandise, she was suddenly contrite about the fuss she was causing. Swallowing an angry lump in her throat, she made her way to Master Martin and curtsied. "I'm sorry sir," she said in her most respectful voice and curbed the urge to add the "buts" that tingled on her tongue.

Her father, John Howland, and Richard were crowding now around the warehouse door, and her father motioned for her to come out. She read the appreciation in Richard's eyes, and detected a twinkle in John's as she joined them.

"You and your mother had better go back to the room," her

father said reproachfully. "You can wait until we finish loading the Speedwell's cargo to sort our things out."

Her mother took her arm and Elizabeth went dutifully up the street with her. When the men were out of earshot, Elizabeth drew a deep breath and let it out in a disgusted snort.

"That man makes me so mad," she burst out, "I could kick him."

"Elizabeth, for shame," her mother said sharply. "What kind of an attitude is that for a Christian woman to have? I thought we had taught you to respect your elders. Master Martin was right. You never should have interfered in the first place."

When Elizabeth pointed out to her mother why the shoes were so important, she replied, "You should have let Richard and your father handle it."

Still disagreeing with her mother, but unwilling to disturb her further, Elizabeth fell silent as they picked their way up the cobblestone street.

That evening her father brought the news that the shoes had been stowed in the hold of the Mayflower.

When Elizabeth and her mother went back the next day, she was shocked to find her parents bedstead abandoned by the warehouse. Was their comfort the cost of the shoes, she wondered. But when they boarded the Mayflower she understood. The shallop had been dismantled, and boards were loaded into their common quarters. They were stacked as well as possible, but along with the baggage of the seventeen Leydeners, and the barrels of supplies coming from the Speedwell, there was scarcely room to move.

Soon she was caught up in the decisions her mother was making. They, too, were allotted one less box. Her mother dug through the housewares. "Most of these will have to be sold off," she said. "We don't need extra pewter." Elizabeth knew how pleased her mother had been when they had been able to buy three more platters and eventually add porringers and mugs for guests!

"We don't need this trencher or rolling pin. We'll be able to make those things over there, if wood is as plentiful as they say." The rolling pin had belonged to her grandmother. The sacrifice her mother was making hit Elizabeth again.

As Elizabeth watched in dismay all of their iron cookware but one pot and a skillet was discarded. Surprised by her sudden practicality, she realized she could have used them when she and Richard set up housekeeping.

As if reading her mind her mother said, "By the time you and Richard marry we should be able to have what you need brought over to us."

How long would that be, Elizabeth wondered, in some ways encouraged that she might not have to keep here promise to Richard for a long time.

"But we have to have the pot hook, the fire shovel and tongs," her mother was saying. "I think I can get them in."

When the packing was done Elizabeth was relieved that at least they had been able to keep their few extra pieces of clothing.

That evening the colonists gathered with their host families in the old stone church on the top of the hill for a farewell service. Elizabeth's eyes filled with tears as she stood between her mother and father listening to the mayor extending the community's good wishes to them, and Master Carver in turn thanking the community for its kindness. How good it was to sail with their prayers following them. How different from the other places where they left almost unnoticed.

After the service Elizabeth was strolling with her parents down to the Mayflower where they were to spend the night in readiness for pre-dawn sailing, when Desire slipped up beside her and took her arm.

"I haven't had a chance to talk to you for a couple of days," she said drawing her away from her family. "I have news."

Elizabeth shivered in the early twilight. A sense of foreboding came over her as she became acutely aware that the shorter days of September were upon them. She didn't want to hear what she expected Desire to say, but resigned to the inevitable, gave her an inquiring look.

"John has asked me to marry him," Desire confided. "I met him the other morning on the dock when I was trying to decide if I should go. He told me he wanted me to, and then asked me to be his wife. I wanted you to be the first to know."

Elizabeth groped for words and said slowly, "I'm so glad for you." It was an honest comment. She was glad for Desire, even if not for herself. What a foolish thought! *It's got nothing to do with me,* she told herself. *I'm supposed to marry Richard Gardiner.* But there were no bubbles of joy inside, only a dull empty feeling as she approached the ship rising black in the gathering night.

The sky above the ghostly white cliff across the harbor was streaked with peach and gold as the Mayflower cast off from the Plymouth dock at dawn the next day. In spite of the early hour most of the passengers were on deck, and many of the towns-people had come to wave farewell and wish them Godspeed as the stretch of dark water between them widened.

Elizabeth found herself almost as excited this morning as she had been when they sailed from London. Many of the same emotions coursed through her; excitement that they would make the crossing at last, fear of the vast Western Sea, tempered by the Mayflower having already been tested on the open ocean. She thanked God for both the ship and its master.

For a few days a favorable wind drove them westward. On one of these bright days Elizabeth stood on the deck with several of the children and turned about in amazement follow-ing the great circle of the horizon. "Look," she exclaimed, "We're in the very middle of an upside down bowl. The only thing in it. How could God not see us out here?"

The children laughed as they all gazed into the deep blue sky above them. But now Elizabeth was staring into the blue-black water trying to fathom its depths when her attention was drawn to a fountain rising a short distance from the ship. A great black hump rolled past.

"Oh, it's a whale," she exclaimed.

All the children rushed to the railing and the two Billington boys, whom she hadn't realized had joined them, shoved their way to the front, climbing onto the belaying bar and teetering dangerously over the sea.

A woman screamed behind them, and Elizabeth grabbed each boy by the seat of the pants before they toppled overboard.

"Wait until your father gets ahold of you," their mother scolded as she dragged them below deck shaking them as they went.

Elizabeth smiled to herself. *Wherever the Billington boys are there seems to be trouble,* she thought.

Suddenly a stream of profanity was spewed on Elizabeth and the children from the top of the forecastle where several sailors were loafing. Elizabeth clapped her hands over Humility's ears and hustled the children to the other end of the deck. Raucous laughter followed them, and the cursing began again just as Capt. Standish and William Bradford came topside.

"That's enough of that," Capt. Standish barked up at them.

"You going to make us stop, Capt. Shrimp?" Elizabeth recognized the sailor who had promised to feed her to the fish.

"If you have no respect for women and children, what about God?" William Bradford challenged. "Some day you'll have to answer at the judgment seat for your words."

There was a second of silence, and then the same fellow answered with blasphemy and spat down at Bradford.

The captain appeared on the poop deck and shouted an order that temporarily quieted the rowdy sailors as they scrambled to obey him.

While the sailors caused Elizabeth and many others grief with their offensive language, at least Master Martin was no longer troubling her. As the ship bounced jauntily along with a jumping motion that hadn't improved much over the English channel, seasickness struck many, including him. He had already been subdued by Master Carver's arrival on shipboard, and he hadn't appeared since they had gotten well under way.

With strong winds keeping the ocean choppy day after day, more and more became ill. All Elizabeth's family had taken to their bunks as well as Richard and Desire. John and Elizabeth were kept busy tending the sick, but she found it hard to identify with them when she felt such exhilaration each time she went on deck. John was always on hand to help her carry the slop buckets to the railing. The sea air smelled so fresh, and the wild breezes, hurrying them westward, felt so clean whipping her hair freely about her face. She sometimes felt guilty at how often she and John found things to laugh about when they escaped from the sick below.

"Better hold on to my hat," John said more than once as the wind hit them. "Need it to hold my brains in."

"At any rate they'll work better if they're warm," she would tease.

Now that so many were down, the sailor that had baited

Elizabeth called down the hatchway every time he passed that he would soon be feeding them to the fish and making merry with their belongings. Elizabeth was holding Desire's head as she was throwing up when he jeered at them again.

"He's right," Desire gasped as she retched, "I'm ready to be fed to the fish. I don't care if I live or not."

Elizabeth laughed at her, "You'll be all right. Nobody's going to make fish food of you." Then she sobered realizing how demoralizing his comments were to the sick souls clinging to their bunks in the 'tween deck that was becoming rank with vomit on top of the foul odors beginning to rise from the bilge.

Suddenly Elizabeth couldn't wait to escape to the deck again, and almost before she knew what was happening she was sick too. So sick, she thought she would die. In fact death looked very inviting. To be with Jesus, what a welcome escape from this foul place!

Far above the sailor laughed cruelly and jibbed, "Hunt up the burial sacks. We'll need 'em right soon."

She heard John Howland begin to remonstrate with him, "You should be ashamed of yourself, making fun of...." his words broke off.

Elizabeth felt herself falling. When she managed to open her eyes, she saw John kneeling beside her with a worried look on his face. "Elizabeth, what happened?"

"I'm so sick," she moaned as she reached for a bucket. When the retching stopped, she felt herself being lifted from the decking and placed gently on a pallet. Soon there was a cold cloth on her head. She heard Desire calling plaintively, "John, John, help me." But the firm hand continued to hold the soothing cloth in place.

By the next morning Elizabeth was well again. When she and John took their biscuit and cheese on deck to eat away from the continuing stench, Master Jones joined them.

"Master Heale is attending one of the seamen who became violently ill last night," he said looking with concern toward the forecastle cabin where off duty seamen ate and slept.

Elizabeth was aware that Master Giles Heale was the ship's surgeon, though Deacon Fuller who had come with the Leydeners was tending the colonists when he was able to be about.

"Who is it?" Elizabeth asked realizing ruefully that she could scarcely tell one crew member from another.

"One you might well want out of commission permanently," Master Jones answered. "The fellow who's been harassing your sick. It almost looks like the hand of God on him."

"That fellow," John snorted. "He'll be fine. I've never seen a more able bodied young man. Besides the Devil himself wouldn't want him."

It was with a great sense of awe, a few days later, that Elizabeth witnessed the committal to the sea of the "able bodied young man" in the canvas sack he was hunting up for her. Elder Brewster, who conducted the service, was too kind to say it, but she heard more than one passenger quoting, "Vengeance is mine. I will repay, saith the Lord." She felt sure that none of the crew would mock them again when they were ill.

Briefly everyone seemed to improve. Then, with land so interminably far away that Elizabeth began to wonder if it really existed, a storm swirled down upon them, launching a violent attack on their tiny floating world. The waves roared and slashed at the hull as Elizabeth imaged a forest full of lions about to devour them. The wind in the rigging screamed like an alley overflowing with tomcats. The ship leaped and plunged from mountain to valley in violent seas.

Elizabeth, like everyone else, tied herself in her bunk when she wasn't staggering about ministering to those too sick to be up at all. John was usually close by to break her falls as they were thrown about, and she seemed to draw strength from his presence.

The captain climbed down the ladder by the helmsman to admonish the terror-stricken passengers to stay where they were. "You'll be swept overboard if you venture onto the deck," he shouted over the raging storm. He tried to reassure them explaining, "We've taken all the sails off and put out the sea anchor. Keeping her headed into the wind. Nothing to fear. The Mayflower is a seaworthy old girl."

Elizabeth heard what he said, but she suspected that few others did for his words must surely have been lost in the banshee shrieking of the wind. She had struggled back to get Desire a drink from a barrel lashed to the mainmast. One of her biggest fears was that the barrels straining against their ropes would break lose and crash into someone in the dimly lit 'tween deck. She already had a bad bruise on her ankle from one of the sand-filled braziers sliding into her. Richard had seen it happen and tried to get up to help, but he collapsed again, and it was John Howland who lashed it to a cargo ring.

As the captain left, the moans of the passengers competed with the wind. Elder Brewster who had lurched forward to greet the captain began to sing. It was a familiar tune from the Ainsworth Psalter based on the forty sixth-Psalm, "God is our refuge and strength ... though the waters roar and be troubled..." Slowly it was taken up and passed from throat to throat, from bunk to bunk until the wind's sounds blended with the music. Elizabeth felt her fluttering heart steady again as she was pitched down the narrow aisle making her way back to Desire.

Desire wasn't singing. She was crying. "We're going to sink," she sobbed.

Elizabeth tried to reassure her by repeating what Master Jones had said.

"Then we'll be like Blackwell's two hundred; fifty left. Oh, I'd rather drown and get it over with."

"Don't say that," Elizabeth ordered, but had to admit that she too had been thinking of Francis Blackwell's party. Every Separatist knew his story. They had set sail in the autumn two years ago, and their ship had been driven off course by a storm, as they were now being driven. Water and beer had run out, the captain and the crew had died, and it had taken the survivors six months to find land.

Was this one of the reasons her father had wanted to back out of the voyage? But many believed that catastrophe was God's judgment upon Blackwell. He had been an elder in one of the Brethren Churches in Amsterdam that had decided to colonize in the New World, but when he went to England to arrange passage he was arrested. At his trial he denied being a Separatist and betrayed another man as well.

"You can be glad we don't have the same baneful blessing on us that he had," Elizabeth said, reminding Desire that the archbishop of Canterbury had blessed that venture, tantamount to a blessing from Satan in any Separatist's eyes.

"Yes, but...Oh, I'm getting wet," Desire interrupted herself with a wail.

That's hardly new, Elizabeth thought. Her own feet had been wet most of the time since the storm began. There was always a certain amount of water splashing in around the tiller and sloshing across the deck until it drained into the bilge. But as the ship tilted on its side again, Elizabeth hanging onto Desire's bunk, felt water pouring down her arms. The smoky taper over Desire's head was extinguished, and in the sudden darkness Elizabeth was sure the ship was turning over.

All around her cries arose from prostrate souls, "God help us! Lord have mercy!"

But as suddenly as the vessel was thrown to her side, she righted again, seemed to shake herself like a drenched dog and labored on.

"John! John!" Desire's scream rose above the storm.

With relief Elizabeth made out his shadowy figure in the doorway. "I'm going up for help. She's leaking all over."

As John was leaving, Desire pulled herself from her bunk and grabbed his arm. "Don't leave me," she cried. "Hold me. We'll drown together."

John turned to Desire just as another wave tossed her against him. She clung to him, circling her arms around his neck. Elizabeth watched his arms go about her and draw her close as he seemed to be whispering in her ear. Desire turned her face to him and her lips searched for his. Just as they met a lurch of the ship threw Elizabeth against them. Quickly she pulled away. On top of the fear churning inside, her stomach suddenly knotted. Once, twice, she had been in John's strong arms. How she longed to feel those arms about her now! That's coveting, she scolded herself. John belongs to Desire.

"I've got to go now," he told her and started for the hatchway.

Desire collapsed again on her bunk, and Elizabeth, following John, suddenly realized that he was going in the wrong direction.

"John, not that way! You'll be washed overboard. Use the ladder."

He paused and considered, "You're right," he said and turned back to the common cabin.

She staggered after him. Someone had to go up there, but why John? Foolish question, she knew that he was one of the strongest men on the ship as well as one of the few on his feet.

Elder Brewster was waiting for him, but over the howling wind and crashing waves, she couldn't make out what he said to John.

"Oh, be careful, be careful," she called as he began climbing. She wasn't sure he heard, but before he stuck his head out he turned briefly and looked back at her. With a wink and a grin he settled his hat firmly on his head. She gave him her best smile before he disappeared above.

Chapter 7

I'm waiting right here for John to return, Elizabeth vowed as he disappeared. "Oh, Lord, take care of him" she was praying over and over.

For the space of a few long-drawn breaths the ship seemed to steady and the wind quieted. Then abruptly Elizabeth was being flung against the steps as the Mayflower was heaved onto its beam-ends.

"John!" Such was her terror that she never knew if the scream escaped her lips or not. She only knew that every sore muscle was attuned to sounds from overhead. Did someone shout "Man overboard?" She had to know, and began scrambling up the ladder.

Elder Brewster caught her on the first step. "Stay here," he commanded. "Pray!"

Clinging to the rungs she began to pray, "God, save John!"

But as the words formed they caught in her throat. She remembered how God had punished the people on Blackwell's ship for his sin. She too had sinned. She had refused to pray with Master Martin when they were sailing, and how many times had she defied him?

Jonah had been thrown overboard to appease the wrath of God that he recognized in the fury of the storm. Was this storm God's judgment on her? Was John paying the price of her sin? It's I who should be thrown into the sea. I'm the sinner, not John, she despaired.

"Oh God, spare him! Take me!" she groaned swaying with the rolling ship and listening intently for sounds above.

Suddenly she found herself sobbing, "Jesus! Jesus!"

The next thing Elizabeth knew two sailors were lowering a soaking wet man with heaving chest and chattering teeth into the 'tween deck. John had been thrown into the sea! By what miracle had he been saved? Or was he?

As he was lowered onto the decking his heaving chest slowed, and his breathing stopped. Oh God, Elizabeth pleaded, don't let him die now. As she watched his breath came again in a long sigh, but great chills convulsed his frame.

Elizabeth, bracing herself against the roll of the ship, grabbed for one of his wrists and began rubbing it. In a minute Deacon Fuller, dropping to his knees by the unconscious man, fell against her as the ship pitched. "I'll take care of him," he shouted just as the howling wind quieted momentarily. "We've got to get these wet clothes off. Elizabeth, toddy," he ordered.

"How can we heat a drink?" Elizabeth asked her mother who, hanging onto a partition, had helped Elizabeth to her feet. No one had had anything hot since the storm began. It was too dangerous even to build the smallest charcoal fire in one of the open sand boxes.

"We can't, but I have some medicinal brandy." Her mother lurched into their own cubicle to get it. Elizabeth braced a pewter mug against their door frame. Her mother uncorked the bottle and put the neck into the mug before she sloshed out a few swallows of the precious liquid.

When Elizabeth staggered back with it, she found John had been lifted into the Carver's bunk and buried under quilts. His eyes were open, but between his own shivering, and the plunging of the ship, he got very little when the deacon tried to lift the mug to his lips.

John Tilley and Governor Carver crowded into the cabin doorway, and the governor asked, "How are you?"

He was shaking so hard he couldn't answer.

The deacon placed his hand on his head. "He's like ice," he said, "Someone needs to crawl in with him until he gets rid of these chills."

Elizabeth opened her mouth, and closed it again. Desire had wriggled in beside John's bunk. "Let me." she said. "It's all right. We're betrothed."

Elizabeth knew that. Why did her stomach tie itself into knots? Because a public announcement made it official? Would they let Desire go to bed with him? Elizabeth looked at Governor Carver.

"That sounds like a good idea, but I'd like Elder Brewster's opinion," he said.

"Certainly, Desire would be the logical one to lend him her warmth," Elder Brewster had come up behind the governor. "You women leave now while we get some clothes on him, and we'll call you.

Desire was going to bed with John! Elizabeth turned away with a choking sensation in her throat. Richard came up behind her, caught her around the waist, and whispered in her ear, "It would be worth falling overboard if I could have you in bed with me."

She jerked away from him, and rushed off to hide in the dark recesses of the tiller flat where John had comforted her on that long ago night. He would never comfort her again. Tears streamed down her face even as she struggled to thank God that he was safe.

Elizabeth never knew how long Desire stayed in bed with John for she crawled into her own ticking, refusing supper and not moving until Desire nudged her. "Move over," she whispered. "I can't get warm alone in my own bunk."

Elizabeth could have screamed, but instead she did as Desire asked. "Oh, Elizabeth it was so sweet to have John beside me," she cooed into her ear. "I can't wait to be married."

"I thought you would sleep with him all night," Elizabeth said.

"No, I'm afraid he has a fever now. He's so hot he doesn't want me. Besides they moved him to his own pallet with the rest of the men."

"But he needs you by him even more now," Elizabeth said sitting up.

"Oh no, he's asleep. He'll be all right."

Elizabeth lay awake long after Desire was still, her stomach pitching with each plunge of the ship. I should go to John, she told herself, but she knew that for her to spend the night in the men's sleeping area under the forecastle would be totally unacceptable. I've caused enough trouble already, she scolded herself.

But when the men clumped past her curtain looking for breakfast, she could stand it no longer and slipped off to see for herself how John was feeling. Through the night the storm had abated. Perhaps God wasn't so angry with her after all. When he saw her he grinned, "Lost my hat."

" Oh John, what did happen?" Elizabeth asked, relieved to see him able to joke.

"I started across the deck, and all of a sudden there was nothing under my feet," he paused, groping for words, "Time just stopped!"

"What do you mean?" Elizabeth couldn't quite understand.

"I can't explain it, but I was just hanging there in space, seemed like an eternity. I kept groping for something, anything to catch myself."

"But you went overboard." Elizabeth was incredulous.

"Oh yes! Waves huge as mountains came rolling at me."

"What saved you?" Elizabeth felt a lump in her throat.

"Jesus!" he spoke deliberately. "I know he did. I remember crying out his name, or hearing his name called, I'll never know which."

Elizabeth couldn't breathe. *Could it be that he heard me?* she wondered.

"But how? What?..."

"A giant wave like some foaming monster gulped for me." John shivered involuntarily. "I saw it then— a dangling halyard line."

"You caught it!" Elizabeth breathed again.

"Well, no, not then. I lunged for it and missed. I was tossed around in the waves. Seems like I rolled over and over. Oh, was it cold! Icy cold. So cold I couldn't breath." He shivered again.

"Dear Lord, it's a miracle you're here!" Elizabeth gasped.

"Sure is," John agreed. "Seemed like I was lifted up almost out of the water on great wings. There it was again. I grabbed with all my might, and this time I caught it. Almost didn't. It slipped along my wrist and then just sort of fell into my palm. And I hung on!"

Elizabeth sensed John's agitation as she noted the blanket over his foot moving up and down. "Thank the Lord, you hung on," she whispered.

John held out his hands and Elizabeth shuddered. Each palm had been rubbed raw and dry blood still clung to them. She extended a finger and gently touched one hand. She must get him some bacon fat, but she couldn't move until she heard the rest of the story.

"Wasn't easy. The rope burned even in the icy water, and the waves pitched me up and down. Sometimes I was under, sometimes dangling in the air. Tried to gulp some air every time I was up. Felt like my chest was paralyzed."

"How long was it?" Elizabeth still had questions.

"No idea, probably not as long as it seemed. Seemed like I lived a lifetime bobbing along like a cork. Thought about my mother and father and brothers, and..." here John broke off and looked at Elizabeth.

"Desire," Elizabeth finished for him.

John smiled a crooked smile, and she continued with her questions, "Did you pull yourself up the rope?"

"I tried to pull myself up, but the ship kept plunging up and down and ducking me again and again. I kept wondering if I would ever be rescued. Had anyone seen me?" John's teeth were chattering as he spoke, and the blanket took on a life of its own bouncing up and down over his feet.

"How did you get out of the water?"

"Someone spotted me. Thank the Lord! At last I felt something scraping along my back. I think I got pulled up with a boat hook."

"Like a big fish," Elizabeth laughed with relief.

John laughed, too, long and hard, and the blankets stopped moving.

Then he spoke meditatively, "You know, it was strange when I was under the water. Scared as I was, it was sort of peaceful. It was such a deep green, beautiful really underneath those rolling waves. I guess I was numb by the time I'd been ducked a couple of times. If I hadn't been jerked up with the roll of the ship I could easily have given in. Not be too bad a way to go to be with the Lord."

Elizabeth suddenly realized that Desire was standing there holding a steaming bowl. Someone had gotten a brazier going in the respite from the storm.

"Brought you some hot oatmeal, even added molasses. You don't get burgoo every day," she said kneeling beside John and attempting to spoon feed him.

"I can feed myself," John said, propping himself up on his elbow and reaching for the spoon.

"Not yet, you get served today," Desire said.

A dip of the ship put burgoo on John's chin. "You should see yourself. You look just like a baby," Desire laughed as she tried to scrape off the mess.

He caught her hand, "That's enough," he said swinging himself around on his pallet to a sitting position.

But Desire wouldn't relinquish the spoon and a minor tussle resulted in much laughter and Desire falling into his lap.

She's behaving like a child, Elizabeth thought. *Why doesn't she grow up? Can't she see John doesn't appreciate being babied, especially after all he's been through?* At the same time she realized that she should back off and leave them alone.

At that moment Master Jones appeared. "John Howland, I'm glad you're able to sit up and take nourishment," he boomed.

"Thank you or your sailors, whoever it was, for rescuing me."

"I was on the poop deck and saw you go, but it was the quick action of one of my men that saved you," Master Jones said.

"Did he use a boat hook?" John wanted to know.

"That was how he did it. I'd just sent him out to lash down the halyard lines that had broken loose. First he tried to hook the line with it, but it was easier to grab you. How are your hands?

John held them out and opened them slowly, "My fingers are still tingly," he said.

"Not much wonder. I'll never know how you hung on in the first place. We had to peel your fingers free from the line. Remember that?"

John shook his head no, and looked at his hands with awe.

"I've never heard of a man falling into the North Atlantic and surviving," Master Jones shook his head in disbelief. "It had to be a miracle."

John's eyes met Elizabeth's as he nodded yes. Wonder flooded her again. Yes, it was a miracle of God's grace.

Now John was asking about the leaks, and she must get some lard for those sore hands. On her way to the common cabin she was assailed by children wanting to know what had happened to John and how their friend was.

When she had shared his story, she realized that with calmer seas this might be a good time to continue their lessons. She sent Henry for the lard, and went for her paddle book.

The lesson in the tiller flat had barely begun, when the storm was upon them again with all its fury. The ship rolled and plunged. Suddenly a violent shudder racked it from bow to stern. Water poured in around the tiller flap. The flame of their small lamp sputtered out.

Cra-a-ck! The thunderous sound of splitting wood rumbled through the darkness.

"We're breaking up," Elizabeth gasped.

Instinctively she reached for Humility and clasped her to her. She could feel the child quivering even as her own teeth chattered.

Swaying back and forth with her, she cooed in her ear, "We'll be safe with Jesus. We'll be with Jesus."

Suddenly it hit her. *I won't be with Jesus!* Great sobs engulfed her. *I'm the sinner who refused to pray. I defied Master Martin. Now the whole ship is condemned because of me. Why didn't I ask Elder Brewster to throw me overboard when John was saved? I must. I must do it now if there is any hope of the rest surviving.*

Suddenly a shaft of light broke into the fore end of the 'tween deck. It took Elizabeth a second to realize that someone was climbing down the ladder with a lantern swinging shadows through the common area.

"Master Jones, over here," she heard her father yell above the storm.

Curious to know what had happened, she put Humility down and pressed forward. Perhaps they weren't going to sink after all.

Close to their cabin door she found Master Jones lifting a lantern to explore a jagged crack over their heads. A beam had splintered and was beginning to sag in the aisle. Her teeth chattered harder than before. How long could the rest of the ship hold together? Their reprieve couldn't last long.

"We'll never make it!" screamed one of the crew, who had come down with the captain.

The men of the proposed colony, tumbling against each other, crowded around staring up at the broken beam.

"There must be some way to brace it up," her father said, struggling to keep his balance.

"But what about the rest of the ship. Is it weakened too?" John Carver voiced Elizabeth's fears.

"The next beam will snap, and the next," Edward Dotey predicted.

"And the next, and the next. They'll all go!" cried a sailor.

The ship's master, swaying with the ship, held the lamp near the break studying it without comment. Elizabeth tried to read his face in the flickering light, but the shadows played tricks, and she couldn't tell what he was thinking.

"We've got to turn back," one of the sailors declared.

"Never should have tried it this time of the year. Crazy to dare the sea demons," another sailor cried.

"Let's run for home," the first proposed.

"Turn back now? Oh, no!" Elizabeth wanted to scream, but bit her lip.

"We're in God's hands," Elder Brewster spoke up, and for a few seconds the wind quieted. "We must ask His guidance before we decide."

"You pray while I look over the rest of the hull," Master Jones said at last. Working his way the length of the 'tween deck, he studied each beam and inspected the ribbing of the ship while every eye followed him. Then he let himself down into the hold and the flickering light disappeared.

Everyone knelt now, and Elder Brewster's voice was raised in petition to God. As he prayed, Elizabeth's guilt overwhelmed her again. When he finished she stumbled back to her bunk, and threw herself on the damp tick.

Teeth chattering uncontrollably, she abandoned herself to despair. God was punishing everyone because of her irreverence, just as he had punished Jonah's shipmates. If she, like Jonah, were thrown into the sea perhaps the rest would be spared. Then, remembering Pastor Robinson's letter, she realized she'd sinned many times over in defying Master Martin.

Great sobs shook her, even as the storm shook the ship. *I*

don't want to die. Will God have a great fish swallow me like it did Jonah? That would be awful! Then she remembered what John had said about peace under the waves. *Maybe drowning won't be that bad.*

Finally she got to her feet, wiped her eyes with her apron, lifted her chin, and groped her way back to Elder Brewster.

When she reached the men, they were arguing whether they should continue the voyage or return to England.

"But the immediate problem is how to support the broken beam," Richard Gardiner said. "Maybe it could be nailed together with a few strips of iron."

"But how do we get the beam back in place?" her father asked.

"Pile barrels under it," William Bradford suggested.

Elizabeth knew that wouldn't work. Someone would be killed when they fell on them.

Her father voiced her fear, "No way to steady them."

"Are there any extra beams in the hold?" Master Carver asked.

"We'd need a way to brace it," Edward Tilley put in.

Momentarily forgetting her mission, Elizabeth spoke up, "The screw, Uncle Edward, what about your screw?"

"Of course," her father exclaimed, and hurried off to the hold.

"What will I do with my cloth? Suppose it's ruined anyway," Uncle Edward's voice trailed off. "Might as well throw it overboard."

Overboard! Elizabeth remembered her mission. As the company crowded toward the hold, she tugged on Elder Brewster's sleeve, and insisted that she talk to him alone.

Sensing her distress, he led her back to the tiller flat where she poured out her confession. "So you see the only way for you to be saved is for me to be thrown overboard," she ended bleakly.

Reaching out and taking both her hands in his, he replied, "No, Elizabeth, you don't understand. We all deserve death. We have all done wrong, but Christ died in our place on the cross. These storms may be part of God's purifying process for each of us, but there's no need for us to sacrifice anyone."

Tears were streaming down her cheeks, and her chest

which had felt as though the beam had fallen on it felt lighter. It was hard to believe what he said. She always thought that she had to be good to go to be with Jesus.

Elder Brewster patted her arm, "It's all right."

She followed as the elder made his way to where Richard Gardiner was knocking the bottom beam off the big screw. When he finished, Edward Tilley helped him turn it onto its top bar. Some of the men angled the sturdy frame ready to push it under either side of the shattered beam when Richard and Uncle Edward turned the screw.

The frame slid into position, but the screw stiffened as it crunched into the splintered wood. With great grunts Richard and Uncle Edward twisted the iron handle.

John Howland lurched from his bunk to help, but was shoved aside by William Bradford. "I'll do it. You mustn't strain yourself yet," he yelled.

Only then Elizabeth realized that the storm had quieted after her decision to die. It was rising again. Was the elder right about Christ's death taking away the need for hers? If they got the beam in place, she would know for sure.

Could they do it? Every muscle in her arm and back strained with Richard as he bent and tugged with heaving chest at the resisting bar. She could see beads of sweat reflected on his forehead in the light of the lamp held high by the master.

The beam would not budge. She held her breath as she glanced from the struggling men to the beam. It still sagged.

She jumped as someone elbowed past her. It was her mother with a tin cup that she handed her father. "Bacon grease," she said. "That screw is rusted from all the salt water."

Goodman Tilley pressed forward, and calling a halt to the two men's exertions, he rubbed the grease on the curling pin.

They bent their backs to the bar again. Elizabeth couldn't take her eyes off it. Did it move? William and Richard grunted with the strain.

Yes, yes, it was moving. The bar had come all the way around now. She glanced up. The beam was almost even with the others. Just a little more. The wood crunched into place.

"Thank you, Jesus," she breathed. Suddenly her legs would hold her no longer. She staggered into her cabin and collapsed on her bunk.

Through the curtain she heard the controversy raging again.

"Go on..."

"Go back..."

"Please, Jesus, you have saved us. Let us go on," she prayed.

Chapter 8

The heated discussion that was going on just outside Elizabeth's canvas curtain came to an abrupt halt. "I've inspected the ship and the rest of her is sound." Master Jones was speaking. "The beam is well supported, and by dead reckoning we're at least half way across the ocean. It would be no better to go back, so we shall continue."

Elizabeth sensed the men dispersing, and was about to return to the common area when she overheard Edward Dotey mumble, "He's `master' now, but it mightn't always be that way."

"Don't forget what almost happened to Master Hopkins," the second Edward said.

"I know, he near got himself hung, but in the end, he got away with it," Edward Dotey said with a low chuckle.

So that was the rest of the story that Edward Leister didn't want to tell Constance that night on the shore at Southampton. Was mutiny in their minds too? She must tell her father what she had overheard.

Her father's brow was knit in a worried frown by the time she finished sharing their comments with him. "I don't like the implications of Dotey's remarks," he said. "Master Hopkins was an aid to the chaplain on a ship that was wrecked on a voyage to take a new governor to Virginia. By the grace of God no lives were lost, but when the governor ordered the building of pinnaces to go on to the New World, mutiny broke out. He regained control, and Master Hopkins was convicted of being the instigator."

"Why would he do such a thing?" Elizabeth couldn't understand it.

"He claimed he was afraid they would be forced into slave labor if they went on to Virginia, and perhaps with some reason, considering the trouble that the Jamestown colony was having," her father replied.

"How did he escape hanging?" Elizabeth questioned.

"The governor took pity on him because of his family. It was many years ago, and Master Hopkins is a different person now, but I'm sorry that his servants have learned the story. They don't need any ideas like that. I'd better warn Master Carver that there could be trouble."

Elizabeth heard no more about mutiny, perhaps because for several more days waves continued to crash over the Mayflower, rolling her close to her beam-ends, and keeping everyone in their bunks most of the time. But finally the storm subsided and the battered passengers were able to be about again.

Now stories of other hardships the Separatists had faced came out. As Elizabeth gathered with some of the women to collect their daily ration of biscuit and salt pork, Mistress Brewster recalled her experiences when their congregation left Scrooby for Holland.

As Mary Brewster talked, Dorothy Bradford joined the group. Elizabeth was glad to see her take an interest. Even on the good days, she looked frightened and sad.

"We sold all our belongings, and set out to walk to the coast. We knew it was sixty miles, but none of us had any idea what a sixty-mile walk with children would mean. Patience was eight then and Fear only two."

"You mean you have other children besides Wrestling and Love?" Constance interrupted.

"Yes, didn't you know? We have another son also. Jonathon. He's twenty-seven now and the girls are twenty and fourteen. We left them with him in Leyden. I'm not sure who will be taking care of whom. Jonathon's wife and son both went to be with the Lord shortly before we left." Mary Brewster's eyes reflected her sorrow for her son's great loss.

"But you brought your little ones with you. William made me leave my baby with Pastor Robinson. I'll never see him again," Dorothy Bradford said with a mixture of bitterness and hopelessness in her voice.

"Dorothy, you'll see him again," Mary tried to reassure her.

"Yes, when we're all with the Lord, but never here," Dorothy said.

"I know how hard it was for you to leave your only child, but I thought you had agreed it was best. He'll be joining us when the colony is established. He's much better off in Holland for now," Mary Brewster spoke gently but reprovingly to her.

"Tell us how you managed a sixty-mile walk," Elizabeth interjected, anxious to redirect the conversation.

"I'll never forget my aching legs and the blisters on my feet. We took turns carrying Fear who cried most of the time." Mary took up her story again. "In fact the children were all crying. It rained on us, and half of us were sick, but we finally made it to Boston and boarded the ship."

"And then the captain betrayed you," Dorothy said shrilly.

"What do you mean, betrayed you?" Constance asked.

"It wasn't legal to leave the country. They didn't want us, but they wouldn't let us go either," Mary Brewster answered.

"The captain took their passage money, and then turned them in to collect a reward from the crown. On top of that, the soldiers who arrested them stole everything they could. They searched all of them, thinking we had gold. It was the most humiliating thing that ever happened to them."

Mary Brewster let them fill in the details in their own minds.

"Then what did they do with you?" Constance asked, wide-eyed.

"They put them in prison," Dorothy said.

Prison! Elizabeth remembered again the dank stinking Clink where she had gone with her mother. She shuddered.

"But they didn't keep us very long. They couldn't decide what to do with so many women and children, so they sent us back to Scrooby," Mary said. "But as soon as possible we tried again."

"After what you had already been through?" Constance wondered.

"They had to." Dorothy took up the story. "Mistress Brewster didn't tell you that they held her husband in prison in Boston for several months more. When he was released he was still in danger of being arrested in Scrooby. He was on a wanted list for disobedience in matters of religion."

"That's true," Mary continued. "And besides he had given up his place as postmaster of Scrooby. We had nothing to go back to. As soon as he was free, he made arrangements with a Dutch captain to pick us up in a lonely spot on the coast."

"Did he?" Elizabeth was anxious now to hear the rest of the story.

"Yes and no. This time only the men walked. They sent us by boat. Little did we dream what a disaster that would be."

"What happened?" Constance asked.

"When we reached the shore, neither the men nor the ship were in sight. It was almost dark. There we were with young children and no place to go!"

"What did you do?" Elizabeth gasped at their plight.

"We spent a wretched night in the boat trying to keep the children from crying. We didn't dare make any noise for fear we'd be arrested again."

"How awful!" Constance interjected.

"At daybreak we spotted the men on the beach, and the ship just off shore," Mistress Brewster said.

"Then it all worked out all right." Elizabeth breathed a sigh of relief.

"No! The tide was out and we were stuck on the mud flat." Mistress Brewster frowned at the memory. "The ship had sent its jolly to pick us up, so the men went ahead while we waited for the tide to float us. Suddenly a band of soldiers came crashing out of the woods. We watched stunned as the ship sailed away with our husbands!"

"My husband says he'll never forget the horrified look on the faces of the men whose families were still ashore," Dorothy chimed in.

"Did they put you in prison again?" Constance wanted to know.

"No, in the end, the magistrates took pity on us. They put us under house arrest in private homes until they could quietly arrange for a few of us at a time to take passage for Amsterdam."

"The men were almost lost at sea. How many times William

has told me about it." Dorothy took up the story. "A terrible storm came up and the sailors were crying, 'We sink! We sink!'

"'Lord, thou canst save us!' our men prayed over and over. But for those prayers, William believes the ship would have gone down."

"How did you meet Master Bradford? You weren't one of the Scrooby congregation, were you?" Constance asked Dorothy.

"No, my family had come to Amsterdam earlier with another group that fled English popery." She paused and smiled fleetingly. "I remember so well the first time William came to our church. It was the Sunday after that terrible voyage. I was only eleven, but I was so impressed when he stood up and told of their deliverance. He was so very handsome. I think I fell in love with him right then, and when my parents invited him home for dinner after the service I never left his side."

"When did you marry?" Elizabeth asked.

"I was sixteen. Pastor Robinson had moved his congregation to Leyden by then, and William persuaded my parents to let me marry because it was so hard for him to get to Amsterdam to see me. He says he knew how I felt about him from the first. I sometimes wonder..." her words trailed off and suddenly she was far away again.

She was the same age I am now. But William waited five years for her. Richard can wait a few years for me, Elizabeth decided even as she wondered what else Dorothy had started to say.

Later Elizabeth began to question why the Scrooby congregation hadn't stayed in Amsterdam with their fellow exiles. After she put the children to bed that night she asked her mother about it.

"Your Aunt Ann knows more than I do," she hedged as a distressed look passed over her face. "I guess Pastor Robinson was attracted to Leyden because of the university there."

"But that wasn't the only reason," Elizabeth persisted, sensing more to the story.

"The scriptures teach that whatsoever things are good, these we should think upon. On the other hand it doesn't conceal anyone's sins." Dark shadows from the swinging taper played across her mother's grim face as Elizabeth watched her argue with herself. Elizabeth felt that in the end her mother would tell her what she knew because she had always been honest with her.

"You're a young lady now," her mother rambled on.

"Yes, and I'm engaged, don't forget." Elizabeth realized that there were some things that she would need to know before she married.

Her mother sighed, "I guess you should know, though we pray nothing like it will ever happen in our congregation."

"What was it?" Elizabeth urged her on. Just then her aunt carrying her knitting came over to perch on the chest beside them.

"Ann," Goodwife Tilley said, "Elizabeth wants to know why your congregation moved to Leyden. I want her to know the truth."

"It was partly because work was hard to find in Amsterdam, but only partly," Aunt Ann began, weighing her words carefully. "Unfortunately there was a great deal of bickering among the church leaders. The pastor's wife was the cause of some of it. He married a widow who offended many by the extreme way she dressed. But worse than that one of the elders was believed to be carrying on with a widow in the congregation, and he a married man. That wasn't the end of it either. There was some reason to think that he compromised little girls as well, so Pastor Robinson and Elder Brewster felt it was better to put some distance between their congregation and the whole mess."

"And that was the church Mistress Bradford came from. I'll bet she was glad to leave," Elizabeth observed, not entirely understanding what her aunt meant, but getting the general drift of it. She didn't need to know anymore.

"Sometimes I wonder if it had an ill effect on Dorothy," her aunt replied. "I realize that leaving her son was a horrible experience. I saw him screaming and clinging to her before they boarded the Speedwell. His father had to tear him from her skirts and thrust him into Pastor Robinson's arms."

"Oh the poor dears," Elizabeth's mother exclaimed.

"But then there were lots of hard partings, and Dorothy has always seemed preoccupied and dejected. Not the happy soul she had a right to be," Aunt Ann concluded, leaving Elizabeth more concerned than ever for William Bradford's wife.

"You know," Aunt Ann observed to Goodwife Tilley, changing the subject, "I wonder how much longer Mistress Hopkins can hold out before that baby comes."

"Heaven forbid that she deliver on shipboard," Elizabeth heard her mother say as she slipped off to share with Desire her concern over Dorothy Bradford. Desire had missed the conversation this afternoon because she still wasn't feeling well enough to be up very long.

Elizabeth sat down on the bunk beside her friend, but Desire insisted that she crawl into bed with her so they could keep each other warm as they visited. As it turned out, Elizabeth didn't talk very long, for after the many sleepless storm-tossed nights, she soon dozed off.

Sometime later she was roused by Desire shaking her shoulder. "Listen," she whispered in her ear, "It sounds like someone is really sick, maybe dying."

Elizabeth fought off drowsiness and propped herself on her elbow to hear better.

"It's not all the time," Desire buzzed in her ear again, "But someone is really hurting."

Elizabeth, still fighting off sleep, listened closely. First there was nothing but the ships sounds that had become too familiar, and the snores of men in the front of the 'tween deck. She was about to drop her sleep-filled head on the pillow again when a low moan came from the next cabin, and then sounds of someone stirring.

"Do you suppose Mistress Hopkins is having her baby? Come on, let's see," Elizabeth said, suddenly wide awake.

Elizabeth scrambled from the bunk, but Desire chose to stay put. "You're still dressed. I'm not. You go."

Elizabeth found her mother and Mistress Brewster already in the passageway. Master Hopkins met them saying, "The baby is coming. Can you help?"

"We'll take over," Mistress Brewster said. Then, seeing Constance added, "You better take Damarius to the common area."

Elizabeth ducked back into Desire's cabin. She didn't want Constance to recruit her help. She wanted to see the baby born, or at least be as close as possible.

When the aisle had cleared, she crept to the door and pulled the canvas aside enough to peep in.

Her mother, barefooted and clad only in her fustian slip, was kneeling at Mistress Hopkins' side. A long moan escaped from Mistress Hopkins' lips. Elizabeth could see her face whiter than her bedding in the deep shadows.

"You're doing fine," her mother told the writhing woman. "Just rest as much as you can between pains."

"We need more light," Mistress Brewster said.

Elizabeth moved quickly. Unhooking the oil lantern that usually hung in the passageway, she pushed aside the canvas and carried it into the tiny cabin.

Scarcely noticing her, Mistress Brewster grabbed it and held it near the foot of the bed while Elizabeth's mother turned back the covers. Just then Mistress Hopkins let out a loud cry, and groped over her head for the top of the bunk.

"Push now," Goodwife Tilley said. "I can see the top of its head. Next time push hard."

Elizabeth saw it, too, a circle of wet dark hair. Her pulse raced. "You can do it," her mother was saying.

Just then Mistress Brewster realized that Elizabeth was there. "Elizabeth Tilley, you have no business in here. You're too young."

Elizabeth dutifully left the cabin, but continued peeping around the curtain, disappointed that she couldn't see as much now. "It's coming," Goodwife Tilley exclaimed.

Mistress Hopkins moaned again.

"There it is," Elizabeth's mother said, and presently lifted a tiny baby for it's mother to see. "A boy. You have a fine boy."

The baby began crying. "Let me have him," his mother said.

"He needs a bath," Mistress Brewster declared.

"No, just wrap him in the linen that's there on the foot of the bunk," Mistress Hopkins insisted. As they laid him in her arms Elizabeth saw a radiant smile flood her tired face, and Elizabeth stifled an urge to laugh out loud for sheer joy.

Elizabeth couldn't explain it then, but after she had crawled back into her own bed she felt herself throbbing all over with anticipation of bearing a child. How exciting it would be to have a baby! She was certain she would experience the pangs of childbirth as pure joy. She believed Mistress Hopkins felt that way too.

Lost in her own thoughts she was annoyed when she heard Desire whisper, "I can't get warm. May I sleep with you?"

Feeling sorry for her, Elizabeth turned on her side to make room for her shivering friend.

"Are you getting sick again?" Elizabeth asked, snuggling against her to try to share her own warmth.

"No, I guess I'm more scared," Desire confided. "Wasn't it awful? I thought she was going to die."

"Oh, Desire, she wasn't dying. She was living, really living, giving birth to a new life! I can't think of any time when a woman would be more alive," Elizabeth said.

"But it cost my mother her life the second time she had a baby." Desire was still shivering.

"Oh, I didn't know!" Elizabeth became sympathetic.

"She wasn't young anymore, and it was just too hard. Look how hard it was for Mistress Hopkins. How much worse it must have been for my poor mother."

"Sure it's work having a baby, but we're young. It'll be easy for us. We don't have to be afraid." Elizabeth put a comforting arm over Desire.

"You're younger than I am," Desire reminded her. "And we can't be married for awhile. Oh, Elizabeth, I'm afraid, terribly afraid."

"But surely when you marry John Howland you'll want to have his baby," Elizabeth said. How glorious it would be to bear John Howland's baby! The thought rose unbidden and she thrust it from her.

"Maybe he won't want to have children, he's not so young either," Desire seemed to be grasping for straws.

"Desire, when you marry it's your duty to have a baby for your husband. We're going to a new world. God commanded Adam and Eve to fill the world, and we're almost like Adam and Eve. We've got a land to fill. You'll have to have children." Elizabeth fell silent, but her mind raced on with unspoken words. *John Howland deserves children. I could give them to him. But he wants Desire. My best friend. How can I fight for him? I can't. I'll bear Richard's baby,* she thought dejectedly. *But it will be my baby too.* This realization revived her spirit.

"I don't know if I can do it. Even what goes on in the marriage bed frightens me," Desire whimpered.

"Oh Desire, you mustn't feel that way." Elizabeth wasn't quite sure what did go on, but when she was still sleeping on the trundle bed beside her parents she had been awakened on occasion by laughter and joyful sounds from the big bed. "What happens in the marriage bed must be pure pleasure." Especially with John Howland, Elizabeth didn't add.

"I do love John, but I'm so afraid. Maybe I should never have come," Desire said.

"Of course you should have come," Elizabeth tried to reassure her. "If you hadn't, I would never have known you. And you're my best friend, don't forget. Why not quit worrying now and go back to sleep? Things will look different when we all get off this terrible ship, and you are feeling better."

Desire's breathing soon became regular, and her body relaxed. But Elizabeth couldn't sleep. She lay there fearing for John that Desire would refuse to give him a child, and fighting her own terrible hunger to be the one to bear John Howland's baby.

Chapter 9

"The sea gave up the dead...." Elder Brewster's rich voice comforted the band of settlers gathered to commit the body of Deacon Fuller's young servant to the sea. Earlier Elizabeth had heard one of the women moaning that William Butten's fate would be the fate of them all, but everyone stood now in dry-eyed silence as Elder Brewster read from Revelation.

Elizabeth felt as though a chunk of dry biscuit had caught in her throat, and a strange foreboding crept over her as she looked around the group gathered on deck. Was the woman indeed right, would others follow?

"The Lord giveth; the Lord taketh away." A faint sun struggled through the clouds as the stiff canvas bag was lifted to the railing by two young men. It slipped over the side, hitting the water with a dull splash. As the body bag sank out of sight, she rebelled against his death. Even though she scarcely knew him, she was sure he must have wanted to live, too, for he was no older than she.

"Blessed be the name of the Lord," Elder Brewster's words echoed in her mind, and she knew she must agree. It occurred to her then that William's death had already been balanced out by the birth of Oceanus Hopkins. She had to believe God knew what He was doing.

"Be assured that we'll meet again before the great white throne where we all come with robes washed in the blood of the Lamb," the elder ended, and began to sing the 23rd Psalm.

Everyone joined in as the sailors listened quietly from the top of the forecastle, and Master Jones watched from his post on the poop.

Just as singing died away another sound, sweeter than any song Elizabeth would ever hear again, took its place.

"Mew, mew."

A gull! Land! There must be land nearby.

All at once everyone was talking, even laughing. *God has graciously given us hope,* she realized and she thought of Noah's dove returning to the ark with the olive branch. She had a good idea how welcome that bird must have been. To think, they were six months on the ark! Their own two months had been forever.

But search the western horizon as they would no one spotted land that day, or the next. Elizabeth was on deck at dawn the next day, and the next. At last, on November tenth, her vigilance was rewarded.

"Land ahoy!" the cry floated down from the sailor in the working top.

She could smell it before she could see it, a lovely woodsy smell of evergreen and damp earth. Then her straining eyes saw it, a vague line on the horizon, earth separating from the seas as it had at creation. A new world to possess!

John, Richard and Desire had clambered to the deck too, and she swung around to share the excitement that coursed through her. Her eyes met John Howland's just as Desire slipped her hand into his, and reached out the other for Elizabeth's. Richard moved closer and put his arm around her shoulder, and she didn't pull away. She knew they needed each other.

"We've been studying Capt. John Smith's charts, and Master Jones thinks our landfall is Cape Cod," John Tilley told his family later in the day. "We're a good distance from where we hoped to settle."

"You mean we can't go ashore yet?" Elizabeth's mother sounded discouraged. "I was just thinking that I can't stand this ship another minute, and was so thankful that our ordeal was almost over."

"I'm sorry, my dear, but I'm afraid even when we anchor you won't be going ashore for awhile. We'll have to pick a site for a village and put up some kind of shelter for you first," Goodman Tilley answered.

Elizabeth knew her father was right, but she also agreed with her mother. Often when she first came down to the 'tween deck from the fresh air above, the accumulation of smells in the cramped quarters would make her gag.

However, her mother managed a smile as she conceded, "I know, we should be thankful that we have finally arrived safely."

"The master is going to try to get us around the elbow of the cape and land us in Northern Virginia. Hopefully it shouldn't take too long," her father tried to encourage them.

But before the afternoon was over they had reason to think they were in mid-Atlantic again. The ship jumped and tossed unmercifully, and only later did Elizabeth discover how much danger they had been in. Master Jones, by running for the open sea, had saved them from the riptides that raged at the elbow of the Cape threatening to drive them onto the shoals.

The next morning as they were sailing back along the same wild dune-lined coast that they had followed the day before, Elizabeth wondered bleakly if they had come to a desert even though she could usually spot a tangle of green behind the sand hills.

Before evening they turned west again, rounded the hook end of the Cape, and entered the protected waters on the south side. Here at last, they dropped anchor.

Immediately after evening prayers Elizabeth escaped to the main deck to drink in the scent of pines that came from the shore. She was standing in the deep shadows of the forecastle when two dark figures came onto the deck and stopped by the rail close to her.

She started to move, but was stopped by the conspiratorial tone of the one who spoke first. "So we're not going to Northern Virginia after all. Do you know what that means?" Her heart dropped as she recognized Edward Dotey's voice.

"It means I won't be landing where I wanted to." It was Edward Leister speaking.

"Don't you get it? We'll be without a patent, no charter, no law. We'll be our own law. Free of king or anyone else. We can take control, do as we please."

"You mean we won't have to work as indentured servants? We can take the land for our own right away?" Edward Leister's voice rose with excitement.

"Shussh, now you've got the idea, but we have to get the other bond servants behind us. If we stick together when we go ashore we can just tell those old Dutchmen to go jump in the ocean. We'll build our own houses and let them worry about themselves." The malice in Dotey's voice shocked Elizabeth even though she had heard rumblings like this before.

"Yeh, I guess it'll be like when Master Hopkins' ship wrecked and claimed they were outside English law." Edward Leister had gotten the idea.

"Not *Master* Hopkins, just Stephen Hopkins. No man will be our master anymore. Let's go talk to the others," Edward Dotey said, and the two went below deck again leaving a shaking Elizabeth behind.

She must warn Master Carver, who had gone to the Great Cabin earlier.

Approaching it, she paused. *Master Martin will be angry if I infringe on his territory,* she thought. *I don't want to be disrespectful again, but I have no other choice. I must tell Master Carver.* With cold hands, she knocked urgently on the narrow door. *God help me if Master Martin answers,* she prayed. *I don't want to be disrespectful to him again.*

A shred of light appeared as the door cracked and Master Carver was silhouetted in the opening. In relief Elizabeth burst in with her story. She had almost finished before she realized that Master Martin wasn't in the circle of lamp light at the table that reflected on the faces of Master Carver, Elder Brewster, and William Bradford.

"Thank you for telling me, Elizabeth," Master Carver said. "We'll need to make our plans to defuse this scheme tonight." And he sent Elizabeth back to the 'tween deck with a message for her father to bring the rest of the leaders to the great cabin immediately.

When the men had gone Mary Brewster, her mother, her aunt and Desire gathered around her wanting to know what was going on.

"What will happen to us if they refuse to build our houses?" Desire worried.

"Let's ask the Lord to give the men wisdom to deal with this," Elizabeth's mother spoke up.

Mary Brewster held out her hands to those on either side of her, then glancing around the small circle asked, "Where is Dorothy? She needs to pray with us for her husband."

"She's been in her bunk since devotions were over," Desire said.

A concerned look crossed Mary Brewster's face, but she went ahead with the prayer.

Later, when Elizabeth had crawled into her sack, she could hear the voices of the young men in the front of the 'tween deck rising and falling almost like distant thunder. She shivered as she contemplated what might happen. Would her dream of a place to dwell in peace and safety be exploded by Edward Dotey's rebellious spirit? Unable to sleep she sat up, folded her hands and prayed silently, *Oh God, please deliver us from evil.*

When she opened her eyes she thought she heard footsteps on the hatchway, and peeked to see who was coming. She was sure the tall figure was John Howland, and soon heard his voice speaking earnestly with the younger men as he seemed to be moving among them. It was much later before the area grew silent, and Elizabeth had fallen asleep before the rest of the men returned from the great cabin.

Elizabeth could feel the high excitement among the sea-weary passengers as they gathered on deck the next morning for devotions. "Can't wait to get my feet on solid ground," was heard over and over.

As the final prayer died away, Master Carver requested everyone to stay on deck. Elizabeth's fingers sought the tie of her cap as the men who had been summoned the night before moved to stand behind Master Carver and Capt. Standish.

"Since we are landing outside the limits of our charter we have decided that we need a compact to govern us until we can receive further communication from England." Master Carver wasted no words. "Last evening, with our consent, Elder Brewster drew up a concord that we are inviting every man of legal age, who intends to be a permanent member of our plantation, to swear to by subscribing his name before Almighty God and his fellow citizens. Anyone who doesn't agree isn't leaving this ship."

Elizabeth looked around for Edward Dotey who was skulking off with Edward Leister to the shadow of the forecastle. Elder Brewster stepped forward and unrolled a piece of parchment that he had tucked under his arm. Elizabeth's tie was a corkscrew again.

"Attention!" Capt. Standish squared his shoulders, set his feet apart, and rested his musket at ready before him. The men whom he had been training reacted immediately. Even the two Edwards whom Elizabeth had seen whispering together straightened up, and Elizabeth felt her breath escape in relief.

"In the name of Almighty God, Amen." Elder Brewster began reading in his most solemn church voice, "We whose names are underwritten, the Loyal Subjects of our dread Sovereign King James by the Grace of God...covenant and combine ourselves together into a civil Body Politick for our better Ordering and Preservation...to enact just and equal Laws from time to time, as shall be thought most meet and convenient for the General good of the Colony; unto which we Promise all due *Submission and Obedience...*"

Elizabeth caught the heavy emphasis on the last two words. She straightened her cape on her shoulders, and noticed that Edward Dotey was scowling. Even though he stood at attention, he was swaying on his feet like a bull about to charge.

Elizabeth hugged her cape around her, and looked back at Master Carver. He was staring at Dotey as though holding him back by sheer willpower. Meanwhile, Elder Brewster had gone to the Great Cabin after inviting the men to line up to sign.

Finally Master Carver turned and climbed to the great cabin to be the first to put his signature on the document. Elizabeth watched William Bradford, then Edward Winslow and Issac Allerton, two men she hadn't yet gotten to know very well, go next. Miles Standish shouldered his musket and took his turn, followed shortly by John Billington whose two sons clambered to go also and had to be held back by their mother. Soon John Howland worked his way out of the group with a light touch on Elizabeth's shoulder as he passed. Her pulse quickened.

Stephen Hopkins followed John, and shortly John and Edward Tilley took their turn. Elizabeth squared her shoulders and lifted her chin, proud that her father was a part of this pioneer band. Richard Gardiner was among the last to sign, but

Elizabeth couldn't help noticing the bounce in his step as he crossed the poop deck to the Great Cabin. She was proud, too, that the man she was to marry was a signer of the compact. But now she was twisting her ties again. Edward Dotey and Edward Leister still hadn't moved.

Master Jones descended to the main deck and approached the young men. "On land they cool mutineers in stocks. On ship board we keel haul them," he said in a voice that could be heard by all.

The sullen looks on their faces crumpled into resignation, and Edward Dotey took the lead in going up to sign. Elizabeth unwound her ties.

Then for the first time in weeks she saw Master Martin appear in the cabin door as if to make sure they were coming. It was Master Martin, wasn't it? The man wore clothes that hung on him like a sail that had lost the wind. Glancing about at the other passengers, Elizabeth suddenly realized that almost everyone's clothes were looser than when the voyage began. Still his were worse than most. She heard him coughing then, and he quickly disappeared again.

Richard joined Elizabeth. "Isn't this tremendous? I was never able to vote back in England, and here I am taking part in setting up a new government where I'll have a voice. We're going to elect a governor for the colony this afternoon. Who would you vote for?"

Elizabeth turned away. "I can't vote," she said stifling a surge of resentment. Even Edward Dotey who hadn't wanted to sign the compact would have a vote, and she, because she was a woman, never would. John Howland, coming down from the poop deck, overheard her.

"Who would you vote for, Elizabeth? We value your opinion."

"Do you really want women to think about such things?" Desire asked, looking up at John with wide eyes.

"Queen Bess did a good job of governing England," John replied. "Maybe we should listen to women's ideas more, when they have any to offer." There was a twinkle in his eye which softened his final comment.

"You would make a mighty fine governor," Desire suggested.

"Yes, he would," Elizabeth spoke up, "but now we need an

older, more experienced man. I would vote for Master Carver."

"A good choice," John said. "I think he will be elected unanimously."

"Anyway it's only for a year, and then we get to vote again." Richard was still enthused. "Just think, maybe someday even I could be governor."

Elizabeth felt resentful again that she could never entertain such a dream because she was a woman. *Why can't I be as innocent and accepting as Desire*, she scolded herself. She must guard against a spirit of rebellion, or she would be as bad as the Edwards.

She caught a glimpse of Oceanus in his mother's arms. Men might vote, but they could never bear a child. Suddenly she felt sorry for them.

When the vote was taken John Carver was chosen unanimously as John Howland had predicted, and with political matters settled they could consider going ashore.

From the 'tween deck Elizabeth could see the beach ahead of the jolly boat bearing John Howland, Capt. Standish, and William Bradford to shore. Awash in November sunlight, pale as their dwindling supply of butter, the beach appeared inviting this morning. As the small boat grounded, gulls screamed and sandpipers darted back and forth playing catch me if you can with the breaking waves.

A number of the men were on a mission to locate fresh water and firewood. Having studied the weather-beaten shoreline where all of the trees on the top of the dunes pointed inland like a line of flags atop a rampart, John had assured Elizabeth and Desire that wood would be no problem.

"They must get a lot of stiff wind blowing across the bay," he had noted. "It's not likely to be a good site for a village." This was the subject uppermost in all their minds, and in spite of the warm sunshine, Elizabeth knew he was right.

Elizabeth watched with envy as the men tumbled ashore like puppies spilled from a box. Some were stamping their feet up and down in the sand as if to prove to themselves that it was real. She saw John bend and pick up a handful. How anxious she was to do the same thing!

She was glad to see Capt. Standish scanning the tree line,

for while they had seen no signs of life yet, the threat of savages was never far from anyone's mind. Soon he beckoned the men to follow him. As they shouldered their muskets, trooped across the sand and disappeared into the woods, Elizabeth was thankful for the training Capt. Standish had given them.

Knowing the hours would be endless until they returned, and seeing Dorothy Bradford on the deck, she tried to engage her in conversation, but the young woman walked away from her. She thought she heard her mumble, "...wasteland.... die here."

Elizabeth spent most of the day watching the shore for any movement, and was the first to spot the returning company. As they came aboard those left behind crowded around them and quickly learned that the only water was surface water. Eager hands helped them unload the fragrant wood that they had brought.

William Bradford did have some encouraging words. "I poked into the layer of needles and it's good soil underneath," he said. "It reminds me of the sand dune country in parts of Holland, only this is blacker and thicker than anything I've seen there. When we find water it should yield us good crops."

Later, John told Desire and Elizabeth more details of the venture. As he spoke of fluttering leaves and skittering squirrels, Elizabeth sensed his fear of an Indian skulking in every shadow.

"After what seemed like days of walking, I caught the glint of sunlight on water. At first we thought it was a pond, but you know what we'd done? We'd crossed the hook of land that we'd sailed around, and were back on the ocean," he said.

Elizabeth felt the sinking sensation that must have come over them, but he finished by promising they would explore further down the cape when the shallop was ready.

Then Elizabeth became aware of another discussion going on close by.

"...Not tomorrow," William Bradford was saying, "Tomorrow is the Sabbath."

"Surely God would excuse us this once," Capt. Standish growled.

"No, Sir," William Bradford answered. "If we expect God's blessing on our endeavors we must certainly not dishonor Him by breaking the Sabbath."

The Sabbath dawned mild and clear, and Elder Brewster invited the sailors and Master Jones to join them for worship on the deck. Elizabeth was glad to see the ship's master accept. The seamen, however, disdained to attend, making remarks from the forecastle for the benefit of the colonists as they emerged from the hatchway.

"Better get on with unloading 'fore we dump you all on the beach ourselves."

"Gotta get rid of 'em 'fore they eat up all our victuals."

"Time we was on our way home."

"Won't the Mayflower stay until we choose a site?" Elizabeth whispered her to her father.

"Let's not worry about that now," John Tilley replied gently. "Today let's give ourselves to praise and thanksgiving to the Lord. We can trust Him to continue to provide for us."

So Elizabeth tried to join wholeheartedly in the singing of the Psalms and give full attention to the prayers, but somehow that coastline out there was pressing in on her. Not even the children of Israel had faced what they were facing, for the land they entered had houses and towns. This— nothing! Nothing, but raw wilderness on every side, and the sailors were threatening to abandon them.

But now her father was praying, "Oh Lord, as your forgiven remnant we have come to these strange shores. We have separated ourselves as you have commanded, recognizing that we must not be unequally yoked with unbelievers. Now separate us from the sin that does so easily beset us that we might love one another, and work together in harmony. Help us remember that nothing can separate us from your love in Christ Jesus."

He was using many familiar Bible passages, but today they took on fresh significance. Elizabeth found her spirit reviving. What had they expected? They knew they were coming to plant a colony in undeveloped land. By the grace of God they would tame this desolate place and make it home.

Still, as the wind swung to the northeast and the sun was blotted out by gathering clouds she had a premonition that the cost would be far greater than anyone had yet guessed.

Chapter 10

"You must choose a site for your colony without delay," Master Jones said to Elder Brewster when the service ended. "We've been so long in crossing that unless we start back soon we won't have enough supplies to make it. I want you to bring up the shallop and get to work reassembling her this afternoon."

Elizabeth expected Elder Brewster to go along with him, because surely this was a work of necessity. But the elder's forehead wrinkled and his kindly mouth formed into a stiff line. Shaking his head, he clutched his Geneva Bible and quoted the fourth commandment, "Remember the Sabbath Day to keep it holy." The subject was closed.

Elizabeth was ashamed that she had ever thought that he might compromise the Sabbath, but would Master Jones agree?

The sea captain shrugged his shoulders. "Do it your way and we'll manage somehow," he said with a note of resignation in his voice.

The afternoon meditations, questions and discussion on the sermon ensued as usual. Because the weather had grown colder the evening prayers, scripture reading and the hymn sing were held below.

Tonight Elder Brewster seemed to be in a reflective mood, and his meditation took a personal turn, something Elizabeth had never heard him do before.

"I shall never forget how important I felt when William Davison, who was Queen Elizabeth's envoy to Antwerp, placed in my keeping the great bronze keys to the city of Flushing. That very day the prince of the Netherlands had turned them over to Master Davison in a grand ceremony," he reminisced.

"How young I was then! What dreams of grandeur I had! As a clerk for Envoy Davidson I saw a great political future before me, but the Lord had something better."

Elizabeth listened eagerly, wondering why Elder Brewster, if he had been attached to the Queen's court, wound up as a refugee in Holland.

"I always thank God for my years at Cambridge where I came to know many who later risked their lives for their faith. Seeing the sacrifice they were willing to make for a pure church gave me the courage later to break with the Church of England.

"But I would never have done it if my career with William Davidson hadn't ended so cruelly. He rose to be a member of the Queen's privy counsel and I rose with him. But it was a dangerous place to be. There was always intrigue about the queen, and he was tricked into getting her to sign the death warrant for her traitorous cousin. No sooner was the Scott executed than Elizabeth turned on my master, threw him into the Tower of London, and put the blame for Mary's death on him.

"I saw then how fleeting was worldly favor, and I went home disillusioned, but glad to be able to escape into obscurity. The Lord met me then with the promise of an eternal kingdom, and offered me the key to it, Jesus Christ himself." Elder Brewster paused then, but no one moved.

It passed through Elizabeth's mind that she was glad she had been named for her mother and not for the virgin queen.

"We have a brand-new opportunity to build God's kingdom on earth where His will shall be done as Jesus taught us to pray." He concluded by leading them in the Lord's prayer.

The next morning Elizabeth woke to find her mother already bustling about sorting clothes as if they were going to wash. *There's no water aboard to do laundry,* Elizabeth thought jumping out of her bunk. *They must be going ashore.*

"Did someone find fresh water?" she asked.

"No," Goodwife Tilley replied, "But there's lots of water in this ocean. We've persuaded the men we should all go ashore to do laundry and just plain get the feel of land under us again."

As soon as the men brought the shallop pieces up and towed them ashore, they were ready to take the women in the dory. Elizabeth and Desire were first in line for the "Laundry Ferry," as John Howland laughingly called it.

Bright sun and a mild southerly breeze raised Elizabeth's spirits. The world of beach, sea, sky and forested shore seemed much less formidable this morning. *Was this what it was like when Adam and Eve first awakened to the a brand new world,* she wondered.

Not quite, she told herself ruefully. *God placed them in a garden. But we can make this into a garden.* She brightened. *He told them to be fruitful and multiply. We can do that, too,* she thought, spotting both John and Richard moving about on the beach. Desire had never said anything more about her fears of marriage or childbirth. Elizabeth glanced at the pensive girl sitting close beside her. Did she still feel that way?

I won't think about that today, she promised herself. She began studying the exasperating slow dip, pull, lift of the oars, and could scarcely keep from grabbing them herself. Each deliberate stroke stopped in midair and time hung with it. *Hurry, hurry,* she felt like shouting, *I want to get my feet on land, my land.* Impatiently she began pulling off her shoes and stockings.

"What are you doing?" Desire asked.

"I want to dig my toes into that sand and claim it for my own," she said.

Desire laughed, but soon she and the rest of the girls in the boat were following Elizabeth's example. Even the older women followed suit, all that is but Dorothy Bradford. Elizabeth noticed that while the others were laughing and making ready to wade ashore, Dorothy sat unmoving in the bow staring straight ahead.

At last the dory scraped to a stop in the sand, and hoisting their skirts, the women clambered into the shallow surf. Elizabeth waded back along the side of the boat and offered her hand to Dorothy who still hadn't moved. "Let me help you out."

"Yeh, hurry up," the seamen who had rowed them ashore

prodded, "You ain't the only ones that need ferryin'."

With that Dorothy stirred and handed Elizabeth her sack of laundry while she climbed from the now beached boat.

"Elizabeth," her mother called. "Come and help me."

Soon she was busy with the rest of the women scrubbing and beating clothes in a tidal pool.

"It would be a waste to try to use soap. I suppose things will be stiff from the salt water, but at least they'll be fresh," Goodwife Tilley said as she wrung out a linen nightshirt and looked for a place to lay it to dry.

Elizabeth took it from her and carried it to a long piece of driftwood, a skeleton of a whole tree with broken limbs. There were any number of such silvery smooth derelicts to drape the laundry on.

As Elizabeth passed close to where the men were gathered about the shallop she heard William Bradford say, "There's more work to be done here than we expected. I think we'd better plan to explore on foot again."

Elizabeth couldn't help wondering how long it would take to explore that impenetrable-looking wilderness on foot, but today she was determined to enjoy the fresh air and the freedom of the warm beach.

Just as the last pair of drawers were hung on a contorted driftwood branch, and Elizabeth was laughing at a gull who swooped down to investigate the strange blossoms that had appeared on his perch, Henry came running up. The children, who had been allowed ashore, too, had been racing up and down the beach shouting to each other with each new discovery while Miles Standish stood on guard scowling, but not scolding.

"Look what I found," Henry said holding up a clam with a grey ridged shell. "Do you think it's good to eat?"

Hungry as she was for fresh food, Elizabeth had never liked shellfish. But Richard came over to them, took the clam from him and broke it open with a rock. "Sure it's good to eat," he said gulping it down.

"That was Henry's!" Elizabeth was upset that he would take the child's food.

"There must be lots more. Where did you find this?" Richard asked, and Henry led him to the water's edge.

"I felt it with my toes," he said.

Richard began digging with his hands, but wasn't finding anything when John Howland joined them.

"See all those bubbles in the wet sand?" John said. "There are clams down there." Beginning to dig, he soon turned up another one. "It would be easier to dig with a forked stick," he suggested.

As Henry scampered off to find one, Desire, who had been helping Mistress Carver with her laundry, came to John's side, "Humm, I love clams," she said.

"We'll soon have a sackful," John promised. "Maybe we can roast them right here on the beach."

"Roast them?" Richard exclaimed. "Why roast them? They're good just as they come out of the shell." He swallowed another to make his point.

"Maybe you should listen to John," Elizabeth said. "I've heard of people getting sick from raw clams."

"But that was in England. What could possibly make us sick over here?" Desire sided with Richard as John sought his own stick.

News of the clams spread and before long the whole party was digging furiously for the fresh food. Soon someone discovered the long black muscle and found the shell much easier to break, and everyone seemed to be eating them as fast as they could find and open them. But Elizabeth stood back watching them scurry around the tidal flat, thinking they looked a little like the sandpipers that had darted away as they landed.

"Come on, Elizabeth," Richard called. "Come dig, too."

But Elizabeth ignored him until he came over with an open clam, and pulling it loose from the shell, lifted it to her face. She jumped back and he laughingly grabbed her and tried to shove the slimy mess into her mouth.

Elizabeth screamed involuntarily and tried to free herself, but Richard didn't let go. "Come on. Taste it," he insisted, rubbing it on her lips.

Elizabeth was almost ready to open her mouth when from the corner of her eye she saw John Howland running toward them. As she renewed her struggle, he grabbed Richard by the shoulder and whirled him around. Elizabeth saw John's right hand tighten into a fist and then relax as Richard backed off.

"I was only trying to have some fun," Richard said. "Besides

I'll bet she really would like them if she tried them."

As Elizabeth turned away, shaken by the strength she had felt in Richard's grasp, her eyes met John Howland's and she hoped he could read the gratitude she felt.

Her appreciation was even greater that night when those who had feasted on the mussels began to "cast and scour" as her mother so aptly put it.

"Elizabeth, help me," Richard called out to her clutching for her skirt as she went by carrying a slop bucket for her mother. "I think I'm dying," he moaned.

"Serves you right," she said with satisfaction, whisking her skirt away and leaving him to fend for himself.

Later, when her mother was feeling somewhat better, she patted the bunk beside her and asked Elizabeth to sit down.

"You know you haven't been very nice to Richard today," her mother said.

Elizabeth began crying softly.

"What's the matter? You think you don't love Richard?" Goodwife Tilley said quietly.

Elizabeth nodded and groped for a handkerchief.

"I understand," her mother said. "I didn't love your father either when I married him."

Her mother not love her father! Elizabeth couldn't imagine such a thing. They were as devoted a couple as she knew.

"There was a yeoman that I used to see in the village on market day, blond hair, blue eyes, never a youth more handsome. One day he caught me behind the fish stall, gave me a kiss to set my blood tingling, but it wasn't possible for him to marry me. I had no land to join to his. I was but a servant's daughter. So when your father wanted to marry me, I could do nothing but agree. He was a hired worker like my father. It was right, and I was never sorry. Be good to Richard. You'll come to love him." Her mother's eyes, that had had a far away look when she began, came back to Elizabeth as she patted her hand.

Was her mother right? Elizabeth wondered, giving her a wan smile of half assent. Would she, in time, come to love Richard?

Chapter 11

John Howland felt his pulse quicken with excitement as he waited his turn to climb into the jolly. While the shallop was being refurbished, sixteen of them had volunteered to explore the shore on foot.

As he was about to swing onto the rope ladder, Desire grasped his arm. "Oh John, I wish you weren't going. Please be careful."

"Pray for me," he said, resisting the urge to shake free, and gently removing her hand instead.

"Oh, I will. I will!" Desire answered. John saw Elizabeth nod her head too, and caught a look of concern in her eyes.

When they reached the beach, Capt. Standish ordered the exploring party to move in single file along the water's edge. "Keep your muskets ready," he commanded.

John fell in between William Bradford and Edward Tilley. As they trudged the sunlit beach, John kept glancing up at the dark woods wondering what savages might be lurking there.

There was no sound but the lapping of the bay waters on the shore, and the shussh of boots in the sand. A breeze rippled across the open water and rustled into the trees. John shivered even as he warmed from exertion.

They had tramped a good distance when he spied several figures farther up the beach.

"Was Master Jones taking some of the sailors ashore this morning?" Edward Tilley asked.

"Yes, but they couldn't have rowed past without our seeing them," Capt. Standish replied.

"Look, there's a dog with them," John exclaimed.

Just then the figures, who had been wandering toward them, stopped, poised as hunting dogs. When Capt. Standish waved to them, they turned as one, and loped up a sand dune and into the woods. John had never seen anyone move so swiftly and lightly before.

"Wait," he yelled instinctively, realizing almost immediately that he could better have saved his breath for running. Capt. Standish had started chasing down the beach after then with sword clanking at his knee and musket bouncing on his shoulder.

As John quickened his pace, soft sand sucked at his feet, and his banging musket gained pounds. The natives had no encumbrances, not even clothes. By the time they reached the place where they had disappeared, the only sign of their existence was bare footprints near the water's edge and lines of indentations filling with loose sand where they had scampered over the dune.

"I can track them," Stephen Hopkins panted when they reached the spot where the footprints ended. "I got fairly good at it when I was in Virginia."

"Take the lead," Capt. Standish ordered, relinquishing his position and falling in behind him.

Like the land they had explored on Saturday, scraggly pine and dense juniper cast deep shadows over the needle-carpeted floor. They had more reason now to expect each shadow to harbor an Indian.

"Suppose they are laying in ambush for us." John voiced his fear and felt better for it.

"Don't worry," Capt. Standish said, patting his musket. "These will take care of any ambush."

Trotting was easier on the firmer soil, but seeing any distance was impossible. Everything blended together. From which dark patch were they being stalked? John could feel a prickling sensation at the back of his neck as his eyes shifted constantly and his head pivoted from side to side. He needed eyes like a toad, set high on his head so he could see behind as well.

That shadow! Was it moving? Just a breeze ruffling some oak leaves.

The space between John and William Bradford lengthened. His ears strained for any sound beyond their own quiet footfalls. A branch snapped echoing in his chest. Thump. Thump. His heart pounded in his ears. He swallowed hard.

At last he realized what was happening. Fear was taking control. A verse from the Psalms surfaced. "It is Thou, Lord, only who makest me dwell in safety." *God has brought us across wild seas, and lifted me out of raging water, and now I am afraid walking on dry ground.* He almost laughed at himself.

"Forgive me, Lord," he prayed silently. Squaring his shoulders and taking longer strides, he caught up with William Bradford.

Just then Master Hopkins veered back to the shore. There were footprints again, but going both ways. Apparently the Indians were retracing their steps. Hopefully they would either catch up with them or find their village.

But they trudged on for hours more until John could no longer ignore his gnawing stomach. They had eaten nothing all day. The sky was ablaze with sunset. Night was upon them and they were miles from the ship.

Only now did Capt. Standish call a halt. "It'll soon be too dark to see," he said.

"We'll have to make camp for the night," William Bradford said, stepping forward. "We'll need a fire. It's much colder already."

John gratefully laid down his gun and began collecting driftwood.

"Better drag down some branches, too," Stephen Hopkins suggest. "We can build a barricade."

When a pile of dead limbs was collected, Stephen Hopkins heaped pine needles and twigs under them and sprinkled on gun powder. Capt. Standish struck his flint, once, twice. On the third try a spark sizzled onto the powder. A tiny flame flared.

Soon a roaring fire blazed up, driving back the dark and warming John's weary frame as he munched on hard biscuit and dry cheese. Everyone had carried a small parcel of food with them, but, hoping to find water, they had only one bottle of Dutch aqua vitae among them.

Edward Tilley passed it to John. He felt fifteen pairs of eyes on him, even as, before it came to him, he had watched each person take the one swig Standish had allotted. John raised the bottle slowly to his lips. Letting the liquid run into his mouth, he held it there moistening his dry tongue. When he finally swallowed, his parched throat cried for more, but he lowered the bottle and passed it on.

Not only was he thirsty, but his arms ached from carrying the musket. Most of all, his feet hurt. How he longed to take his boots off, but had a strong suspicion that if he did he might never get them on again. He was just stretching out on the sand, sighing with relief when Capt. Standish called him to take the first watch.

Groaning inwardly, John dragged himself to his feet and shouldered his musket.

"Howland, keep a lookout in the woods. Bradford, up the beach. I'll watch down," Capt. Standish barked.

This is ridiculous, John thought as he turned from the fire and took his post. *I can't see a thing.* But gradually his eyes adjusted and he could pick out black trees and bushes from the dark grey surrounding them. *If something moves, I guess I will see it. I'm glad Capt. Standish taught me how to use a gun*, he mused, his eyes roving up and down the edge of the forest. "Lord, help me stay awake," he whispered. "Please watch over those we left behind."

His thoughts drifted back to the ship. Was Elizabeth praying for him? Was Desire? It was she he must think of, not Elizabeth.

He relived that fateful morning on the dock at Plymouth. Rising early, unable to sleep because he had heard John Tilley might not be going, he had wandered down to the wharf. Knowing that Desire had come expecting to marry him, he was struggling to decide if he could honorably ask to marry Elizabeth.

A cloaked figure was already there, and he wished it might be Elizabeth. Not tall enough, and too slight, it was Desire.

Hurrying up to him, she said, "Oh John, I'm so glad to see you. I've been trying to decide whether I should go or not." Then with a flutter of her lashes she added, "I'm not that young anymore. I need a good reason to continue this awful voyage."

Looking up at him, she asked, "Do *you* think I should go?"

John felt doomed. He knew what he must do. Mistress Carver was counting on Desire coming with them, and Master Carver had made it clear that they expected him to marry Desire.

After all, she was pretty and appealing. Surely he could love her.

John sighed as he remembered what he had said. "Desire, I'd like you to come. Carvers want us to marry."

"How wonderful! I'd love that!" she had exclaimed.

But when she had stepped toward him with lifted face, he had put her off saying he still had work to do. He would not kiss her until he could put Elizabeth out of his mind.

"Yes, there is much to do now," she had acquiesced. "The wedding will have to wait until we are settled in the New World, but now I have a reason to go."

Resolutely he pictured her dainty hands, but Elizabeth's long fingers took their place instead. He shook his head, studied the night shadows more closely and prayed for the success of their expedition.

Someone was moving behind him. He spun about to see Capt. Standish tending the fire. John ventured over to warm his hands and stretch his cramped legs. In the circle of firelight the rest of the men were sprawled like battle casualties, some snoring, some groaning in their sleep.

"Our watch is up. I'll waken the next shift," Capt. Standish said as William Bradford joined them.

John collapsed beside Edward Tilley and knew nothing more until he awoke chilled and stiff in the cold grey dawn. After kneeling for prayer led by William Bradford, and eating their hard biscuit washed down by a mouthful from the same bottle they had shared the night before, they began following the trail again.

At first every step was painful, but John gradually worked out his stiffness. What was unbearable was the thirst. His mouth was sticky and his lips were parched, dry as the sand they had clambered through to enter the woods. He wiggled his tongue and licked his lips, but there was no saliva. *Have we landed on a desert*, he wondered. *No water Saturday, none yesterday. No sight nor sound of any but the ocean today.*

The tracks led around an inlet and into scrubby woods which gave way to a thicket that tore at John's breeches and scratched his leather breastplate. Stephen Hopkins persisted on the trail, laboring up hill.

John was becoming skeptical of his tracking ability when Hopkins stopped and confessed, "I seem to have lost the Indian tracks. I know it's rough going, but this looks like a deer trail. Perhaps it will lead to a water hole."

Everyone agreed to press on. The trail plunged down hill, but they stumbled on twisting free of the brambles that clawed as if to imprison them. Just like evil, John thought. "Deliver us," he prayed.

Just then Hopkins turned abruptly to the right and made his way along the side of the hill. Suddenly he called, "Water! There's a spring over here."

"Water, water!" The word sang in John's mind as men stumbled over each other to reach it. When his turn came to kneel by the little pool that bubbled out of the ground, he dipped his hand in the water and let it trickle through his fingers, remembering how David had offered to God the water that his servant had brought him from the well at Bethlehem. "Thank you, Lord," he breathed as he drank deeply. Never had any drink tasted so good.

Refreshed and with their bottle filled with sweet water, they made their way back to the shore and tramped on. Their goal was to reach the spot which from the Mayflower looked like the mouth of a river. They hoped it might lead to a good village site.

Coming to a hollow running back from the beach, John thought he caught the glint of water through the trees. Could it be a pond? When he pointed it out, they decided to investigate. A good tramp brought them at last to the bank of a brown lake whose quiet surface reflected the surrounding trees. Brackish or fresh? John stooped, scooped up a handful and lifted it to his mouth. God be praised! It was fresh. A water supply at last. This was the news those on the ship were waiting to hear.

Rejoicing, the weary band angled back toward the beach. Shortly they stumbled onto cleared ground. Something had been growing here this past summer. But what? Remains of slender stalks similar to bamboo stood on hillocks through the field.

"A corn field!" Stephen exclaimed as he came out behind John, having let Capt. Standish take the lead again.

"Corn?" John echoed doubtfully. Corn left straw, not stalks.

"Maize. The Indians have been growing their grain here," Master Hopkins explained.

John had heard about maize. Curious now, he looked around for a sample, but couldn't see a single head.

Meanwhile the party crossed the field and ranged about the wooded area on the far side.

"Looks like the remains of a small building," William Bradford called.

As the men gathered to look at a pile of rotting boards, John, who was still looking for corn came on a rusted iron pot such as sailors used in the ship's galley. Had some English sailors wintered here?

Perhaps, but that didn't explain the still fresh-looking corn stalks.

Foraging on, he spotted a strange mound much larger than the hillocks with the broken stalks. *What's that,* he wondered and went to explore. Sand had been deliberately piled up. He could still see the handprints of whomever had built it.

Could this be it, the site for the plantation? Apparently the Indians didn't live here. They might be willing to sell the land. If only they could overtake them! His breath became shallow at the thought.

"What do you suppose this is all about?" he called to the men who had finished speculating about the decaying boards.

"Could it be a grave?" Edward Tilley wondered as the men collected around it.

"One way to find out," Stephen Hopkins said, beginning to dig into it with his bare hands.

"Wait a minute," William Bradford spoke with authority, "If it's a grave we have no right to violate it."

"But how will we ever know?" Capt. Standish reasoned. "We can fix it up and leave it as it was. But it makes sense to find out what is buried here."

William Bradford reluctantly agreed. John dropped to his knees beside Stephen Hopkins and both dug furiously while the rest kept watch. Soon John's fingers hit something rough, and scrapping away the sand he exposed a bit of woven straw.

Working around it, they brought to light a beautifully woven basket. Buried treasure?

No, the mound was too obvious. Still John's pulse quickened as he lifted the lid. Bright yellows, dark reds, purplish blue colors shone in the dim interior. Beads? No, he could see that they were attached to small tapered cylinders. He reached in and lifted one out.

"Corn. Indian maize," Stephen Hopkins announced.

So this was what grew in the field over there. More precious than jewels. Seed that will grow in this soil. Food. Life itself. All this raced through his mind, and then he realized that it must belong to the savages, perhaps those they had seen on the beach.

The importance of the find seemed to hit all of them at once. "Seed. Seed corn." John heard the words all around him.

"But we must buy it," William Bradford reminded them.

"What if we can't find anyone to buy it from?" Capt. Standish challenged.

"We don't need to worry about stealing from the natives. They'd steal us blind if they got half the chance," Stephen Hopkins said.

"It doesn't matter what they would do. We answer to God for our actions," Bradford replied.

"But surely God has given this to us. As soon as we catch up with the Indians we can pay for it," Edward Tilley spoke up.

The men were still on their knees around the basket looking at William Bradford. He considered briefly and nodded his head slowly, "Perhaps Goodman Tilley is right." He smiled. "Since we are in the best position for prayer, why don't we give God thanks for providing both water and food for us in our new land?"

After the prayer he carefully counted our thirty-six "ears" as Stephen Hopkins called them. The basket still held more.

"We must leave them seed, too, " William Bradford declared.

When he replaced the lid and began recovering it, John helped. It seemed more like child's play than work. John was fascinated that each thump of his hand gave back a soft hollow ring as they reshaped the mound. Soon it was covered with fresh handprints, just as they had found it. Only this time it bore the prints of Englishmen.

The wall at South Hampton

Citadel on the harbor at Plymouth, England

The shallop

Replica of the original settlement at Plymouth Plantation in Massachusetts

Author with actress Elizabeth Tilley

Typical cottage at Plymouth Plantation

Father of the Billington boys

Reenactors of the original Pilgrim settlers

Chapter 12

"Elizabeth, you should be knitting too," Goodwife Tilley admonished.

While the men left on the ship had gone ashore to work on the shallop, the women had gathered on deck in the pale fall sunshine. Elizabeth and Constance were hanging over the side watching for the men who had disappeared into the woods the day before.

"The tie on your hat is going to break if you don't find something else to do with your hands," Elizabeth's mother said. Suddenly Elizabeth realized why the older women and even Desire were clicking away furiously. All except Dorothy Bradford who stood alone, looking vacantly across the water.

"I've used up my wool," Elizabeth answered, not sure she could think about knitting anyway.

"Go down in the hold, and find our extra chest," her mother directed. "There's plenty of yarn in it."

Elizabeth glanced at Desire and Constance, but neither seemed inclined to come with her. She went below, picked up a candle in the 'tween deck and climbed down the ladder into the hold.

As she descended into the depths of the ship, she became aware that someone already had a light down there. Who could it be? Wasn't everyone on deck or ashore? Might it be one of the sailors? Was it wise for her to go on alone?

Just then she recognized the voice of one of the Billington

boys. *Guess I haven't seen them for awhile*, she thought.

Suddenly she caught the odd smell of flint being struck, as if someone were trying to build a fire. Then she heard Francis Billington say, "Almost got it that time. Try again."

Why are they striking flint when they already have a light, she wondered. Then a horrible thought stuck her.

Gunpowder! The boys had been fascinated by the men loading their guns. And there it was, just as she feared, a barrel labeled "black powder."

Quickly blowing out her candle, she scurried around the barrel. Elizabeth surprised the two boys who were chipping away at a flint as they leaned over a generous pile of black dust.

"Stop!" she screamed. "You'll blow us all to kingdom come!"

Francis jumped and his brother dropped the flint.

"What on earth were you trying to do?" she gasped.

"Just wanted to see how this stuff works," Francis said.

Elizabeth's knees were shaking as she tore into them, "You should have better sense. If that pile had caught you could have blown up the whole ship. Get back on deck."

When the rest of the women heard the story they gasped in horror. Only later, after their mother had taken them in hand and promised that their father would give them a real thrashing, did Elizabeth give thanks that they hadn't had wit enough to put their candle to the powder.

Hard as it was to concentrate, she gathered the children around her to listen to stories from Fox's *Book of Martyrs*. That way everyone knew where they were.

When the men returned from working on the shallop, and heard the story, Goodman Billington whisked the boys off to the 'tween deck.

The cracks he administered and the howls of pain could be heard topside. Elizabeth listened with satisfaction, and hoped they had learned their lesson.

As the mast of the ship cast a long shadow shoreward, Elizabeth was back at her railing watching the distant beach. At last she thought she spotted movement far off on the curving line of sand. In the evening shadows it was hard to be sure. Then she heard it

Three shots! The signal she had been waiting for. Others had heard it too, and Master Jones immediately ordered the sailors off to pick up the explorers.

As the bedraggled men clambered aboard, everyone crowded around, full of questions.

"We found the place for our village," Edward Tilley began. In excited bits and pieces the story spilled out.

But there was disagreement over whether Corn Hill was the right place to build. Some feared the pond would dry up in summer. Others felt the landing spot was too shallow. Still it was a water supply and tillable land. So the argument went back and forth.

While Elizabeth grew more and more impatient to go ashore permanently, the leaders decided to send out yet another expedition. The shallop was ready and they could easily sail down to explore the feasibility of landing near the site and appraise it again. Both her father, uncle and Richard volunteered to go.

Elizabeth found herself twisting her ties again. Each day there was less light and the weather was growing steadily colder.

"I wish I were a man so I could go too," she said to Richard the next day as she wrapped biscuits for him. "This waiting is worse than being there, no matter what happens."

"At least John's not going this time," Desire said, coming over to them.

"He's not?" Richard said in disbelief.

"My uncle's going again," Elizabeth said.

Desire shrugged, and tucked her hands under her cape. It was cold even in the 'tween deck. "It's his choice, but I don't know how your aunt can take it."

Her aunt, who had overheard the conversation, looked up from mending a snag in her husband's cloak and spoke softly, "There's more than one way to love, my dear."

Elizabeth joined in seeing the men off the next morning under lowering skies. A wet, but favorable wind blew from the northeast, and the loaded shallop went skittering off down the coast.

"I know it's going to rain," her mother predicted. "But there's no stopping them now."

Her mother was right on both counts. Before noon the rain started. Shortly it turned to needle-like sleet driven by a rising wind. Those left aboard closed the hatches and huddled around their braziers attempting to keep warm.

"Surely the men won't go on in this storm," Elizabeth's mother's tone betrayed her anxiety.

By afternoon most people had crawled into their ticks. But much to Desire's dismay, John Howland and some of the sailors insisted on going ashore for firewood. Elizabeth noticed that he had stayed away from Desire after she had extracted his promise not to go.

Becoming very restless cooped up below, and finding both Constance and Desire napping, Elizabeth pulled her cloak about her and climbed onto the main deck. The air was full of dancing snowflakes blowing about like steam from a witch's kettle. Through the lacy white blur she discerned another hooded figure on deck leaning against the rail and staring down into the black waves that were tossing the ship at anchor. She started toward it and was about to speak when the figure turned and moved to the other side.

Oh, it's Dorothy Bradford! Elizabeth recognized the drooping shoulders and shuffling gait. While she was wondering if she should follow, she heard voices drifting across the water. Out of the curtain of snow, the shallop emerged. With a sigh of relief she strained to pick out her father's lincoln-green coat, but couldn't locate it. There were fewer men on board than had started out. What had happened?

Elizabeth couldn't wait for the men to come aboard. She leaned over the railing and called her question into the swirling snow.

"Went ashore," Capt. Jones' muffled voice came back to her.

Elizabeth's teeth began chattering. They would take their death of cold. How could they have done such a stupid thing? But she understood how eager everyone was to settle on a site for the village, and realized that she would have done the same thing.

When her father and Richard climbed aboard the next evening their pockets were bulging with colorful corn and beans, and they were full of tales of Corn Hill. But her father was so hoarse she could barely hear what he had to say. And still, she learned, they couldn't agree on the site.

As the men talked, Elizabeth glanced at John Howland, and read the disappointment in his eyes. She knew he would go next time.

He had learned of a bay called Thievish Harbor from Robert Coffin, one of the ship's mates, who had gone with him to gather wood. She had stood by that evening while Governor Carver drew a candle close and poured over John Smith's map. He had located a place named Plymouth that matched the mate's description, and had decided that if the men couldn't agree on Corn Hill, they should explore it.

Her chest swelled with pride when her father and uncle as well as John were chosen for the Plymouth expedition. But it quickly constricted with fear for her father's health. Would more exposure to this wild weather make him worse?

She was being foolish. He only had a cold. After a hot drink and a good night's sleep, he would be better, she assured herself. But she couldn't help noticing her mother's tight-lipped silence.

At least Desire raised no objections to John's going this time. Elizabeth was relieved that he could leave without being made to feel guilty.

Chapter 13

Zing! Something whizzed past John Howland's head. An arrow quivered in a coat hanging to dry on the brush wall of the barricade.

"Yowl, wa, wa, yowl!" Blood curdling cries rent the air. The same cries he had heard during the night!

"Wolves," a sailor had said then.

No wolf shot that arrow!

"Indians! Indians!" Edward Dotey yelled, plunging into the barricade from his sentry post.

"To arms!" Capt. Standish's command rang out.

John Howland was already grabbing for his musket.

"My gun's on the beach!" John Tilley gasped. Several men had laid down their weapons when they had begun reloading the shallop for the second day of exploration. Elizabeth's father led a dash for the muskets as more arrows winged into the compound.

John Howland, musket ready, pulse racing, popped his head above the flimsy rampart. Several Indians were chasing after John Tilley.

He let go a blast at the pursuing savages. Beside him Capt. Standish's gun boomed. Several men grabbed cutlasses. Wielding them high, they rushed headlong to rescue their comrades just as John Tilley skidded up to his gun.

Boom. Boom. More guns exploded in John Howland's ear.

Terrified, the Indians turned and vanished among the trees.

All but one.

Zing. Zing. Zing. As fast as the brave could string his bow, arrow after arrow flew at the exposed men.

Bang. John Howland's shot was lost in the woods.

Bang. Bang. Bang. Shots echoed from the men on the shore.

The big Indian stood his ground and continued to rain arrows upon them. While John was tapping another round of powder into his musket, he saw Capt. Standish take careful aim. Ready to fire again, he looked up as the captain's gun resounded.

Bark shattered over the brave's head. With a shriek the Indian streaked into the woods.

A great stillness descended, and John, tensing to catch any movement, realized that the wilderness was as empty as if they had only imagined the Indians. His ears rang, his arms ached, blood pounded in his temples, but a strange exultation filled him. He had survived his first battle. Never had he felt more alive.

The men on the beach marched back to the shelter, and an assessment was made of the damage. No one had a scratch.

"It's too bad," John Tilley said, "but it looks like we won't be able to make friends with those Indians."

"But I don't think we'll have to fear an attack from them again," John responded chuckling over the flight of the brave.

A short while later a mild breeze was carrying the shallop across the bay, and John watched the shore of the Cape fade into sky and water. Would that John Smith's Plymouth was like the town they had sailed from in England, he thought wistfully. But he was sure there would be no more civilization there than there was on the barren coast they had just left.

The morning was hazy clear with a mild southerly breeze swinging the Mayflower gently at anchor as Elizabeth and Desire helped several of the children down the rope ladder into the ship's dinghy. Yesterday there had been freezing rain, and she was thankful for the return of mild weather for the sake of the exploring party. With Richard at the oars, they were off to forage for wood.

Dorothy Bradford had been staring into the water again, when Elizabeth had come on deck. Elizabeth spoke to her. This time Dorothy answered brightly, commenting on the pleasant weather. But when Elizabeth seized on her improved mood to invite her to join them, she refused.

"Perhaps next time," Elizabeth said with a smile as she climbed into the little boat.

The children were soon scurrying up and down the beach shouting to each other as they raced to see who could collect the most wood the fastest. When the boat was full the children begged to stay longer, so Elizabeth persuaded Richard to take the first load back while they gathered more.

She had to admit to herself that she was glad to escape his attention. It seemed that his hand was always lingering on hers as she handed him a piece of wood. She was upset with herself because she couldn't respond as she ought. Somehow it was easier to put up with him better when John Howland was around. Was it because John had a way of making any situation more bearable, or was it because Richard seldom attempted to touch her when John was nearby? She wished they had taken Richard along on the exploration of Plymouth, but the men from the Leyden congregation wanted to see it for themselves.

He had asked her before he left to go up into the woods with him to find some green wood to mix with the rest. "Desire will keep an eye on the children," he had said. She had quickly squelched the idea.

Another boatload of silvery wood was piled on the shore awaiting Richard's return. Elizabeth and Desire felt free at last to wander the beach in search of shells. Elizabeth was fascinated by the pearly lining of clam shells, ranging from white to shades of grey and sometimes pink or yellow.

"Look at this," Desire said, picking up a small oval shell. "It has a hole in it."

Humility came running up at the same time with a handful of the same kind. "Can I make a necklace?" she asked.

Just then Henry came charging at them waving a crab. Its claws were clacking at the girls who ran screaming down the beach with Elizabeth bringing up the rear. Henry laughed so hard that he dropped the crab.

As Elizabeth came back to him she realized that the clouds had blotted out the sun, and the wind had shifted. She shivered and looked across the water for Richard. He was just pulling away from the lee of the Mayflower. She was watching the dip, pull, lift of his oars when suddenly one oar stopped suspended in midair. At the same time she became aware of figures on the ship waving frantically at him.

Desire and the children were watching too. "What do you suppose is wrong?" Desire asked.

"Could there be a fire?" It was something Elizabeth dreaded since her latest experience with the Billington boys. "I don't see any smoke," Desire said quickly.

Elizabeth looked the ship over carefully and could see nothing out of the ordinary. Richard was almost back to it, and those on deck were waving him to the far side out of their sight. As he pulled around, they swarmed to the other side too.

Why? Elizabeth couldn't guess.

"Maybe someone caught a big fish, and they want him to bring it in," Henry suggested.

But they weren't prepared to catch the whales that they had seen cavorting near the ship, even though Master Jones had commented on the valuable oil that could be obtained from the them.

Did one of them hit the ship? She didn't voice her fears for the children's sakes. Instead she said, "Maybe Richard forgot something." Yet she didn't really believe it.

The wind had grown colder. They were all shivering as a few wet snowflakes began spitting at them.

"I'll race you for that piece of driftwood down there," Elizabeth challenged. "Last one there is a rotten apple."

No one moved.

"I'm cold" Henry said plaintively. "I want to go back to the boat."

"Why doesn't Richard come?" Humility crowded close to Elizabeth.

Desire and Elizabeth looked at each other helplessly, and then Desire suggested, "If we go up into the woods it might be warmer."

But everyone continued standing there with their eyes glued to the Mayflower.

"I want Richard," Humility said and began to cry.

Elizabeth bent down and picked her up. "Don't cry, he'll be coming soon." She carried her over to the pile of firewood.

Choosing a twisted piece that looked like a bird, she held it for Humility to see. "I'll bet we can find other animals in here too," she said in an effort to divert her.

But Humility wrapped her arms around her neck and buried her face in Elizabeth's rough wool cloak.

"He's coming," Desire called.

The snowflakes were falling faster, making it hard to see across the water, but Elizabeth thought she could pick out three other men in the boat as well as Richard. *Why would they be coming ashore now,* she wondered.

Humility wriggled out of Elizabeth's arms. The little group on the shore stood very still watching the approaching boat. As it beat its way closer Elizabeth recognized Elder Brewster in the stern.

The children ran to meet the skiff as it grated onto the beach. Before Elizabeth and Desire could join them they came rushing back with frightened faces.

Humility threw her arms around Elizabeth's legs and buried her face in the older girl's skirts.

"What is it?" Elizabeth asked through chattering teeth.

"That lady. She's in the bottom of the boat all wet and white," Henry answered, his eyes almost popping from his head.

"What lady?" Desire asked as the color drained from her face.

"You know. The one who's always walking around the deck all alone," he answered breathlessly.

"Dorothy Bradford!" Elizabeth and Desire spoke in chorus. Elizabeth felt certain the horror on Desire's face was reflected in her own.

As they watched, the first man to alight from the boat picked up a shovel, climbed the dunes and disappeared into the woods. At the same time Elder Brewster handed several precious boards to the other two who produced a hammer and saw and fell to work banging together a— a coffin. Elizabeth choked as the word formed in her mind.

Seeing the little group huddled there, Elder Brewster came over to them. "Somehow Dorothy fell overboard," he said quietly. There was a flatness to his voice that Elizabeth had never heard before. "Your mother discovered it when she came up thinking to catch Richard with a little lunch for you," he went on. "She just happened to catch sight of something floating on the water."

"She spent so much time on deck. She seemed to be fascinated by the water. She must have leaned too far over," Desire said quickly.

Why? Why did she do it, was all that Elizabeth could think. She said nothing.

"One of the men will take you back to the ship as soon as they finish the coffin," Elder Brewster said.

"Please, may I stay for her burial?" Elizabeth asked. It was all she could do now. Could she have done more earlier? She would never know.

Elder Brewster studied her face and then nodded consent.

"I'll stay too. There's no need to make an extra trip," Desire said.

When the rough box was finished Elder Brewster approached the beached boat. Elizabeth followed close behind, while Desire held the children back.

"May I help?" she asked. Again he nodded consent.

Bracing herself for a ghastly sight Elizabeth looked over the gunwale into a face of carved ivory with the most peaceful expression she had ever seen. Gently she helped the men lift the cold stiff figure and place it in the coffin.

Little Humility came running up then with a handful of shells, the ones she had hoped to make into beads, and solemnly dropped them into the box before the men nailed on the lid.

The four men shouldered the box and carried it to the top of a dune where a shallow grave was ready beneath the sheltering branches of a weather-beaten pine. The box thudded into the hole and sand was quickly shoveled over it.

Elder Brewster stood silent with bowed head as snow collected on his wide-brimmed hat. Snow blew into Elizabeth's face, mingling with the tears that were streaming down her cheeks. *Couldn't he say something*, she raged inside. But the horrible weight of knowing that anyone who took their own life was a murderer snuffed out the anger in grief.

"God have mercy!" she cried into the wind.

The job finished, the three grim-faced men never glanced at

her as they marched away. But Elder Brewster seemed frozen, as bent as the trunk of the gnarled pine by which he stood. At last he fell to his knees beside the fresh mound of sand, buried his face in his hands, and his sagging shoulders heaved.

Elizabeth turned and ran through the blinding snow back to the beach where the others were waiting. As she faced the snow-swept water, she thought of William Bradford for the first time. He was out there somewhere risking his life to find a place to build a home for his wife, and she did this! Suddenly she was very angry with Dorothy. Somehow it helped.

John Howland clenched his teeth against the biting cold and hugged his greatcoat around him. Snowflakes like tiny arrows pelted him. Freezing spray splashed into the boat glazing everything, even making beads on John Tilley's mustache. John doubled against the icy blast.

He marveled that the sailors could hold the vessel on course, and worried about John and Edward Tilley. They weren't young men any longer. Could they survive this weather? Scarcely able to open his eyes now against the needle-like snow, he turned to Edward Tilley huddled beside him.

Just then Edward slumped sideways and fell against John. Even as he tried to support him, he slid from his seat into the bottom of the boat. *He's dead*, John thought, and bent his ear to the his mouth. In partial shelter from the wind, he thought he could catch a faint breath.

William Bradford and his brother clambered to his side.

"He's passed out," John yelled over the wind. "Get bedrolls."

John reached for one of Edward's wrists. John Tilley grabbed the other. His own fingers were so numb they would scarcely move, but gradually feeling returned as he rubbed.

Someone stuffed bedrolls about him, while William Bradford pulled off his boots and began massaging his feet. John was vaguely aware that he hadn't felt his own toes for some time, and tried to curl them inside his boots as he continued to work on Edward.

Edward moaned and opened his eyes. Someone handed John Tilley a bottle of precious spirits. He lifted his brother's head and tilted the flask to his lips. Edward gulped and struggled to sit up.

"Sit close to each other and put your bedrolls around you," Governor Carver ordered, beating his hands together and blowing on them.

John Howland sat down in the bottom of the boat, snuggling up as close as he could to Edward Tilley while John Tilley hugged against his brother's other side. The gunwales broke the wind, but it was still deathly cold.

Suddenly the sound of cracking wood split the wailing wind. *Or is it my own nerves snapping,* John wondered.

"We've lost our rudder," Coffin cried out.

"We're lost," Edward gasped in John's ear.

Saved from the ocean to die in the bay so close to shore!

"To the oars," Coffin shouted, and two of the sailors scrambled to get oars in the water to control the wind-driven vessel.

"Can we run back to the Cape?" Governor Carver called to Coffin.

"Let's go back," John Tilley pleaded.

"Go back! Go back," others took up the cry.

But as John looked up he thought he could see two arms of land on the horizon outlined through the driving snow.

"Land ho!" Coffin sang out. He had seen it too. "That's what we're looking for."

But it was still a good distance off, and the scanty daylight was fading fast. Coffin ordered the boat about. "Hoist the jib! Give the main full sail. We'll run for it."

Once the sails were tugged into place the ship raced before the wind. John clung to the gunwale to keep from being pitched into the sea.

Again a heart-stopping crack pierced John's ears. Mast and sails came tumbling down barely missing John's head. The wind caught the main, billowing it over the side where it sagged into the water threatening to pull the boat over with it.

One of the sailors yanked out a knife and hacked at the ropes. Water rushed over the gunwale soaking John as he struggled to disentangle himself from the jib that was plastered to him. Suddenly the main's ropes gave way. As the wind finished whipping it overboard, the shallop quivered and righted itself.

Now while the sailors struggled at the oars to hold the ship on course, everyone bailed frantically. Finding nothing else, John took his new hat and splashed away with it. When he looked up again they were riding the in-rushing tide between the two arms of land he had picked out earlier. Praise God, they were entering the harbor.

But the strong seas carried them on out of control.

"There's a beach ahead," the sailor's voice sounded confident. All at once the shallop seemed to be picked up by a mighty hand and tossed into a cove where thunderous breakers rushed them toward the rocky shore.

"Lord, help us," he yelled. "I've never seen this place before. Pull for your lives."

Chapter 14

John Howland, grabbing a free oar, swung it into the sea, and laid to with all his might. Pulling against the tide, the shallop seemed to stand still on the top of each comber, sometimes coming down on the rock-strewn landward side, and sometimes mounting the wave and moving away from the shore.

Lean forward. Pull back. Forward. Back. Again, again. Slowly, ever so slowly, the distance between the shallop and the shore widened.

John's arms and back screamed, but he kept up a steady pace with the oar. Would he ever be able to let go? At least he was no longer cold. He could feel sweat mixing with the snow on his brow in spite of his wet feet and legs.

Once free of the breakers, they rowed along the coast of what was either an island or a peninsula and worked their way to the leeward side. The wind slackened. The waters quieted. At last John was able to relax his grip. Panting, he dropped over the oar, as near to complete exhaustion as he had been when he was pulled from the Atlantic.

He had no idea how long he hung there, but finally he heard Governor Carver say, "We'll have to spend the night right here in the boat." He looked up then at the shoreline that was bleak and forbidding in the gathering night.

"Not me, I'm going ashore and try to get a fire going," Clarke, a mate from the Mayflower, announced.

"But we could be attacked by Indians again," William Bradford expressed John Howland's fears as he remembered the encounter of the morning. This time they might not wait until morning to attack.

"I'd rather take my chances with the Indians than die of exposure," Clarke insisted.

"It's your choice," Governor Carver said.

Rowing on a little farther they discovered a sheltered cove with a strip of sand, white in the deep dusk. John carefully weighed the prospects of a night freezing in the boat versus a fire and possibly Indians. He decided to take his chances on land.

When Clarke jumped overboard to wade ashore in knee-deep ice water, John, Edward Dotey and Coffin followed. Carrying muskets over their heads and cheese and biscuits in their pockets, they slogged onto the beach. Driftwood was plentiful. By breaking dead twigs from the lower branches of hemlocks, and sprinkling them with a little gunpowder, a fire was soon blazing. Building a barricade between two hemlocks where the ground was almost dry, they were protected from the wind.

When John took up his watch with warm feet, he wondered why he had hesitated at all. They would always have to be on guard against savages. It would be a part of life from now on.

Just then his sensitive ears heard the dip of oars, then a big splash and the sound of the boat bottom scraping on sand. He laughed to himself. The others had finally seen it their way.

In the morning the snow was melting and the clouds were being driven away by a brisk west wind. It had been a quiet night with the storm abating soon after they made camp. John, anxious to stretch his legs, cramped from huddling in the boat the day before and having them drawn up to his chest much of the night, was ready to explore the coastline.

When he approached Governor Carver, he agreed saying, "We're going to stay here today and let everyone recover from yesterday. Be on the lookout for Indians, and be sure to start back soon enough to get here before dark."

"Are your boots dry?" Goodman Tilley inquired. "I'd like to go, but my shoes are still so wet I'm afraid my feet will freeze." He began to cough.

"Put your feet closer to the fire," John said, piling on more wood. He had amused himself last night by watching the steam rise from his boots as he had put his feet almost into the flames and felt his toes toasting. "You and your brother need to keep yourselves warm."

"I'm fine," Edward Tilley said lifting his head from his bedroll, and struggling to get up.

John studied his slow movements and pale face and wasn't so sure. "Edward Dotey and Steven Hopkins are coming with me. We'll find out if we're on an island or a peninsula. Probably won't be long. You take it easy today."

"Keep a sharp lookout for Indians," Elizabeth's father cautioned as the three set off with muskets in hand.

He doesn't need to tell us that, John Howland thought to himself, and smiled, remembering the big Indian running from the bullet that shattered over his head. *I guess we do have a slight advantage over them.*

As the three began picking their way along the rocky coast Steven Hopkins commented on the Tilleys, "I'm glad they have a day to recuperate. This weather is hard on older people when you're not used to it."

John shot Steven a quick look. He must be as old as the Tilleys. Was he all right? He seemed to be, but John continued to worry about both John and Edward Tilley.

Shortly after noon they spotted the shallop on the shore, and realized they had come back to where they had started. This was an island. At the encampment, the sailors had cut and trimmed a pine for a new mast, and dug out the spare canvas that the shallop carried.

They were almost ready to set sail for the mainland when William Bradford reminded them the next day was the Sabbath. John suddenly realized how tired he was, and welcomed another day to recuperate, as well as to give the Lord thanks for their deliverance.

Relaxing on the soft sand by the blazing fire, his thoughts turned to Elizabeth. Her beautiful eyes with the long dark lashes were what he always thought of first. Usually clear blue, they seemed to change color with her mood. When she was upset they appeared grey, or even green if she was excited. He curled his fingers into his palm, and closed his thumb over them as he thought how he longed to stroke her rich brown hair away from that lovely face.

Actually when her hat had fallen off letting the sun bring out all its golden lights, he had brushed her hair—with his lips. That was the evening he had rescued her from Richard on the shore of Southampton Water, and the only time he had seen her hair in all its beauty. And that night—oh, the warm memory of it—he had held her in his arms!

Surely her clinging to him hadn't been an accident as it had been on the ship. Why hadn't he had the courage to speak up before they both had committed their lives to someone else?

He shook his head. He couldn't let himself think that way. He must think of Desire. Her eyes were— he couldn't remember, and became angry with himself. "Lord, I must not covet another man's betrothed. Help me to love Desire," he prayed silently.

Monday morning everyone had recuperated and was in high spirits as the shallop pulled off for Thievish Harbor, as the sailors called it.

John felt his pulse quicken when the island fell behind and he surveyed the bay's protecting arms. To the south lay a sand spit and on the north a low-rising peninsula. If only the water supply was as good as the sailor had promised, this should be the place they had been looking for.

As the shallop approached the mainland John could see open land cut through by a stream that poured into the bay. Was the open land abandoned fields? Could it be that God had already prepared the place for them? It was more than he had dared hope.

As the men clambered ashore John's heart pounded with excitement. He charged across the pebbly beach to the bank of a fast-flowing brook. Like one of Gideon's 300, he stooped, scooped up a handful of water and raised it to his lips. God be praised, it was fresh. Here at the very edge of the salty ocean was sweet water! The sweetest he had ever tasted!

He looked up to see William Bradford already tramping across the open ground. Stomping his way through waist-high weeds to overtake William Bradford, John looked down. There among the tangle of dry weeds he saw a blackened stalk. He looked more closely to be sure. Yes, it was the same kind of stalk that they had found on Corn Hill.

"Thank you, Lord," he breathed. Then, waiting for John Tilley to overtake him on the climb up the hill from the bay, he pointed the corn stalks out to him. "A field. An abandoned field. That's what this is." John's voice rose with excitement.

"It looks like several years since anything was planted here." John Tilley's voice was filled with wonder.

"Shouldn't be too hard to get it ready to use again," Edward Tilley said as he caught up with them. "I wonder why this wasn't farmed recently?"

John Howland suddenly became aware of how empty the place seemed. "I wonder what happened to the people who farmed here?" he said.

"We may never know, but we can thank the Lord that we don't have to begin by clearing land. I'm not sure I could have done it." John Tilley puffed, obviously finding the climb difficult.

When everyone gathered on the crest of the hill after foraging widely over the open ground, no one reported any signs of habitation. Capt. Standish declared the spot where they were standing to be an ideal place for a fort, and John agreed with him completely.

"Praise be to God, who does exceedingly abundantly above all that we could ask or think," William Bradford said solemnly. "He has led us to the spot He prepared for us."

Anxious to share the news, John looked down to the shallop waiting to take them back to Elizabeth. To Desire, he corrected himself.

Monday morning, December 25, 1620, Elizabeth Tilley stood shivering on deck watching the shallop beat its way across the waves. She and several of her friends had come up to see the men off who were going ashore to begin building a Common House. She scanned the beach for signs of the few who had landed on Friday to lay it out. Those poor souls had been stranded by a fierce storm. How thankful she was that John Howland and her father hadn't been caught in it. How she hated to see her father leave the shelter of the ship! In spite of spasms of coughing, he had insisted he must do his part.

Richard was in bed below, claiming to be too weak to work, though she doubted he was any sicker than her father. It had already been six long weeks since land was sighted, and if they were ever going to get off this ship every man's help was needed.

She hugged her cloak closer around her and pressed her arms against her stomach to relieve her hunger pangs. No one was eating breakfast anymore. Without the extra protection houses would afford how could they survive on such short rations?

Another thought set her to twisting her hat strings. When houses were ready, how soon would Richard demand that she honor her promise to marry him? He hadn't said anything about it lately. She would forestall him as long as possible by avoiding him as much as she could.

"Do you realize that this is Christmas Day?" Constance Hopkins interrupted Elizabeth's reverie.

"We never celebrated Christmas, did you?" Elizabeth replied.

"Oh yes, we brought in the Yule log and holly, and my mother always baked a special pudding," she said wistfully. Elizabeth remembered that Mistress Hopkins was her stepmother.

"When we began trying to conform our lives to Bible teaching we could find no reason to celebrate Christmas. It's a holdover from pagan times that led to drunkenness and debauchery," Elizabeth said. Indeed she felt no nostalgia for Christmas. As a little girl she found it a frightening time. After they had moved to London, masked noisy people in the street kept her close to her parent's side if they had to go out. Usually they stayed home.

As the chilled girls sought the shelter of the 'tween deck, Desire recalled things her mother had done, too. Thankful that both her parents were still living, Elizabeth suddenly became conscious of how thin her mother had grown.

Her mother's frailness reminded her of Christopher Martin's appearance the last time she had seen him. It occurred to her that he wasn't among the men who had crammed into the shallop that morning.

Just then Capt. Jones' brightly polished boots appeared in the hatchway. He ducked his head down calling, "Do you ladies know that everyone in the master cabin is ill? They could use some help up there."

In the ensuing silence, Elizabeth twisted her cap strings even harder. Was this the way the Lord was offering to prove that she had really repented of her disrepectfulness to that man?

She didn't want to take care of Master Martin. There were enough sick to take care of here below, including Richard.   But she had determined to avoid him.

"Then I'll give you another task." Was that what the Lord was saying?

Mistress Carver, sick too, beckoned to Desire from the bunk where she lay. When Desire came to her side, she said "Would you go? We didn't realize Mistress Martin was sick. She's been caring for the men."

Elizabeth hung on Desire's answer.

"But you need me here," Desire replied.

This was indeed what Governor Carver expected.

"I'll go," Elizabeth said, feeling as if the ship were sinking beneath her.

Looking now for her mother's reaction, she found Goodwife Tilley nodding her approval. "I'll care for Richard," she promised.

Elizabeth turned slowly to the hatchway. Praying silently for God's help, she climbed to the poop deck on leaden feet.

When she entered the great cabin, she had trouble determining where Master Martin lay. Could the wasted figure on the bunk just inside the door be he? She stifled a gasp as she recognized the eyes gazing up at her from the face with flaming cheeks. A paroxysm of coughing hit him, and was echoed from three other bunks.

Elizabeth forced herself to the sick man's side, "Have you had any breakfast? May I get you something?" she asked.

"Can't eat," he rasped, beginning to cough again. "My wife, help my wife," he gasped when he could speak.

Obeying, Elizabeth approached Mistress Martin just as she threw back her covers. "Hot, so hot," she mumbled, "Papa, beautiful hall. Mama, Mama."

She's delirious, Elizabeth thought. *She needs a drink. They all do. But there's nothing left. The men took the last of their beverage with them. Water. It'll have to be water that might make them worse. Maybe I can make a gruel of biscuits.*

She found a barrel into which she had to dig deeply to find any, and crumbled a few into water that she heated over the sand-filled brazier. She had just finished coaxing a few spoonfuls into Mrs. Martin when Desire came into the cabin.

"I thought you might need...." Desire stopped as her eyes came to rest on Master Martin's skeleton-like face. She broke into tears and rushed out.

Elizabeth ran after her and caught her on deck, "Desire, you've got to control yourself. These people need our help. See if you can find something to make a poultice."

Her slight shoulders sagging, Desire climbed back to the main deck and disappeared down the hatchway. Elizabeth returned to the cabin. A strange odor assailed her nostrils. She had heard of the stench of death. Was this it? With a shiver she thrust the thought from her mind. Master Martin needed food too.

She carried a cup of gruel to his bedside and knelt beside him. He shook his head, but she quietly persisted in putting the spoon to his lips, and he finally accepted a few bites.

"A waste." His voice was barely discernible. "Give it to my son."

When she bent over his son there was no response, no sign of breathing. Staring into his chalky face and unseeing eyes, she choked back a scream. He was dead.

As her initial shock subsided, she wondered what to do. Where was Master Jones? Would he take the body ashore? His soul she could entrust to God, but Mistress Martin's son deserved a decent burial.

She found the ship's master in the forecastle where he was supervising the distribution of Christmas spirits to the sailors. The captain agreed to find someone to help her, "if he is really dead."

"Heale," Master Jones called to the ship's surgeon, "Go check the Martins."

Elizabeth knew that the settlers had little use for this man, preferring instead the ministrations of their own Deacon Fuller, but under the circumstances she was thankful for him.

As he went back with her she told him what she had tried to do for them, and he reassured her, "That's fine. I'll give you some medicine."

"If I'm right, can we find a way to take him out without telling Master and Mistress Martin?" Elizabeth asked. "They're so sick I'm afraid the news will kill them."

"Don't think it'll make much difference. Do as you wish," Dr. Heale replied.

It didn't take him long to confirm Elizabeth's fears. After examining the others, he turned to her, shaking his head. "I'm afraid none of them can get well. You might as well let them be. There's nothing you can do that will change anything."

"But surely I can make them more comfortable," Elizabeth protested.

Dr. Heale shrugged. "It's up to you. I'll send a couple of the sailors," he said and left.

After the sailors collected the body, her mother appeared with a poultice, and helped her put it on Mistress Martin when her husband refused it.

"I don't think we dare use more of our onions for poultices. When it cools perhaps you can reheat it and use it for Master Martin. Do you think you can manage here? Desire seems to be sick now too, and I have all I can do below," her mother said.

"I'll be all right," Elizabeth asserted with more confidence than she really felt. "You take care of yourself," she added, suddenly struck by the too-bright color in her mother's cheeks.

Chapter 15

When John Howland returned to the ship that evening, after a quick visit below, he hurried to the cabin on the poop deck. Elizabeth, looking pale and drawn, was just turning away from the lifeless form of Mistress Martin.

"Oh John, I'm so glad you're here," she said wearily.

How he longed to take her in his arms to comfort her! But it would be totally improper, especially in light of the message he was to deliver. Instead he held out a mug to her and said, "I brought a toddy. It's Master Jones' Christmas treat. You drink it while I find someone to help me take Mistress Martin away."

She didn't seem to see the proffered beverage. Finally he took her arm and, leading her to a seat at the table, set the mug in front of her. Pushing it aside, she folded her arms on the table and dropped her head onto them as her frame shook with soundless sobs.

"Elizabeth," John said reaching out a hand to lay on her shoulder, and drawing back again, unable to trust himself to touch her, "Why don't you go down to the 'tween deck now, and visit Richard? Desire sent me to tell you that he's been asking for you all day. It should make you both feel better."

"Richard! Richard should have been out working with the rest of you," she exclaimed sitting bolt upright, then added, "Where's my father? Is he too sick to come to see me?"

"No, no. He insisted on staying ashore tonight to help guard our supplies and the lumber we cut today. We thought we saw some Indians and after lunch when we went back to work several tools were missing."

"Indians!" Elizabeth's eyes were frightened.

"Don't worry, we put up a snug hut of branches and turf for the men that will protect them from any arrows, and remember how afraid the Indians are of our guns," John sought to reassure her.

"But how is he?" Elizabeth's eyes showed her continued concern.

"He worked all day with the best of us."

"Is he still coughing?"

"Some," John confessed, "But he says lots of people are coughing."

"You can tell Richard for me that if my father can work, so can he. I'm all right now. Please, do something," and she gestured toward Mistress Martin.

John was about to say that she must go back to her own bunk tonight when Master Martin's wracking cough took her attention. Elizabeth rose and moved lightly to the sick man's side where she offered him a spoonful of some kind of dark liquid. A warm feeling spread through John as he saw how gentle she was with this man who had so infuriated her in the past. He sensed that it was useless to remonstrate with her further and went to do her bidding.

Richard went ashore the next day. Part way down the ladder he lost his hold, and John broke his fall as he tumbled into the boat. John looked up to see Elizabeth watching from the poop deck. He hoped she was pleased with the effort Richard was making to do what she asked, though he would gladly have done the same thing for her.

Richard picked himself up slowly and waved to her as the shallop pulled away, but she had already turned back to Master Martin's cabin.

Ashore John was impressed with the way Richard made the chips fly from the trees he was assigned to cut at the edge of the clearing. He must be feeling better, John decided.

But each time John returned to carry a load of hewn wood to the building site, Richard was working more slowly, though none the less doggedly. John was relieved when a wet snow began falling, causing Governor Carver to call a halt in the day's work. Elizabeth's father, too, could use an afternoon's rest, but John couldn't dissuade him from staying on shore.

"I'm sure I'll be better off right here," he said. "You tell the family I'm all right." But he could scarcely finish what he was saying for coughing. John wondered if he felt too sick to make the extra effort to climb aboard the Mayflower.

Back on the ship, after helping Richard below and finding Desire much better, John climbed to the cabin on the poop deck. He shoved the door open quietly so as not to disturb the sick and slipped quietly into the semi-darkness. As he stood still waiting for his eyes to adjust from the murky whiteness outside, he heard moans and violent coughing above the rising wind.

"Drink," Martin was pleading in a surprisingly loud voice. John made out Elizabeth kneeling beside him holding a cloth to his head. Apparently she was unaware that he had come in, and he stood transfixed watching her care for the dying man.

She rose with her back to him and moved to the table. He could see her strong hands white in the dim light reach for the mug he had left the night before. Her long fingers closed about the handle, and she lifted it almost to her mouth. Her tongue moved across her lips as she lowered it again and stood gazing into its depths. John's own mouth watered as he visualized the liquid shimmering in the light of the single lamp above the table. Surely it was the last they would see of the master's spicy brew.

It was hers, she should drink it. This man was dying. It would do him no good. But he watched in silence as she turned slowly back to Master Martin, and then with determined step carried the mug to him.

With one graceful hand she supported his head as she lifted the mug in her other hand to his lips.

"Bless you." Had Master Martin spoken, or were the words formed in John's mind? He took several steps toward the bed. With every fiber of his being he longed to swoop up this beautiful woman and carry her away from this wasted man, but he dared go no farther.

The dying man drank slowly savoring every drop, his eyes, seemingly on fire, never leaving Elizabeth's face. His strength briefly renewed, he spoke to her. "I deserve nothing from you.

Can you forgive me for the way I treated you?"

It took Elizabeth a long time to answer, and John saw her swallow hard before she said, "Of course. I forgave you long ago, or I wouldn't be here now. Master Martin, it's I that need to ask your forgiveness for the times I have been disrespectful to you." She went on to confess how she had escaped from his prayer the day the Mayflower sailed from London.

It all seemed so long ago, and yet when she spoke of it the scene came to John's mind as fresh as if it were yesterday. How funny it had seemed then, how serious now. Would Martin forgive her? *Please God, let him be reconciled to her. Grant her this peace of mind,* he found himself praying.

"Your hand." Martin's voice was a whisper now that John strained to hear. Boney fingers groped across the counterpane. Elizabeth took them and dropped her face on his claw-like hand. John sensed that he was witnessing a moment too sacred to desecrate by making his presence known. He let himself out quietly as she continued to kneel beside the man who stood at the gate of eternity.

As December gave way to January, Elizabeth eagerly watched from the ship as the Common House took shape. Most of the men, including her father and Richard had stayed ashore since the work began, but John Howland came regularly with reports of them. He claimed that both her father and Richard seemed to be no worse and were working hard. Still, Elizabeth was deeply concerned for them. Whenever she thought about how Richard had fallen when climbing down to the shallop, she felt a twinge of guilt.

Last evening her mother had had a nosebleed, and this morning she hadn't been able to get out of her bunk. When Elizabeth begged a little extra oatmeal for her from their reduced rations, her mother refused it. "I'm not hungry. You eat it," she said.

Elizabeth was suddenly aware how often her mother had claimed not to be hungry lately. She would take a few bites and pass her ration to Elizabeth who was too hungry to refuse. She pressed the extra porridge on her, but her mother turned her head away.

"You've got to eat to keep up your strength," Elizabeth pleaded, very conscious of how pale and sunken her mother's cheeks were.

Her mother turned her face to the plank wall dividing their cabin from the next. Elizabeth, who had been taught to obey her parents, found it impossible to insist. Perhaps Aunt Ann could persuade her to eat.

"I'll try," her aunt promised when she found her. "But I think you better get the ship's doctor."

"She wouldn't let me call him last night. She wants to wait for Master Fuller," Elizabeth said.

"He's needed on shore. She must have help now," Aunt Ann said.

Elizabeth went to find the doctor, but was met by Master Jones who told her that the doctor was busy with one of the seamen and would come later. She was about to lift the curtain to her mother's cabin when she heard her mother's voice rising almost hysterically, "Elizabeth must have my food. She needs it. I don't."

Then it hit Elizabeth what had been happening. Her mother had been deliberately saying she wasn't hungry so she could have more. A huge lump formed in her throat, and she fled to the tiller flat. "Lord, what can I do?" she sobbed aloud. Indeed, she was hungry all of the time, but she couldn't eat at her mother's expense.

I'll have to say I'm not hungry. But that's deception, a small voice whispered. Her mother and father had both taught her to be truthful. But her mother deceived her. There must be a higher law! Then she remembered Jesus' words about denying self, and taking the cross. *Is hunger my cross*, she wondered. "Lord, help us," she prayed.

When she tried to feed her mother again, she still couldn't persuade her to eat. Even though Elizabeth denied being hungry herself, she feared her growling tummy gave her away.

Finally the ship's doctor poked his head around the canvas flap, and Elizabeth stood by as the wisp of a man examined her mother's gums. He shook his head. "Scurvy," he pronounced.

"What can we do?" Elizabeth asked, not sure what the disease was.

"Nothing," her mother interjected. "I told you not to bring him."

"Some think it can be cured with fresh vegetables," the

doctor said. "Onions might help."

Onions? When she had made the poultice for Master Martin there were very few left. Mistress Brewster shook her head even as Elizabeth asked for some. Elizabeth then remembered how her mother had insisted she eat onions and refused them even though she had always liked them. Elizabeth turned away in despair.

Desire, some better after her own illness, came to her side. "Let's go up on the deck for a breath of fresh air," she urged.

As they stood by the railing, Elizabeth poured out her feeling of guilt over her mother. When she had finished berating herself, Desire said gently, "Wouldn't you do the same for your child?"

Elizabeth looked across the water weighing Desire's words. Of course she would, but...

She felt a bump against the ship. She had scarcely been aware of the shallop approaching.

John boarded in good spirits. "The Common House is finished. The men want their women to come ashore for worship service. We're ready to begin our cottages," he announced.

"I must tell Mother, " Elizabeth said, and started for the hatchway.

"Wait, there's something else you need to talk over with her." John stopped her. "Richard has picked the site for your cottage, but your parent's house will be built first." John paused, and as Elizabeth waited for him to continue, it seemed as though a shadow crossed his face. "He wanted to know if you could be married as soon as their place is ready and live with them while he builds your cottage." He finally got the words out.

"How can he talk about marriage when my mother may be dying? Taking care of her and the rest of the ill is all we can think about now!" Elizabeth felt her face flush with anger.

Since Master Martin's death three more had died in December, and two had died already in these early weeks of January. A chill ran through Elizabeth as she realized what she had said about her mother. Would she live to see her married? Her mother, who had always talked of a celebration when Elizabeth wed.

In spite of her outburst, Elizabeth knew she wouldn't be able to put the marriage off much longer, even if her mother wasn't there. Her only hope lay in telling her father how she felt, and asking his permission to break her engagement.

John Howland cut into her thoughts with more disturbing news. Two of the party had disappeared about noon, and the rest of the day had been spent searching for them. It was feared that they had been carried off by Indians. Elizabeth felt a cold hand twist her stomach as her thoughts turned to her father.

"None of us is going to survive," said Desire who had moved close to John.

"Don't we believe that God is stronger than even the wildest savage? He's promised to never leave us or forsake us," John said reprovingly.

But the next morning their worst fears were confirmed. When she came on deck to reassure herself that all was well on the shore, flames were licking the roof of the newly completed Common House. Figures were dashing about the building. Indians closing in to massacre! Her scream brought every person who could stand running onto deck.

"God help us," Elizabeth's plea went up in silence as Desire stood at her side wringing her hands and crying.

Colonists and seamen alike scrambled into the shallop. But as they tried to push off from the Mayflower, a strong wind pinned it to the side of the larger vessel.

Would they get to shore at all? If they did, would they be in time to rescue her father? Every muscle in Elizabeth's body strained as if she were pushing the shallop away.

For a moment there was a line of water between the two ships, but it disappeared again as the shallop banged against the hull of the larger vessel. At last black water churned between them. In the driving west wind and the foaming surf the small boat pitched up and down. Waves splashed over the men, but the expanse of water slowly widened.

Elizabeth, clutching the railing, found herself pulling on it each time John's oar hit the water. "Oh, hurry, hurry," she called after him.

Before the shallop could reach the beach, the roof was consumed by flames that gradually gave way to a column of grey smoke. When the wave-battered vessel reached the shore, black figures ran toward them. Indians? Her teeth chattered.

As Elizabeth, shivering, continued to watch, the figures

moved together back to the Common House where the walls still stood. They appeared to be examining the damage. Her hands relaxed their grip, holding on now just enough to steady herself on the rocking ship. Thank the Lord, they must not be Indians after all!

Throughout the day, when she would come up on deck, she continued to see purposeful movements on shore. She was able to reassure her mother that work had already begun on replacing the roof.

The wind continued blowing so hard that no one dared the choppy bay that evening, Elizabeth explained to her bedfast mother. She breathed easier the next day when she finally spotted the shallop setting out from shore!

The returning sailors brought the good news that the missing men had returned. They had become lost while hunting, and had seen no Indians. The Common House had caught fire from a spark fanned by the wind, but even the sick had helped roll out the barrels of gunpowder before they exploded. The green lumber and wattle and daub walls had not burned, since the mud used for plastering the woven branches was still damp. John Howland had stayed to work as late as possible cutting sedge for reroofing. By the next Sabbath the men hoped to keep their promise to bring in the women for services.

One of the sailors had brought a note from her father requesting them to bring their Bible. Elizabeth wondered if her mother could part with it. She had kept it with her continuously since she had been sick. But when she saw the note she said Elizabeth must take it. "I have the verses well in mind that are my comfort," she said.

The Sabbath dawn brought misty sun that promised a fair day. When Master Jones assured them there should be no trouble returning in a few hours, Elizabeth agreed to leave her mother to visit her father.

"Tell him that it's time you and Richard were married. I know you don't agree, but promise me you'll give him my message," Goodwife Tilley said before she left.

"I will," she acquiesced, *but I'll also tell him how I feel*, she added silently.

"Ann, you help John see that I'm right." Goodwife Tilley had appealed to her sister-in-law as her last resort.

Clutching the Bible, Elizabeth dropped from the bottom of the ladder into the shallop and made her way to the prow. As they pushed off from the Mayflower she gazed at the building on the far-off shore. How small it looked, but how welcoming set in the midst of the empty fields along the water's edge.

Her eyes traveled on to the dark hills that surrounded the harbor, and back over the waters of the bay ruffled by a pine-scented breeze from the land. Land, her land, that better country they were seeking lay just ahead. She leaned forward in her eagerness to touch it. But another girl was in a better position to be the first to leap onto a big rock at the water's edge as the shallop pulled in beside it.

A small group of men met them. John Howland and her Uncle Edward were there along with Richard who offered her his hand as she climbed onto the rock. She spurned it, jumped onto the beach, and ran to seek her father.

She found him, pale and weak, on a pallet in the corner of the Common House with other sick lying close by. At first she was too distressed over his appearance to do more than fight back tears as she laid the Bible beside him and clutched his hand. She whispered, "Oh Papa, Papa."

"Can I do something for you?" she asked at last.

He shook his head, and beckoned her closer. She had to bend over him to hear his reply. "I'm going to be with our Lord," he said. "Uncle Edward will take care of you and your mother. I don't want you to marry Richard too soon. He has only now accepted the faith and he needs time to grow, and so do you. There is much I hoped to share with him from this." His hand went to the Big Book at his side.

She was glad that Richard had come to the faith, but it didn't change her feelings about him. "Mother told me to tell you she wants us to marry right away," Elizabeth said, keeping her promise. "But Papa, I don't want to marry Richard ever. I don't love him. I only agreed to marry him so I could come here when you said you weren't."

Her father nodded gravely, "I thought as much, but you've given your word before God, and you must keep it."

"Even if I don't love him?" As she protested, Elizabeth remembered too late how important a promise was in the Bible, and knew how her father lived by God's word.

"My daughter," he said hoarsely, "love is a matter of the will, a matter of obedience. You will learn to love Richard with God's help."

The small band of colonists had gathered in the Common House, and Richard summoned her to join them for the service. But Elizabeth had a hard time joining in worship. How could they sing so joyfully in the face of death all about them? The thought of losing her father turned her heart to stone in her chest.

Elder Brewster read his text, "Rejoice evermore, pray without ceasing, and give thanks in all circumstances, for this is the will of God for you in Christ Jesus."

I'm cold and hungry and perhaps dying, and if I live, I'll have to marry Richard. How can I thank God in these circumstances, she rebelled.

"We all came of our own free will," she heard the elder saying. "We came knowing that there were many dangers involved. God has indeed gone ahead of us to prepare this place, fields that for some reason are no longer used by the Indians, but the normal vicissitudes of life are still with us. We become sick, we are cold and hungry, but so was Paul, and he had learned in whatsoever state he was to be content, and even more to give thanks to God in all circumstances of his life; stoned, ship-wrecked, beaten, he could still sing praises in prison, because he knew that nothing could separate him from the love of God in Christ Jesus."

Elizabeth bowed her head contritely and prayed silently, "Forgive me, Lord. I do have much to thank You for, especially the assurance that if my father can't live here, he'll go on living with You, and I'll see him again at the resurrection. Lord, I'll keep my promise to Richard if You'll help me."

When the service was over the little band broke bread together and gave thanks for the scant portion of food that they shared. Kneeling by her father's pallet Elizabeth fed him. When it was time to leave, she took his hand, kissed him, and whispered, "I love you, Papa."

"My dearest daughter," his voice strengthened, "I leave God's blessing with you and your children. Be fruitful and multiply. Build Christ's kingdom in this new land. I have no regrets. We did right to come. Tell your mother I love her." His grip on her hand relaxed, and worn out from speaking, he closed his eyes.

Elizabeth looked up to find John Howland standing nearby watching them intently. "Be fruitful and multiply," the words lingered between them. John too should be fruitful, but would Desire bear him children? Tears came then, and she bent quickly over her father kissing him again and bidding him good-bye. "I'll see you in heaven," she whispered. Stumbling to her feet, she went out from the shadowy room into misty sun.

There was no need for words, when John Howland climbed aboard the Mayflower the next morning. Elizabeth was waiting, and when their eyes met, he knew she knew. She turned from him and stood staring across the bay toward the land where her father lay dead.

John had also brought Edward Tilley, who had fallen ill, back to the Mayflower for his wife to care for, and he felt compelled to help him aboard. Then too, he seemed to be the one to break the news to Goodwife Tilley. He sighed as he went about his tasks.

Elizabeth's mother turned her face to the wall when he told her and silent sobs shook her wasted frame. Desire rushed to help Ann Tilley with her husband, and feeling helpless, John climbed to the deck again.

Elizabeth was waiting for him. "I'm going ashore with you for my father's funeral," she said with her lips set a straight line very like the expression he had sometimes seen on her mother's face.

"There will be no funeral," John felt a lump in his throat.

"No funeral for my father? Why not?" Disbelief showed on Elizabeth's face.

"Too many are dying, and we're afraid the Indians will realize how weak we are if hold funeral services. We're burying the dead at night in unmarked graves, but I promise I'll remember where your father is, and when things are better we'll mark the spot. He was my friend, and I'll never forget him." John swallowed hard.

"My father is dead, and he won't even have a funeral," Elizabeth turned away from him again.

A pain formed in John's chest as he looked at Elizabeth's

drooping shoulders. "I'm so sorry," he mumbled, feeling as if he were to blame.

"It's my fault, all my fault," he heard her say. "He would be alive if I hadn't insisted on coming."

John turned her tear-streaked face to him. "Don't say that," he said sternly, "He wanted to come. He only tried to back out for your sake and your mother's. He said he had no regrets. Don't ever forget that."

She studied him without seeming to see him, but at last she smiled through her tears, like the sun coming out after a rain. "Thank you," she said. "Thank you for helping me remember his words. I'd better go to Mother now. How selfish I've been, wrapped up in my own grief."

She left him to return to his work with redoubled efforts. For the first time he had noticed bright red spots in her cheeks. She and her mother needed a warm cottage to move into soon. Judging from the look of her mother, perhaps it was already too late for her, he thought sadly.

Chapter 16

Elizabeth moved like one in a dream. She looked around the empty 'tween deck scarcely able to believe that she was going ashore to stay. For eight months the Mayflower had been home!

She shook her head to clear it. Father, Mother, Aunt Ann and Uncle Edward all gone! And how many more? She had lost count. Were the dying times over? Only God knew. She too had been ill, but was better now.

Elizabeth pushed herself to roll up her tick and load her cooking utensils into the wooden chest. Her hope for a home with her parents in the new world was no more, but she had come to accept it as God's will, realizing that His ways were beyond her understanding.

"Elizabeth, I'm so glad you'll be living at the Carvers so we won't have to be separated." Desire was bubbling this morning. "At least not until we are both married," she added.

"I'm thankful they offered to take me in, and I hope I can be of help. Mistress Carver doesn't seem to be recovering very fast," Elizabeth replied. Involuntarily her thoughts turned to John Howland. He, too, would be living with the Carvers. Was the pleasure she derived from this thought wrong?

"Let's go," Desire interrupted before Elizabeth could examine the question.

Collecting her bedroll Elizabeth carried what she could to the deck, leaving the heavier things for the sailors to bring. There they found Master Jones supervising the loading of a cannon into the shallop. Cold chills ran up and down Elizabeth's spine.

"Have Indians attacked?" she asked when the minion was settled in the bottom of the boat.

"No, and I certainly hope they won't, but with you women going ashore, I think you need this protection. I'll feel better about leaving you when it's installed," Master Jones replied.

Leaving? Elizabeth's stomach churned with the same sensation that the ship's dropping off a wave had given her. She glanced toward the open sea. When the ship was gone their only link with civilization would be totally cut. No escape from the Indians! She swallowed hard, but concern for the returning ship took precedence. "Can you get along without the cannon?" she asked realizing she had scarcely noticed them before.

"Certainly better than you can. No pirate is going to want my cargo on the return trip," Master Jones laughed.

"I hope you can make our backers understand why we haven't sent them anything." Elizabeth suddenly thought of Thomas Weston and his demands.

Master Jones shrugged, "That's not my problem. Come on. Let's get you women loaded."

As the shallop sailed toward shore, Elizabeth could see the men of the colony swarming about on the high ground just above the Common House working on a platform for the cannon. Five cottages, reminiscent of the one she had lived in before they moved to London, lined the beaten path that marked the street. Remembering that she had once heard they planned to build nineteen, she sighed. They didn't need them now.

But there was hope in the air. The wind on this cloudy March day had moderated bringing the promise of spring and the new year. As the shallop beached, she tossed her bedroll and clothing bag ashore, clambered over the rock, and jumped onto the sand.

Boxes, trunks and pieces of furniture that had been unloaded on an earlier trip stood on the beach. Elizabeth and Desire helped Mistress Carver sort out her things to carry up to the grey wattle and daub cottage. Once inside the one-room dwelling with a dirt floor and a square fireplace overhanging one corner, Mistress Carver took charge of arrangements.

"You girls can unroll your ticks at night and sleep down here with us," she said. "Henry can sleep up above with John." They looked up to discover a half loft under the steep thatch roof.

"It'll be fine if they don't fall off," Elizabeth laughed to cover the tears she felt like shedding as she thought about Humility and Henry having to get used to a new set of foster parents.

"They'll have to build a partition to put our bed behind," Mistress Carver decided as a sailor carried in the heavy oak bedstead she had brought all the way from Leyden.

Someday Richard and I will put up a bed in our own house. She sighed, but didn't shudder anymore when the thought came to her. Yes, she would be Richard's wife before long. In the meantime she would be glad to be part of the Carver household with Desire and John.

She set to work helping Desire put the Carver's bed together in the corner away from the hearth. Just as she was fluffing up a pillow a cry rang out.

Had she heard right? "Indians?" She dropped the pillow and ran into the street, paying no attention to Desire's cries of alarm. Whatever was happening, she didn't want to miss it, and she might be able to help.

A bronze-skinned man came striding up the dirt track carrying a large bow, and wearing nothing but a fringed string about his hips. Elizabeth's eyes opened wide. Her cheeks grew hot. Never had she seen so much of a man's body before. Fascinated she watched the flow of powerful muscles as he passed, then fixed on the quiver of arrows slung on his back. Wondering what he intended to do with the bow and arrows, she found her teeth chattering in the March breeze.

The men, a few carrying muskets, were moving down the street to meet him. The Indian stopped as they approached, folded his arms and stood statue-like. As they came closer, he raised a hand, and in a deep resonant voice said, "Welcome."

She felt her jaw go slack with astonishment and was vaguely aware that John Howland as well as Governor Carver and Elder Brewster, were standing with mouths agape. Capt. Standish, who had stopped with his gun half raised, slowly brought it back to rest across his arm.

Regaining his composure, Governor Carver squared his shoulders, and stepped forward to greet the Indian with as much dignity as the red man was showing. "Thank you. Welcome to you," he said bowing slightly. "Do you speak

English?"

"Ittle" the Indian nodded. "Me Samoset. Squanto, speak much."

The men now crowded around full of questions, and Elizabeth heard Mistress Carver whisper behind her, "We'll have to entertain him."

At the same time she noticed Mrs. Brewster, who had come to her doorway, duck back into her house. She returned shortly with a long red hunting coat that her husband quietly took from her and offered to Samoset. White teeth gleamed as the big Indian smilingly accepted the coat, pulled it on, and struggled to button it across his broad chest. The sleeves ended well above his wrists, and it barely came to his knees.For a second Elizabeth was sorry to see this creature, who was almost like a wild animal, clothed in such a ridiculous manner, but her sense of propriety quickly banished the thought.

Instead of bringing the Indian to their cottage, Governor Carver led him to the Common House. Mistress Carver breathed a sigh of relief.

"We better send some butter and biscuits up for him," she turned to Elizabeth and Desire who had come out with her.

"I'm not going up there," Desire said, her eyes dark with fright.

"I'll be glad to go," Elizabeth said quickly. The Indian apparently intended them no harm, and certainly he was outnumbered.

When she entered the Common House she found the men seated in a circle about Samoset firing questions at him.

"Do you know what happened to the Indians that farmed here?" Governor Carver was asking.

The red-brown face seemed to grow darker as he struggled to find words. "Patuxet die. Much moon pass."

"Why?" the question was almost a chorus.

He pointed solemnly to his head, legs, and stomach, "Fire. Dark," and dotted his finger along his arm.

Fever and spots. Smallpox, Elizabeth guessed. She glanced at her own scarred hands, and felt for the pockmark near her hairline. She had been fortunate to escape more scars. But everyone had said that outbreak had been mild. Then she noticed that he, too, was pockmarked. To think a whole village wiped out! Poor creatures.

Samoset went on then in his broken English to tell them about his friend Massasoit, the Big Chief, sachem of the Wampanoag, who lived on Narragansett Bay. He now laid claim to this territory.

"Was it his men who attacked us on Cape Cod?" John Howland asked.

Samoset shook his head. "Them Nauset. Bad people. Make much war." He struggled to tell of their chilling forays as he sipped his drink and spread generous amounts of butter on the hard biscuits.

How providential that they hadn't decided to stay on the cape. They might all have been wiped out by now. Elizabeth shivered at the thought. As the room grew darker she suddenly realized how late it was and felt guilty that she had neglected her duties.

How are they going to get rid of him, she wondered. *Were there more lurking nearby waiting for nightfall to attack?* Every shadow filled her with foreboding as she hurried back to the house.

When the governor and John returned she learned they had finally sent Samoset to spend the night with the Hopkins, feeling that Dotey and Leister could handle him better than anyone else, should trouble develop.

Later that evening, unable to unroll their beds until John and the governor retired, Elizabeth and Desire waited quietly as the men talked by the dying embers of the supper fire.

They needed so badly to have something to send back on the Mayflower, but there was no way to catch and prepare any quantity of fish at this season. Lumber would be a possibility in the future, but now it was almost more than they could do to cut enough for their own needs.

"We need so many things from home," Governor Carver said. "But I'm afraid the Adventurers won't send us any more supplies if they don't see some return on their investment."

"Perhaps the Indians have some pelts on hand," John suggested.

"We've been hoping to open trade with the Indians, and this may be our opportunity," Governor Carver said. "But it's more important to sign an agreement of peace with them. We must learn to trust each other."

Elizabeth prayed fervently for everyone to be kept safe

before she fell asleep that night. When the whole village appeared to give Samoset a send-off the next morning, she gave thanks for God's care.

Presenting Samoset with a knife, Governor Carver stressed, "Tell Massasoit we have have come in peace," and added, "We have more knives and even jewelry to trade for skins."

As the red-coated Indian disappeared into the woods, Richard, who was staying in the Common House with several of the single men, moved sluggishly to Elizabeth's side. Not having been close to him since he had come ashore, she was shocked at how colorless and sunken his cheeks were, even though his eyes lit up as he looked at her.

"I promised to help Dr. Fuller build his house. We're planning to start today, but I'm afraid it won't go very fast if it depends on me. I guess I'm not much of a worker after all." Richard's voice was flat.

Elizabeth felt a sudden stab of compassion for him. "You're a fine worker when you're well. I don't think you've gotten over your illness yet. Maybe you shouldn't even try to work until you are stronger," she said.

"But I thought you were angry with me for staying on the ship that first day all the men came to work. I didn't do my part, and I want to make up for it." Richard searched Elizabeth's face as he spoke.

There was a weight on her chest as she struggled to answer him, "Oh, Richard, perhaps I was angry with you that day, but I'm sorry. I was wrong. You are sick, too."

"But not as sick as your father. If I had taken his place maybe he wouldn't have died," Richard said.

"Richard, do you think I blame you for my father's death?" Elizabeth asked. Such a thought had never occurred to her.

When he nodded his head she hastened to assure him that she didn't, adding, "We know that death is part of life. It comes to all of us in God's own time. Richard, my father told me that you had come to accept and understand our faith, and this is part of it. Death is only the door to eternal life with Christ."

A radiant smile spread over Richard's face, even as he began coughing again. "Yes, I've read that Jesus is preparing a place for us," he said. "I must return your Bible, but since you taught me to read, I've been spending any time I can get in the Word. Your father told me to take it."

"And Richard, you shall keep it. Some day you will use it as my father did— to read to your family morning and evening. While I am with the Carvers, I don't need it, because the governor reads to us just as my father did," Elizabeth said.

"But don't you want it for your own personal use?" Richard asked.

"That's why I was taught to read, but I'm afraid I have never read it on my own very much," Elizabeth confessed, suddenly feeling ashamed. "But you must go back to bed now."

Elizabeth looked for her mistress, but everyone had gone about their business leaving the two young people standing in the middle of the street. Impulsively Elizabeth grasped Richard's hand, and led him to the Carvers' cottage, over his feeble protests.

"I'm going to ask Mistress Carver if I can put you down on my bed for now so I can take care of you," she said.

Agreeing as soon as she saw him, Mistress Carver helped her unroll the pallet.

After Elizabeth had made him comfortable, she sought out the doctor. "Did you really expect Richard to work today?" she flared. Immediately, she regretted that. Once again, she had been disrespectful.

But Dr. Fuller took no offense. "I've been giving Richard the best medicine I have," he said. "He seemed better for a time. I realize he is weak, but I thought it was important for him not to give up."

"I'm not going to let him work. I want my future husband to get well." It was the first time she had said the words "future husband" aloud. Caring, possessiveness, and fear for his well-being suddenly overwhelmed her. He represented her hope for family in this new world, and she wanted him to live. Suddenly determined to fight for his life, she turned abruptly and hurried back to him.

When John Howland came in at dusk with Governor Carver, he found Elizabeth and Mistress Carver arguing with Richard over where he should spend the night.

Richard turned to the men. "I'm going back to the Common House. I can't take Elizabeth's bed."

"But he shouldn't go out in the damp of evening," Elizabeth fussed.

"I don't think it will make any difference," John said, then offered to spend the night with him.

"John, we need you here with Master Carver to protect us. Suppose that Indian comes back in the night," Desire broke into the discussion.

"I'm feeling better. I don't need you," Richard insisted.

"John, you walk up with him." Governor Carver settled the matter.

John was prepared to catch Richard if he stumbled, but Richard took each step with determination. Making it safely to the Common House door, he leaned panting against the frame, his face grey in the early spring twilight. John was anxious to see him safely to his bed, but Richard wanted to talk.

"John, don't tell Elizabeth, but sometimes I don't think I'm going to live. You'll take care of her for me, won't you?" His sunken eyes reached out to hold John.

"By God's grace, you'll get well. Surely the dying times are over," John affirmed.

"But Elizabeth?" Richard's voice was weaker now, and John realized he couldn't stand much longer.

Elizabeth. How eager he was to care for Elizabeth, always! To have her for his own. He pushed the thought aside. Desire would be his wife.

"Of course I'll take care of Elizabeth." He hoped his tone was casual, but reassuring. "Now let's get you to your own bunk."

The next day being the Sabbath, Richard left his bed to sit for worship on the rude backless benches with the Carver household. John knew he was no better when, at noon, Richard declined Mistress Carver's invitation to sup with them. Elizabeth seemed willing to let him go back to his bed.

She was taking food up to Richard and they were waiting for her to return before the Carver household ate its cold meal. Suddenly the alarm bell on the cannon platform rang out shattering the Sabbath quiet.

John's stomach knotted. Elizabeth! Elizabeth was in danger!

Chapter 17

John grabbed his gun, and rushed out to look for Elizabeth. He found her standing transfixed, just outside the Common House, staring across the field. Following her gaze, he spotted a band of five Indians carrying... what were they carrying? No matter now, he must get Elizabeth to cover, and take his place as a soldier. Capt. Standish was already running up the street barking muster orders.

When he tried to escort her back to the cottage, she refused. "I want to see what's going to happen," she said shaking his hand off of her arm. "Look. There's Samoset. And the men with him are carrying axes, and shovels."

Axes and shovels! John stared in disbelief. The tools that had disappeared! Did they think they were weapons? He tightened his grip on his musket.

As the tall bronze men came closer, he saw that each was carrying a small packet of pelts as well. A mission of trade? They were returning the stolen tools? He felt his shoulder muscles relax just a little though he still clutched his gun.

By now the men had assembled, and John took his place beside Governor Carver. His finger sought the trigger of his musket as Samoset strode up to them carrying an axe. John, watching intently, felt his breath rush out of his lungs as the tall Indian bent and dropped the tool at Capt. Standish's feet. One by one the four others followed, first laying down the tool each carried and then the packet of furs.

Governor Carver stepped out from the line, and said gently, "Thank you for returning our tools, and bringing furs to trade. This is the day set aside to worship God. He has commanded us to do no work on this day. Come and eat with us now." He turned to Elizabeth with instructions for the women to bring what they had prepared, along with anything else that they could spare, to the Common House.

John gulped. As little food as they had, how could they afford to feed these men? Yet could they afford not to? They had to make friends with them, and what better way?

Capt. Standish led the militia in escorting the Indians to the Common House. In a surprisingly short time, the women came carrying their meal up the hill. John hated to see Elizabeth, Desire and Mrs. Carver stay. What if there were trouble? But after Elder Brewster blessed the food everyone sat together on the floor to eat.

The women served the guests first, and John thought he caught a look of dismay on Elizabeth's face at the quantity of food the red men gobbled up. He watched the Indians so closely that he ate almost nothing.

No sooner had the bronze men eaten their fill than they jumped to their feet. Motioning the settlers aside, they formed a ring in the middle of the floor, and began a frenzied swaying, stomping and twirling. The hair at the back of John's neck prickled as their antics gained momentum.

Why were they carrying on so? To what might it lead? John got quietly to his feet and went outside to bring in his musket. Governor Carver was too trusting. What if this was a ruse for others to steal their guns? But the guns were still leaning against the wall by the door where they had left them, and no other Indians were in sight.

Would there be trouble if he brought his in? John decided to risk it. He set it against the inside wall near at hand before he sat down again. No one appeared to notice but Capt. Standish, who nodded approval.

The whirling and jumping had increased in speed while he was gone. Finally, with a great swooping motion, the Indians dropped to the ground at Governor Carver's feet.

"Much thank you. Good food." Samoset beamed even as he panted.

Governor Carver got to his feet now and led the way outside. Picking up the pelts that the Indians had brought, he handed them back to Samoset saying, "Tell them to come again with more furs and we'll be glad to trade with them any day but the Lord's Day."

Samoset translated his message, and the men left. All but Samoset.

Later when Samoset had been taken to the Hopkins again for the night, Governor Carver reproved John for getting his gun. Capt. Standish defended John's action, remonstrating with him as to the wisdom of letting Samoset stay. "How can we be sure he isn't a spy for one of the tribes?" he asked.

"We have to trust that the Lord has sent him to help us," the governor replied. "We must show him every kindness so that he'll know we want to live in peace with our Indian neighbors. After all, we can't trade with enemies."

John understood Governor Carver's point of view, but he was nonetheless relieved to see Samoset leave a few days later. He went off wearing his parting gifts: a hat and a shirt, as well as a pair of shoes and stockings, that surely were too small. *What ever happened to the red coat?* John wondered as he watched him go. He prayed that whoever had it would see it as a gift given in friendship, and wouldn't become so covetous that they might decide to kill them all for their possessions.

The day following Samoset's departure, when John went to the woods to cut lumber, he found Richard limply swinging an ax at a log. He shouldn't be trying to work, John told himself. He knew his appraisal was correct when before long he saw him sprawled on the damp ground gasping for breath.

"Come on, let me help you back to the Common House," John offered.

"No, I'll be all right in a minute," Richard insisted.

"Why are you pushing yourself so?" John asked. "You must let yourself get well."

"I've got to work. The Bible gives us the rule that if a man will not work, he shall not eat. I can't keep on eating our scarce supplies and not do my part." Richard's voice seemed to gain strength as he spoke.

"But it doesn't mean when you are sick. We've all been sick this winter. The work was at a total standstill for weeks. We kept on eating or we wouldn't have survived. Even now William Bradford can scarcely walk, and no one expects him to drill with the militia," John reasoned.

"But he's been working on Dr. Fuller's house, and I'm going to work, too." Richard pulled himself away from John, and began hewing again.

As John turned away from the determined young man he sent up a silent prayer, "Oh Lord, please let him make it." Anyone with that kind of courage was certainly worthy of Elizabeth, yet the thought caused odd prickles to run through him. He stomped off to continue his own chopping, biting his axe deep into a big tree.

Two days later they were working again at the edge of the forest when John's always watchful eyes caught a movement in the shadows. His axe froze in midair. Two Indians! The axe came slowly down as he recognized Samoset. Who was with him? How many more were following? Was he on a trade mission or...?

John whipped out a handkerchief, a prearranged signal, and waved it toward the watchman on the cannon platform. Did he see him? In a second the ships bell was ringing. Thank the Lord!

John had started running to assemble with the militia, when he remembered that Richard was scarcely able to walk, let alone run, and turned back to be sure that he was coming. Before he could reach Richard, Samoset and his friend overtook him, and the three approached John together. They had no weapons, but John still wished for his gun.

"Squanto," Samoset said, indicating his friend.

Squanto, the one Samoset had spoken of. The Indian who could speak better English! There should be nothing to fear from these two.

Squanto had come as interpreter, and told them in amazingly good English that the great sachem, Massasoit, wanted the governor to come for a powwow.

John prayed Governor Carver wouldn't trust himself to the Indian chief and was glad to see the militia assembled to meet them. With introductions over, Squanto delivered his message, and John breathed easier when Governor Carver refused. Instead he sent an invitation to Massasoit to come to the village.

As Samoset and Squanto strode away a band of Indians far outnumbering the militia suddenly materialized on the hill. John dashed off to the Common House for his and Richard's muskets.

He ran back to find Capt. Standish organizing a reception for the chief. "We'll show these savages how things are done in civilized lands," he was saying. "We're representing the king, and we'll do it right. Ah, there you are John, you take three men for an honor guard to escort the governor to the conference. Dotey, Leister, Gardiner." The captain paused, looked at Richard, and frowned. "Not Richard. You're not standing straight enough." With a heave of his chest, Richard pulled himself up, and Capt. Standish gave his approval.

"Does anyone have a drum?" John asked.

"Good idea," Governor Carver said. "I have one that I think Henry could play."

"You can use my house to entertain him," Deacon Fuller offered. "It's not furnished yet, but I can put down a rug and some cushions for you to sit on."

For a time John wondered if their plans were useless. Samoset returned with word that Massasoit wouldn't come, and looked meaningfully up at the squat cannons overhanging the end of the street.

Just then one of the Separatists, Edward Winslow, stepped forward and asked permission of Governor Carver to approach the great chief.

"Him like knife," Samoset suggested.

Governor Carver nodded and motioned to John. Quietly he sent him to the Common House to get a knife and a piece of jewelry worthy of a chief. From the wooden chest filled with items to trade John chose a bright red stone dangling from a copper chain.

When he returned with the gifts, he knew by the big smile on Samoset's face that his choice had been right.

"Tell the great chief that we want to be friends and desire to make a treaty of peace with him," Governor Carver told Samoset and Squanto before they set off with the negotiator.

As soon as they were gone Capt. Standish barked, "Governor Carver, go get dressed in your very best, something with lace at the neck."

"I have a trumpet," Richard said to John." I could play it with the drum. We'll have a royal procession yet." John wondered if he would have breath enough to play.

It was with a sense of satisfaction later that day that John paraded in Governor Carver's retinue behind Richard and Henry's band. John had watched as Capt. Standish marched the militiamen, wearing every available helmet, breastplate and sword, out to meet a tall powerfully built Indian. He was followed into the village by a band of Indians that made every eye bulge. Draped with deerskin fastened on one shoulder and taller than any of the Englishmen, their faces were grotesque with colored crosses, circles and lines.

Why were they painted, John wondered, fearing again for the women who gathered to watch the procession. At least they hadn't brought bows and arrows, and there didn't seem to be as many as he had thought there were when he first saw them on the hill.

One, two, three... John counted twenty. Surely there were more. Edward must have arranged for a number equal only to their own forces to come to town. Still, in any hand-to-hand fighting they were unequally matched. All the Indians were taller and stronger looking than any of them. And Edward? Where was Edward? John realized that he was nowhere to be seen. He must have let himself be held hostage until Massasoit returned.

Capt. Standish had approached Massasoit then and escorted the warrior to the house prepared for his visit.

John marveled at Capt. Standish's composure. The big Indian could have picked him up and carried him off like a child, but Capt. Standish, never blinking, treated him with the stance of a conquering commander. While the militia had stood at attention forming an honor guard, the Indian chief and Capt. Standish turned into Dr. Fuller's almost completed house.

It was time for Governor Carver's appearance. John hoped that Massasoit was as impressed with Henry's drumbeats and Richard's blast on the trumpet as he was. The braves had certainly looked surprised as the company processed behind the governor up to the house.

While the militia and the braves waited outside, John accompanied Governor Carver into Deacon Fuller's green-carpeted cottage. It was John's turn to be surprised. Massasoit rose to his full height as they entered, strode up to Governor Carver, reached for his hand, bent formally, and kissed it.

What would his master do? The thought of returning the kiss on the greasy looking dark skin of their guest made John squeamish. Yet so much hung on this visit.

John noted one of the governor's eyebrows raise slightly, but nonetheless he bent and brushed his lips across the back of Massasoit's hand with equal dignity. Then he motioned for the chief to be seated, and settled himself on the floor opposite him, ordering John to bring a pot of hard liquor to toast his guest.

Together Samoset and his friend Squanto acted as interpreters and when John left they were exchanging greetings. By the time he returned Governor Carver was expressing his desire for a peace treaty. John tried to read the Indian's face, but it remained expressionless.

Taking the tankard from John, Governor Carver raised it as a toast to his Indian counterpart and took a sip. John then carried it to Massasoit who repeated the gesture, but lifting the big mug he drank long and deeply from it. His face immediately flushed, beads of sweat broke out on his forehead, and he wiped his brow before he gave his answer to Squanto. It seemed to John that everyone in the room was holding his breath as they waited for the interpreter to speak.

His people, too, were interested in peace, Squanto told them. John began breathing again as they settled down to hammering out a treaty.

Soon John was sent for pen and paper to record the agreement. Sitting cross-legged on the floor like the guests, John wondered briefly how he would manage, but the articles were short and simple. No wigged judge would be needed to interpret them.

They should not hurt each other, but if anyone did hurt another he should be punished. If anything was taken, it should be restored. They would help each other should either be attacked in an unjust war, and finally when they met together the Indians should leave their bows and arrows behind as they had this day.

Once it was completed John was asked to read the document aloud. After each point he kept glancing at Massasoit's solemn face, and was gratified to see Massasoit's consenting nods as Squanto translated. When he finished, the chief conferred quietly with Squanto who then came to the table and asked to see the paper. He examined it carefully, and whether he actually was able to read it or not John Howland never knew, but when he finished he turned to the sachem and seemed to grunt his approval.

John Carver reached for the paper, and dipping the quill in the ink that John brought him, signed his name to the bottom of the document. It was now up to John to take the treaty, pen and ink to the bronze giant.

John hated to get that close, but remembering that the governor had kissed his hand, he proffered the material and didn't flinch when the Indian's sweaty hand touched his. Can this man write, he wondered. Massasoit dipped the quill in the ink, dribbled it onto the paper, and pushing so hard that the quill broke, made a cross.

The chief spoke then in measured tones and turned to Squanto who interpreted his words. "Now we friends. We work with the king of your country and you, his people. Mark magic from my hand. Never take back."

John wondered as he studied this strange uncivilized creature if they could really trust him. Then he scolded himself for his skepticism. They could trust God. They would have to leave the outcome in His hands.

Governor Carver ceremonially escorted Massasoit and his braves to the edge of the village. Massasoit again kissed Governor Carver's hand and marched away.

However, they hadn't seen the last of the Indians that day. Later another band of Indians marched down the hill with Edward Winslow and let it be known that they, too, wanted to sample the strong water that had been given to the chief. John didn't rest easy until they all left but Samoset and Squanto. At least they could communicate with these two.

After Desire and Elizabeth served supper to all of them, Governor Carver instructed John to take the two Indians to the Common House for the night, and get the Edwards to stay with them.

Tomorrow, John suddenly realized, as he led the group up

the hill, would be the beginning of the new year. 1621. The spring equinox had passed and twilight lingered on this last day of March. In the moderate weather the Indians squatted on the ground outside the Common House, and produced a long pipe and tobacco from one of the pouches each carried. John and the Edwards dropped down beside them and Squanto offered them his pipe.

The idea of taking smoke into his lungs didn't appeal to John, but he didn't want to refuse the gesture of friendship. He gingerly took a puff, and stifled a cough as the acrid smoke stung his throat. Handing it back to Squanto, he asked the question that he had been wanting to ask all afternoon.

"How did you learn to speak English?"

"This is my land." He began tapping the ground he was sitting upon. "I be a Patuxet, the only one left," his voice carried a deep sadness.

"What happened?" John asked. Several of the young men had joined them now. Richard came to lean in the doorway, but he soon began coughing, and disappeared inside again.

"Six springs gone Capt. Hunt's men stole me and many braves from my people. Make us work on fishing boat. They say, sell us in Spain, but go to England. I run away. Kind man help get me on other boat. I come home. No one be alive in village." Squanto's voice was husky.

All at once John was filled with compassion for this man whom he suddenly comprehended as a fellow human being, not the savage he had perceived before.

"This be my land." Squanto drew meditatively on his pipe. "I be glad you come make things grow again. I help. Show you how."

John gazed across the rippling bay, grey white in the evening light. Fluffy clouds floated in an azure sky turning pink in the reflected rays of the setting sun. *It looks as though tomorrow will be a good day,* he thought, *the beginning of a better year for all of us.*

He rejoiced quietly in the goodness of God who had brought them to this spot and brought a man who knew the land to help them establish themselves in it. His thoughts turned to John Tilley, who wouldn't be sharing in this. He drew comfort from the certainty that he had entered into the rest prepared for him, and gave thanks that his daughter was still here.

Chapter 18

"I can't imagine the harbor without the Mayflower." Desire listlessly piled her bedding on top of the chest in the corner. Early April sunshine lighted their tiny window, but it didn't seem to lift Desire's spirits.

"We're going to miss Master Jones," Elizabeth felt the sadness too.

"It's so final. Our last link with England." Desire faced the wall.

Even John's cheery good morning as he swung down the ladder didn't seem to rouse Desire. Governor Carver and his wife emerged from behind the partition that shielded their bed, "Desire, it's still not too late to change your mind if you want to go back," the governor said.

Last night as the villagers gathered with the captain and his crew for a farewell meal, Master Jones had offered passage back to England to anyone willing to work. The killing sickness had depleted his seamen too. "Any woman is welcome without charge," he had concluded.

Elizabeth had looked anxiously at Desire and John. John wasn't free to go, and she was sure he wouldn't want to anyway. But what about Desire? She had talked so much lately of Holland and especially England where she had been born. Sometimes Elizabeth grew impatient with her. There was too much to be done here to waste time being homesick for the land they had chosen to leave.

Then Desire had looked at John with an expression that told Elizabeth she was still planning to marry John Howland though nothing had been said about it for weeks.

Somehow Elizabeth had never come to terms with the idea. Fond as she was of Desire, she didn't feel she was the right person for John.

The longer she knew her the more fears she discovered: Indians, of course, but also spiders and bugs, even the crabs on the beach. But worst of all, childbirth, though it was never mentioned after Oceanus' birth.

John needed a brave wife for this new land, one who looked forward, not backward. She might even try to make him return to England if he married her. The thought had made Elizabeth cold all over. Somehow knowing John was close by gave Elizabeth strength and courage to go on.

Was that wrong, she wondered, as her eyes turned toward Richard. Would Richard go back? Perhaps he should. He didn't seem to be much better, though somehow he persisted in working. His eyes met hers, and she knew he would stay.

There was a long heavy silence in the Common House. At length, Elder Brewster rose to thank him and pray for travel mercies for them.

Elizabeth had noticed the Carvers talking earnestly to each other when the meeting was breaking up. Then they had drawn Desire aside as the rest were leaving. Elizabeth's guess about what they had said to her was confirmed by Governor Carver's words to Desire just now.

"Are your letters ready?" John Howland asked. "I'll be taking them to the Mayflower as soon as I check to see if anyone else has mail to send."

Elizabeth had taken dictation from a number of the women over the last few days, including Desire and Mistress Carver, but she had written to no one back in England. Her life was here now, a life no one over there could possibly understand. She knew John had written to his brothers encouraging them to join the colony, and she wondered if he had mentioned Desire.

As she looked at the packet of letters sealed with red wax that John picked up from the table, Elizabeth thought briefly about Desire's optimistic letter to her father, and wondered how honest she had been. Strangely, she had made no mention of her plans for marrying John Howland.

No one said anything about eating before John left. With the few supplies that remained, they made do with duck broth at noon, and a biscuit with it in the evening. Elizabeth looked forward to the day when her stomach wouldn't nag at her most of the time. *Thank the Lord for the good water from Town Brook,* she thought, as John stopped by the bucket and drank a ladle full. Water quieted the hunger pangs, and gave a feeling of fullness that helped.

Elizabeth followed John to the bucket, and he handed her the ladle when he finished. "John," she said, "Call us before you go out to the ship."

"I will," he promised. "Governor Carver and Elder Brewster want to go too, so I'll be back in a few minutes."

Elizabeth followed him into the yard. She needed to bring in wood for the tiny fire they built for cooking. The house was cold, and a fire helped when there was no food.

Soon he was back with both hands full of letters, and the Carver household followed John and the governor to the beach where the rest of the colonists were gathering. Elizabeth, standing between Desire and Mistress Carver, never took her eyes off the shallop as John sailed out to the ship. Behind her one of the women sobbed quietly, and glancing at Desire, she saw tears coursing down her cheeks.

When John climbed onto the Mayflower, in her mind's eye Elizabeth stood with him again on the familiar deck. She had a special feeling for the sturdy ship that had brought them here, but how glad she was not to be making the return voyage!

Lord, take them back safely, she prayed silently, remembering the violence of storms at sea. Master Jones had assured her, when she was bidding him Godspeed, that the crossing at this season should be an easy one. She fervently hoped so. The day was encouraging. Sunbeams sparkled like tiny crystals on the crest of each little wave.

But by the time John and the governor climbed back into the shallop Elizabeth noticed dusty clouds gathering on the horizon. Before the men reached the shore again the sun had disappeared and a haze was rising over the water. Elizabeth was shivering now.

She felt every ear attuning to the groaning of the hawser as the ship weighed anchor, and every eye watching as the sails were hoisted to catch the light breeze that brought the ship to life. *How beautiful it is, like a great bird,* she thought. *So beautiful it hurts!* Her eyes filled with tears.

Elizabeth brushed her eyes, and raised her hand in a farewell salute. She could see the sailors leaning over the railing waving. The captain on the poop deck faced shoreward briefly with a final lift of his arm, then turned to oversee the ship's course toward the mouth of the harbor. The wind and tide were favorable, and as she watched, the Mayflower soon passed between the long stretch of beach to the south and the higher promontory on the north, and out into Cape Cod Bay. Once outside of the bars, only the tops of the masts were visible.

In front of Elizabeth the waves were empty. There was no sign of human life but the beached shallop, and their own small group clustered silently at the water's edge, as if gathered for a funeral.

A lone gull swooped over the water mewing bleakly. Suddenly Elizabeth was overwhelmed by a sense of desolation, rising as a great swelling pain in her chest. Behind them lay the vast wilderness, before them the empty ocean.

Then Elder Brewster's voice broke the eerie silence. "Remember what the Lord said to Joshua after Moses left, `I will be with thee: I will not fail thee nor forsake thee. Be strong and of good courage.' The promise is for us, too."

Richard, who had come up behind Elizabeth unnoticed, said quietly, "And I'll be with you, too. Can we marry soon?"

She turned and faced him squarely, "Yes, Richard," she said and held out her hand to him.

Before he could take it Squanto came running up the beach from the direction of the brook. "Alewives run. Alewives," he exclaimed breathlessly.

"More come soon. I show you how catch them. They be good to eat, good to plant with corn," he went on. Elizabeth, along with everyone else, turned her attention to him. "Be time to start hills in fields."

Elizabeth wasn't sure what he was talking about, but she was caught up in his excitement.

"What are alewives?" John asked. "And how do we make hills in the fields?"

"Come," Squanto said. He led the men over to the edge of the Town Brook, pointing to a few small fish darting about in the mouth of the stream.

Elizabeth, who had trailed along behind the men, lingered, watching the flash of silver in the clear water. "Alewives," she repeated the name to herself. *What do alewives have to do with hills in the field,* she wondered, and started reluctantly back to the house. The sun had come out again and was warm on her back. The air was sweet with the scent of growing things. She'd love to tarry, but she had a wild duck to dress.

At least, I can walk back along the stream, she thought. *Perhaps I can find some May flowers.* As she wandered, she came on a large patch of succulent, dark green plants.

Chives? She bent and pulled up a handful of small bulbous roots. She sniffed. Definitely a kind of onion. Peeling away the layer with the dirt she bit one off and crunched into it.

Had anything ever tasted as good? Dropping to her knees, she pulled more and more, scarcely able to peel them fast enough as she popped one after another into her mouth. Satiated at last, she yanked up a great handful, and started for the house. Her mouth watered at the thought of the flavor they would impart to the fishy tasting duck soup. Only stark hunger had made it possible for her to eat the smelly mess day after day.

She looked up now to see Desire waving frantically to her. "Come quick. Richard is bleeding," Desire cried.

"But he was all right just a few minutes ago," Elizabeth said when Desire reached her. Had she dawdled longer than she realized?

"John said all the men were on their way to the field to learn about making hills when Richard started to cough, and then blood rushed from his mouth. He got so weak he couldn't go on. Hurry, Elizabeth, I don't think he can live much longer," Desire urged her on.

The last thing Elizabeth wanted to do was to hurry. She had witnessed too many deaths already, and now Richard? *No, God, please, not Richard. You've taken my father and mother, please let me keep Richard.* Even as she begged, she knew she was wrong. God's will must be done. Her stomach churned with the glut of green onion, but she forced her feet to pick up speed.

Coming into the dimly lit cottage Elizabeth could scarcely

see, but Richard was nowhere in sight.

"Here in our bed." Mistress Carver motioned Elizabeth around the partition.

Elizabeth's heavy feet took her around the wall to Richard's side. His breath was shallow; his eyes closed. She picked up his hand. It felt cold in her warm one. She looked into his face and remembered Christopher Martin's servant. Her hand grew as cold as his, and she wanted to drop it. But she held fast, rubbing her fingers against his in an attempt to bring warmth to both of them.

What could she say to him? This man who was to have been her husband. This man she had agreed to marry under duress. She had promised God and herself to be a good wife to this man. Did she love him? Perhaps, but certainly not in the way she had dreamed of loving when her mother told her fairy tales of princes carrying off lovely maidens. Fairy tales were just that. Life was different.

Certainly, in honesty she could tell this dying man that, by the grace of God, she loved him.

She bent her face over his grey one, and brought her lips close to his, but seeing the blood trickling from the corner of the mouth, she drew back as he struggled to breath.

"Richard, I'm here," she said. "I love you."

His eyelids flickered, and there was the slightest pressure on her hand. Then with a strange gurgling sound his struggle for breath was over. Richard lay still.

It was only then that she became aware of John Howland behind her. He took her elbow and gently led her away. Outside she broke free of him and ran to the far side of the cabin. Clutching a young tree, her stomach turned inside out as she vomited green onions, sobbing all the while.

But Elizabeth's service to Richard was not over. She knew it was part of her duty to help prepare his body for burial. When she had collected herself, she returned to the house.

"There's wood on hand now for a coffin," Governor Carver told her.

"I'll get started on it right away," John Howland offered.

"No," she said, "Richard would want to be buried as the rest of our people have been. With hills to make and fish to catch, there is no time even now for coffin building. Please both of you, go back to work."

"Elizabeth is right," the governor said. "John, you can dig the grave after dark, and we'll bury him tonight as we did the others."

Later Desire went with her to choose Richard's best clothes from his limited wardrobe. The first thing Elizabeth saw was the Bible beside the pallet where he had slept—the Bible that had been such a part of her father's life. She picked it up reverently and clasped it to her as tears filled her eyes.

Desire silently placed a gentle arm around her, and Elizabeth wept openly. But she soon regained control and shared with Desire how the Bible might not have been here, but for John Howland. Both were able to smile at her story.

Later Elizabeth helped Mistress Carver wash and dress Richard's wasted body for burial. To her surprise, she found a strange comfort in these simple preparations for committing Richard to the ground from which they had all been made. She discovered she almost felt like singing a hymn of praise to God because she knew that it was only his body that was returning to the earth. His spirit was with the Lord. Richard was among the blessed who were already standing in the presence of Christ, sharing in the joy of being eternally with Him. His pilgrimage was over.

With the Carver and Hopkins households, Elizabeth stumbled up the hill by the light of the waning moon to stand by while John Howland buried the young man who was to have been her husband.

The next morning Elizabeth begged Governor Carver to allow her to take Richard's place in the preparation of the field for planting. "Desire and Humility can help Mistress Carver here. I'm as strong as most of the men," she pleaded.

Governor Carver studied her with his kind eyes, and smiled as he nodded his head, "Yes, I believe we could use you. Many a woman has worked in the field beside the men. But there is one other thing you need to think about. The box of shoes that Richard brought are yours now. Do you want to leave them in the Common House or bring them to ours?"

"I suppose I better look at them." She was reluctant to handle anything more of Richard's, but since it must be done, she would get it over with.

Richard's pallet was rolled on top of the box in the corner of the Common House, the box that Master Martin would have left in England. She glanced at her bare feet, and wondered if there were any shoes in it that would fit her. She and many of the others would need new shoes for winter.

"Let me help." It was John Howland. He rolled the pallet from the lid and stood back while she looked inside.

"Bless Richard! Look at these," Elizabeth said softly, lifting out wooden-soled shoes with leather tops. "Clogs. Just what we need."

"That's what I always wore as a boy," John said.

He peered into the box then, "Look, there are his tools, the clogger's knife, and the groover, and that small box probably has rivets in it. What a happy legacy! None of us should have to go barefoot next winter."

"And there is even leather in here," Elizabeth said, dropping to her knees and rooting to the bottom.

"Well, young lady. You shouldn't go barefoot to the field now," John declared.

"I love going barefoot in the warm weather," Elizabeth said. *Besides, who knows when we'll get more shoes or leather to make them,* she thought. "But, I suppose, if I'm going to dig my foot will need support," she added, choosing a pair of clogs before she closed the box. "We'll leave them here for now. There's no need to clutter up the house with another box."

John went to the wall by the door and shouldered two shovels. He grinned at Elizabeth as she followed him and reached for one, too. "Beat you to it," he said. "I got yours."

But Elizabeth chose one and shouldered it as John had done. "There's likely someone less able to carry their own shovel than I am," she replied.

Squanto met them as they followed the rest of the men up the hill, and said to Elizabeth, "Me show you what to do."

But John Howland dismissed him. "I can show her. It's the first day some of the men are well enough to work. They'll need your help."

Elizabeth didn't know whether to be glad or sorry for John's interference. Too often she found breathing harder when he was nearby.

"We're turning over the earth, breaking it up, and mounding

it into little hillocks," John explained stepping on his shovel, and digging up a spadefull of brown soil.

"How far apart?" Elizabeth asked, glancing across to the mounds already made. "About like this?" She stepped ahead of him and dug her spade into the ground.

She looked up to find John beside her.

"I was going to help you get the feel of digging," he said almost apologetically, "but I guess you don't need me."

Elizabeth wondered why John fell to work turning up the earth and beating on the clods almost as if he were angry. But she didn't think about it again as she began work in earnest.

How good it felt to be active in the fresh air. A whiff of some fragrance came occasionally on the morning breeze, and the sun was warm on her back. This was so much better than being confined to the house, and what a joyous freedom after the cramped quarters of the ship. Once or twice she glanced out to the harbor. Empty. But it was all right. They were going to make it now.

Her thoughts turned only briefly to Richard. He was safe with the Lord, as were her parents and aunt and uncle. No need to grieve for them. She remembered how David in the Bible story had washed and eaten after his son died. He had sat in sack cloth and ashes, refusing food while the infant was sick and suffering, but his son's release was also David's. This was a new year, a new world, a time of new beginnings. She struck her spade into the earth again.

As the sun rose higher the day grew uncomfortably warm, and work turned to drudgery. Elizabeth's face felt as if it were on fire, and under her wool skirt creepy crawly sensations moved up and down her legs. Her back ached, and her hands were blistering, but remembering how Richard had worked to the very last, she persisted.

Once she glanced up to see Governor Carver remove his hat, mop his brow with a kerchief and pause briefly to rub his temples. When he turned back to his work there was an unusual listlessness about him. Is it just the heat, or isn't he feeling well, she wondered.

At mid-morning Elizabeth looked up to see Desire trudging toward them with a bucket. She paused to watch her approach, and stood quietly by as she went first to John and raised a ladle to his lips. Desire smiled and leaned into him as his hand closed over hers to steady the ladle. An odd feeling hit Elizabeth in the stomach, and she turned quickly back to her work.

It's all right, Desire is going to marry John, she told herself, and unaccountably, found tears flowing down her cheeks. *Please don't let Desire come to me next!* What a foolish prayer, she thought, brushing the tears away. But it was answered, for Desire went next to the governor. Again Elizabeth saw him hold his head as he dropped his shovel.

Elizabeth was too far away to hear what was being said, but she could tell Desire was remonstrating with him. Finally, he picked up his spade and started back to the village with shoulders hunched forward, and head down. As she watched him go, a shiver went through Elizabeth in spite of the heat.

"The governor is complaining of a bad headache," Desire told her when she brought her the bucket.

"I'm glad you persuaded him to go back to the house," Elizabeth said. "I pray he'll be all right."

"I'm sure a little rest will make him feel better. It's ghastly hot out here. I don't know how you're standing it," Desire replied. "You're face is beet red."

Elizabeth smiled and wiped her forehead, "It's not so bad," she insisted. *If John can stand it, I can,* she thought to herself.

"I'll go check on the governor, and help Mistress Carver with dinner." Desire picked up her bucket and started back. Elizabeth noted that she stopped again to speak to John and offer him another drink on the way. She supposed she might do the same thing if she were going to marry John, but her thoughts turned again to Governor Carver. She didn't like the way he hung his head as he left. Governor Carver always held his head high.

She shared her concern with John as they trudged back to the village at noon. John agreed that he, too, was worried. Entering the dark cottage they found the table set and the pot boiling on the hearth, but neither Mistress Carver nor Desire were in sight. Heavy breathing came from behind the partition.

Elizabeth looked questioningly at John. Normally they wouldn't go back there, but John led the way and Elizabeth followed. They found Mistress Carver bathing the Governor with cool water as Desire wet and wrung out cloths for her.

Mistress Carver hardly seemed to know they were there, but Desire looked up shaking her head.

John turned immediately back to the kitchen side and ordered Henry, who had just come in, to go for Doctor Fuller. Elizabeth stood for a moment, stunned by Master Carver's appearance. He stared at the rafters with unseeing eyes from a face white as death.

The weight that had begun to lift from her chest as she had chopped away at the earth this morning suddenly descended again. How many more would the Lord require of them? How many more losses could they survive? "God give us strength," she whispered.

Chapter 19

As she stood at the foot of Governor Carver's bed, the hunger pangs in Elizabeth's stomach suddenly became unbearable. John must be hungry too, she realized. They had to eat if they were to go on working. They had to go on working if they wanted to eat later on. The children must be fed as well.

She turned from the sick man, and walked purposefully to the hearth where the pot was bubbling. Taking the long-handled black ladle, she dished up hot broth for them all. Mistress Carver refused food, but sent Desire to eat.

The doctor arrived just after John had returned thanks, and disappeared behind the partition. He came back looking very grave.

"It's a stroke of some kind," he said. "We'll just have to wait and see if he regains consciousness."

"Can't you do something?" Desire begged.

Henry and Humility stopped slurping their soup, and looked wide-eyed at the doctor.

Elizabeth turned her face to the wall, not hungry after all.

"You know he would if he could," John reprimanded Desire as gently as he would the children.

Elizabeth gave John an appreciative look. They didn't need any scenes now. If Desire started to cry she couldn't stand it.

The doctor left and they finished their meal in silence except for the heavy breathing that came from behind the partition. Then John and Elizabeth with one accord rose from the table and started back to the field.

The labored breathing continued through the night and all the next day. At John's insistence, Elizabeth and Desire spelled off Mistress Carver in attending the sick man. By the next night everyone sensed that the end was near. The breathing grew more shallow, and his wife absolutely refused to leave her husband's side.

Elizabeth lay a long time on her pallet watching the flickering shadows on the rafters from the candle behind the partition and listening for each rasping breath of the man who had become her second father. But she had worked in the field again that day, and her weary body overcoming her mind, she finally slept. John Howland had volunteered to keep watch with Mistress Carver at the bed of his master throughout the night.

There was a faint grey light outside the tiny window when Elizabeth woke again. The candle had gone out, and the room was in deep shadows. She listened instinctively for the harsh breathing that had become as pervasive as the swishing of the waves on the shore. Silence. The silence of death.

Then a strangled sob. She sat bolt upright. Sprawled at the table with head on arms was a big figure, blacker than the shadows. John, crying? Every fiber of her body strained toward him. How she longed to put her arms about him! He needed comfort, the warmth and life that she could give him in his loss. She must be strong now for him....and Mistress Carver.

It was Mistress Carver, not John, that Elizabeth took in her arms in the greyness of the early morning.

Standing by Governor Carver's grave the next day, Elizabeth was thankful that he hadn't had to be secreted off in the dark of night as her father had been. The whole community had processed to the grave site behind a proper coffin. After words of comfort from Elder Brewster, the militia saluted their fallen leader with a round of gunfire. Along with grief, pride swelled in Elizabeth's heart to think that she had been privileged to live with this highly esteemed man.

The same evening, while the men met in the Common House to choose a new governor, Elizabeth stood with the women outside awaiting the news.

"William Bradford will be elected," John had predicted as they shared biscuits and water at the evening meal.

"But he isn't well," Elizabeth objected. Besides, how could she ever think of anyone else as "governor"? Still since it had to be, shouldn't Governor Carver's mantle fall on John, his faithful servant?

Desire voiced Elizabeth's sentiment. "You ought to be governor."

"No," John asserted, "Bradford is as much a son to Elder Brewster as I was to Governor Carver, only he wasn't a servant. He'll work closely with him, but the civil government will be separate from the church, as we want it to be."

"You could work with Elder Brewster too," Desire persisted.

"Not the way William does. After all, they have known each other since William began attending Pastor Robinson's church in Scrooby. It's only right that the Leydeners keep control of the plantation, since it was their dream."

Elizabeth had seen John's point, and was ready to accept William Bradford as their new leader when John brought the word. But she didn't linger in the long twilight to congratulate Governor Bradford. Instead, she hurried back to be with Mistress Carver, who scarcely seemed aware of what was going on around her.

Through the next few weeks the ration of food for each of those in the Carver household increased slightly, Elizabeth noted, feeling somewhat guilty. Mistress Carver took less and less and finally refused anything at all, taking to her bed with no specific complaint. Dr. Fuller stopped regularly to see her and brought his last supply of catnip to brew in hopes of reviving her appetite.

It didn't help. In early June Elizabeth stood by an open grave while Mistress Carver was laid to rest beside her husband. It was hard for Elizabeth to understand what had happened to her. Why had she not made more of an effort to live when there was so much to be done and she was so badly needed?

On the painful journey back from the grave to the house that was now John's, Elizabeth faced the fact John and Desire must soon marry. Elizabeth's stomach turned over. She couldn't stay where John and Desire would be sharing a marriage bed. The very thought made her nauseous. She suddenly faced the fact that John meant more to her than was right for a man about to marry someone else.

Her steps faltered and she fell behind the group that had become family to her. Nothing could ever be the same again. John and Desire had their life to build together, and she must find another place to live.

June melted into July and as the days passed nothing in the former Carver household changed. Elizabeth couldn't bring herself to ask Mistress Hopkins if she might move in with them, and neither John nor Desire broached the subject of their wedding day. Instead, as the corn began to grow, and Squanto instructed them in hoeing weeds, Elizabeth once again fell to working beside John in the field. Desire managed the house and the kitchen garden with the help of Humility, and Henry worked in the field like a young man.

The Hopkins household seemed the logical move for Elizabeth. But she was reluctant to ask because trouble seemed to be brewing between the two Edwards. Elizabeth knew that Constance was part of it, and she wasn't anxious to become involved any more than she could help.

Constance, too, had begun working in the field, and took delight in playing one Edward against the other. One day she would walk with one to work, laughing and rolling her eyes at him, and the next it would be the other. Elizabeth could see that Edward Leister was particularly disturbed by her fickleness. He would glower at Dotey if he offered to carry Constance's hoe, and seemed to make a point of trying to beat Dotey to her side.

But even when he arrived first, Constance was apt to say sweetly, "Thank you so much for offering, but it's Edward Dotey's turn today. I'll walk with you tomorrow."

One day when he was beat out again Elizabeth saw him heave his hoe across the field with all his might. She shuddered to think what would have happened if it hit anyone. The next day Constance elected to walk back with her, ignoring both of them.

Elizabeth felt compelled to speak up. "Why don't you make up your mind which Edward you like best, and stop leading both of them on? I'm afraid there's going to be trouble if you don't."

Constance laughed. "But it's fun to have two fellows competing for you. Just like in the days of knights when they would fight over a lady."

"Do you really want them to fight?" Elizabeth asked.

"It would be kind of fun." Constance crinkled her nose and shrugged.

"Constance, do you care about either one of them?" Elizabeth stopped and turned to face her squarely.

"It doesn't matter whether I do or not," she replied. "My father says I can't marry until I'm at least 18. What else can I do? I'm afraid they'll both be interested in someone else by that time, and I won't have anybody," she answered.

Elizabeth could sympathize with Constance's plight. After all she had been absolutely serious about marrying Richard, and she hadn't expected to wait two years. "But that doesn't make it right to keep leading them both on. You should choose one, and if he really cares about you, he'll wait," she said.

"But I do like them both, and since I don't have to decide, why should I?" she retorted. Seeing Edward Leister catching up with them, she turned from Elizabeth to him.

"What happened to you? I missed you," she said, giving him her sweetest smile.

But Edward Leister didn't smile back at her. "I want you to be my girl, and I don't want you walking with anyone else," he thundered at her.

"Oh Edward, if you really want me to be your girl, I will be," she declared.

"And you won't walk with Dotey anymore?" he asked brightening.

"No, I'll always wait for you," she promised blithely and giving him her rake, she tucked her hand in his arm and went off down the hill with him.

She did what I suggested, Elizabeth thought, but somehow she wasn't comfortable about it.

As soon as Elizabeth was free after supper she slipped away to walk by the water. She had come to cherish a quiet time on the beach after the heat of the day. The bay lay still and luminescent under the evening sky. Enjoying the water gently lapping on the shore, she went farther than usual. She reached a spot where sand dunes rose between the shore and the trees, and was about to turn back when she heard voices and laughter. Indians? No, distinctively English. Curious, she slogged her way through the soft sand following the sounds which died away as she approached.

Coming into a dip between the dunes she discovered why it had become so quiet. There were Constance and Edward Dotey wrapped in each other's arms, totally absorbed in a kiss.

That crazy Constance, she thought as she backed away, her footfalls silent in the sand. *There's going to be trouble for sure.*

When Elizabeth stepped outside to rinse her face before bedtime a dark figure was waiting for her. "Oh Elizabeth, I'm glad I caught you," Constance Hopkins spoke in a whisper.

"What's the matter?" Elizabeth asked trying to make out her friend's features in the gathering night.

She took her arm and pulled her away from the house. "Promise you won't tell anyone what I'm going to tell you." Her voice was low.

As Elizabeth debated the wisdom of making such a promise Constance pleaded, "Please, please, I need to talk to someone."

Recognizing her distress, Elizabeth reluctantly gave her word.

"Edward Leister and Edward Dotey are going to fight a duel over me!" She sounded both frightened and gratified.

"We can't let them do that. One of them will be killed," Elizabeth exclaimed.

"Shussh," Constance said, "We can't stop them now. They're determined to let God choose between them. Nothing but a duel will do."

"How did it come to this?" Elizabeth asked, though she could guess the answer.

"I sneaked off and met Edward Dotey down in the dunes tonight, and Edward Leister found us. He claimed that Dotey had compromised me and that since I had promised to be his girl he must have justice. Dotey just laughed at him and said I loved him and that he was going to marry me. He called Leister a bloody freak to think I cared a rap for a puny runt like him. Leister was furious and challenged him to a duel."

"What are they fighting with?" Elizabeth asked. "They don't own any weapons."

"There are pistols with the militia supplies in the Common House," Constance answered. "And Leister vowed he'd get them."

"But they've never used pistols before, have they?" Elizabeth shuddered, expecting them both to be killed.

"Maybe not, but they'll figure them out. They are meeting down the beach after the moon comes up, and I've got to be there. Please come with me," Constance begged.

"I think I better tell John Howland about this," Elizabeth was having second thoughts.

"No! You promised." Constance's voice rose sharply, "If they don't fight the duel, I'm afraid Leister will kill Dotey in his bed. He's furious enough to do it."

Elizabeth remembered the flying hoe, and knew she was right.

"But what if someone hears me leaving?" Elizabeth was already shivering in the cool night air, torn between the wisdom of staying away from the scene and the need to be there with her friend.

"Haven't you ever gotten up in the night before?" Constance asked archly.

The way her stomach was already churning, *it would probably be necessary*, Elizabeth thought as she agreed.

She positioned herself in her bed so that she could see out the little window and keep watch for the rise of the waning moon. In spite of her day in the fields, all thought of sleep was banished, and every muscle was tense. *I should never have given Constance my word not to tell*, she told herself over and over. *Our plantation can't spare another person. Even if they don't kill each other, one is bound to be hurt, and may die of his wound. I hope Constance has learned her lesson.*

But Elizabeth wasn't sure that she had. She suspected that she was relishing being the center of a duel.

At last moonlight filtered through the window, and Elizabeth crept from bed and slipped into her clothes." Desire stirred and Elizabeth paused, with her skirt pulled part way up, until her breathing became regular again. Then, without shoes, she tiptoed around the partition and through the kitchen to the door. *The door squeaks*, she thought, but her stomach knotted and she remembered her excuse. Quickly she opened it, and let herself out.

They were all to meet at the bottom of the street by the water.

As she made her way down the dark tracks the moon made a sparkling path across the bay leading her on. Soon she made out five figures waiting.

Constance came to her immediately. "Good, you're here. Edward Winslow's and Elder Brewster's servants are going to act as seconds for them. They'll watch to see if all is fair."

Elizabeth noted the set of the opponents shoulders and saw that words were useless. Moonlight glinted from the burnished pistol barrels as the grim party trooped up the softly lit beach. There was no sound but the crunch of pebbles under the men's boots and the slapping of the waves in the rising night wind. The pebbles bore into Elizabeth's bare feet, but she scarcely noticed. They had become quite hardened from going barefoot much of the time. Her eyes were on the stiff backs that preceded her.

Pebbles gave way to sand and she could make out black hills on the land side. She knew they had reached the spot where Edward Leister had discovered Constance in Edward Dotey's embrace. Here the duelists stopped and whirled to face each other.

The tense silence was broken by Edward Winslow's servant. "Twenty paces?" he suggested.

She saw both heads nod.

"George will count," the other servant spoke. "Remember, your honor is at stake if you turn sooner."

Again a silent nod. Then Leister spoke in a strangled voice, "God will show who is a puny runt." And Elizabeth caught the gleam of metal as Leister accepted the pistol from his second.

When she looked toward Dotey she could see the outline of the pistol in his hand.

Then Constance whispered in her ear. "Isn't it exciting? I wish I had a rose for the winner. I did bring a handkerchief for him."

Elizabeth felt like shaking her, but she was shaking too badly herself to shake anyone else. "God help us," she breathed.

George was positioning the duelists back to back in the soft sand. She had never seen anyone stiffer or straighter than those two as their shadows blended into one on the moonlit beach.

George moved back to stand with the other servant beside Elizabeth and Constance at what they believed to be a safe distance from the line of fire.

"One," the two figures broke apart, "Two," the distance widened slightly, "Three" one pace further apart, "Four, five, six, seven, eight, nine, ten, eleven, twelve," the space between them grew greater. Elizabeth's mouth was so dry that she knew she couldn't have said thirteen if she had to. "Thirteen" the servant boomed, and now the time between the numbers slowed until Elizabeth thought he would never reach twenty. "Nineteen,"....time stopped...."twenty!"

Fire blazed from each gun. Elizabeth felt something whizz by her head as the blasts rent the air, echoing into the dunes and rolling back from the forest wall. Looking at Leister she saw him still on his feet. She turned to Dotey expecting to see him crumpled on the ground, but no, his shadowy figure was as straight as before. She looked back to Leister. Surely he must be down by now. Instead, he raised the gun again, but nothing happened. With a rush of fresh air into her lungs Elizabeth realized that these pistols carried only one shot. Both men had missed.

"No one gets my hankie," Constance sounded disappointed.

"Give us another shot," Edward Leister demanded rushing up to them.

"We don't have any more," Winslow's servant answered evenly.

Leister grabbed him by the shoulders. "You didn't bring any more!" he screamed in frustration, shaking him and tossing him aside.

Elizabeth had a great urge to kiss the far-thinking servant. "It looks as if God has given you all another chance," she said, but no one was paying any attention.

"I'll have my satisfaction yet," Edward Leister stormed and started up the beach just as several lanterns bobbed along the water's edge, and excited voices drifted down to them. Villagers were on their way to investigate.

"Come on, Constance," Elizabeth said moving away from the men, "We better go meet them and explain what happened. The shots must have wakened the whole town."

"Oh, do you think there'll be trouble?" Constance wailed.

"It's a little late to worry about that," Elizabeth replied, starting up the beach after Edward Leister who strode defiantly toward the flickering lights.

By the time she met the colonists with the lanterns Capt. Standish, who was in the lead, was giving Edward Leister a tongue lashing. "It was a totally irresponsible thing to do. Risking two lives over a point of honor. And you nowhere near to being gentry," he ended scornfully.

"I have my honor to protect too, even if I'm not gentry," Leister said, his voice surly.

"Young man, if the community had stocks we'd put the two of you in them side by side, but since we can ill afford to spend time building stocks, or lose your labor while you sit in them, we will devise another punishment for you," Governor Bradford declared.

"Don't you realize there was as much likelihood of your killing Constance or Elizabeth as there was of killing each other?" Capt. Standish ripped into Edward Dotey as he came up.

"What do you mean?" Elizabeth asked, suddenly remembering the whizzing sound she had heard just after the shots were fired.

"There's nothing harder to handle than a pistol, the slightest twist of the wrist can send the ball flying off in any direction, and without experience you're more apt to hit a bystander than what you're aiming at," Capt. Standish was still upset.

"Our General Council will meet in the morning and decide how to deal with you men. In the meantime Dotey, you come to my house for the night, and Leister, you go with Captain Standish," Governor Bradford ordered.

Then the governor turned to Elizabeth. "What are you doing here?" he asked.

Elizabeth quickly told of her role as Constance's confidante, and then he turned to Constance for her explanation.

"Well I guess they both want to marry me. And somehow both thought I had promised them, and well...." she trailed off, too embarrassed to continue.

"All right, young lady, you come home now and you can figure on staying at home for a good while to come." Stephen Hopkins stepped forward and claimed his daughter.

"Elizabeth, I think you better get to bed, too." John Howland emerged from the shadows, holding out a hand to her as if she were a child.

Spurning it, she started up the street, but he soon overtook her. "Elizabeth, can you imagine how worried I was when we discovered you weren't in the house after we were awakened by the shots? We had no idea what was going on," John spoke reasonably to her.

Suddenly, all her fears and misgivings came together. Stopping, she turned to John, studying the strong face made even stronger by the shadows from the lantern. "I'm so sorry," she said, "but I had given my word, and father always taught me to keep my word. That was why I was prepared to marry Richard, when I didn't really love him." She stopped short, realizing that perhaps she had said too much. Would John guess her reason for not wanting to marry Richard? He must never know.

Chapter 20

The next morning Constance hailed Elizabeth from her doorway, "I'm not allowed in the fields anymore ever," she said petulantly, "and the Edwards are forbidden to see me again. They'll both be staying where they were sent last night."

By now Elizabeth had determined that the Hopkins household was not for her. When the time came to move she would definitely need to look for another place.

But the days continued in their usual pattern. John seemed too busy to plan a wedding, and Desire didn't talk about it either. Elizabeth was content to let things drift.

One evening in late July, John came in with some disturbing news. Young John Billington was missing. He had wandered into the woods after the noon break and hadn't returned.

"He's been stolen by the Indians," Desire gasped, and Elizabeth saw her hand was trembling as she drew a thread through a skirt she was mending for Humility.

"Surely not," Elizabeth tried to quiet Desire's fears. And her own. "Massasoit wouldn't let anyone do that."

"We can't trust those savages," Desire said her voice rising. "Some night they'll murder all of us in our beds."

"I don't think so," John spoke with conviction. "Not as long as Miles Standish has someone up there manning that big gun. I think they will keep their covenant with us. From what I know of that Billington boy, he'll probably show up tomorrow with a string of fish."

But Billington's older son didn't show up the next day nor the day after that, and Elizabeth had to fight to keep Desire's fears from becoming her own. *Surely the Lord won't let the Indians wipe us out now*, she told herself.

By this time the Governor had sent Squanto to see what he could find out about the missing lad. More than a week passed and Squanto returned with no word of him.

Then one day as Elizabeth was hoeing corn, her heart skipped several beats as she looked up to see an Indian brave standing nearby. Squanto saw him at the same time, and laying down his hoe approached him with measured steps. They conferred briefly while Elizabeth strained to hear what was said over the pounding of her heart. But she couldn't understand them anyway. Soon Squanto led the young brave to Governor Bradford. The governor tapped several men, including John Howland, and led them down the hill.

He might at least have told us what's going on, Elizabeth thought as she watched them go. But it occurred to her that as scattered as the workers were it would have been hard to do. *Patience*, she said to herself, and dug her hoe deep into the ground.

When she went in for her bowl of soup, John wasn't there, and Desire was stirring the pot excessively hard with both hands.

"Oh Elizabeth," she burst out as soon as she saw her, "They sent John with the shallop to try to get that no-good Billington fellow back. Some of those Indians that shot at our men over on the Cape have him. They'll keep John, too, if they don't kill him first." With that Desire dropped the spoon and turned sobbing to Elizabeth.

Elizabeth took her in her arms and tried to find words of encouragement. "No, no, John will come back. Governor Bradford wouldn't have sent them unless he had reason to believe they would be all right."

"They took their guns and Miles Standish went along. There could be a battle," Desire said, wiping her eyes with her apron as she pulled away from Elizabeth.

"They're in the Lord's hands," Elizabeth said quietly. "We have to trust them to Him."

In spite of her brave words to Desire, Elizabeth was thankful for hard work to do the rest of the day. That night sleep was a long time coming. She missed the comforting presence of John in the loft overhead. Involuntarily, her thoughts would turn to him if she stirred, and she would chide herself for the impropriety of the feelings that coursed through her young body.

This night was especially black. Was she being punished? *God forgive me,* she prayed, *and oh, please take care of John. I'll try to keep my thoughts pure,* she promised as she tossed and turned.

Elizabeth was never sure that she slept, but somehow morning came. Now the day stretched interminably before her. She got very little hoeing done because she stopped so often to look toward the harbor.

At long last Elizabeth made out a vessel between the two points of land that protected their bay. It had to be the shallop. There had been no other ship there since the Mayflower sailed. She watched it slowly grow larger. Tacking back and forth against the prevailing breeze, it finally came close enough for her to pick out John.

Elizabeth could contain herself no longer. Dropping her hoe and calling to those working nearby that the boat had returned, she ran down the hill. She almost bypassed the village, but a sudden pang of conscience took her to the door of their cottage to call Desire.

Young Billington was the first one ashore, followed by his scowling father. Both were greeted by a scolding Goodwife Billington. John was the last to debark, and suddenly, eager as Elizabeth was to see him, she was overcome by a feeling of shyness. She didn't dare rush up and throw her arms around him as she would have liked. Oddly enough Desire seemed to be infected with the same disease. But the awkward moment passed as John launched into the story of the trip.

A hunting party of Indians from the Cape had found John Billington wandering in the forest, and had taken him along with them. "They turned out to be the tribe who had fled from us. They were afraid we would carry them off for slaves. That's what white men had done to them before. That's why they hid and then attacked us when we came too close," John went on. "They're also the Indians from whom we borrowed the basket of corn. We told them we wanted to pay for it and asked them to come for a visit. I'm sure they'll be here soon," he concluded.

Two days later a delegation of Indians from the Cape paraded into the village to be entertained, and receive knives and trinkets in payment for their corn. Elizabeth heaved a sigh of relief and prayed fervently that that would be the last of the Indian visits. Much as she had come to appreciate Squanto, she had to admit to herself that she didn't like to have a group of them so close.

Her prayers were answered. Except for one other unpleasant incident, they had little contact with the Indians the rest of the summer. Since it didn't involve John, she wasn't too concerned. In fact Capt. Standish's decisive action made her feel more secure.

Squanto had been gone for several days, when word was received that he had been taken captive by a neighboring tribe who resented his close friendship with the English, and that his life had been threatened. Declaring the settlers dared not desert their friend, Miles Standish prevailed on Governor Bradford to let him lead a rescue mission.

Before they learned that Squanto had not been killed, the captain had led a night raid on the chief's dwelling. Three braves were injured and, to make up for the mistake, Captain Standish brought them back for Dr. Fuller to care for. When the red men recovered, they were profuse in their thanks, and were sent back to their tribe, each bearing a prized knife.

Elizabeth agreed with John's appraisal of the incident. "I should like it better if we didn't ever have to fight with our neighbors. Perhaps, if we show them immediately that we will stand up to them, we may have less trouble in the long run," he had said.

Elizabeth's main concern was what she would do when Desire and John married, even as the summer days settled themselves into a routine that made them pass quickly. When the work in the fields was done there were wild berries to pick to supplement their food supply. In mid-June Elizabeth marveled at the tiny sweet strawberries that nestled in the tall grass in the uncultivated field. By early July flavorful black raspberries were ripening followed by plump blackberries that exacted their toll on the pickers, but were worth every scratch.

Before the blackberries were gone Squanto reported a stand

of huckleberries. The whole village carried their lunches to the patch to spend the day picking. Mingling with the scent of juniper and pine, the bushes, soaking up the August sunshine, exuded a fragrance that reminded Elizabeth of honeysuckle. She soon got the knack of stripping the delicately flavored fruit into the leather bucket, and challenged John and Desire to a race. The delighted children wanted to join as well.

The work started off with much bantering back and forth, but soon each settled to picking in earnest. Elizabeth's fingers flew from one cluster of berries to the next, peeling them adroitly into her leather bucket. Her arm and shoulder muscles strained with the effort, and the sun grew hot on her back, but she worked doggedly on until at last her bucket was brimming with frosted blue berries.

"I'm done!" Her shout rang victoriously across the huckleberry patch.

Ready for a break, everyone gathered to check her claim. Elizabeth was basking in John's admiration when she saw Desire working her way toward them through the waist-high bushes. Suddenly Desire went down. Berries splashed into the air as a cry of pain arose from the spot where she fell.

With a pang of remorse Elizabeth shoved her way toward her friend. *I shouldn't have embarrassed her this way,* she thought. *A contest is no good if anyone is humiliated, or worse yet, hurt.* Perhaps she had been showing off for John. She slowed to let him pass her to help Desire.

That night Elizabeth lay for a long time listening to the chirping of the crickets that blended into one continuous note, very aware of Desire lying stiffly beside her. Along with Humility, at John's insistence, they now shared the Carvers' bed.

At last she whispered, "Desire, are you awake?"

There was a faint stirring at her side. "Desire, I'm so sorry about this afternoon. I never should have suggested a contest. Does your ankle hurt very much?" Desire had limped the rest of the day on a swollen ankle and had had little to say to anyone.

There was no answer.

What am I going to do? Elizabeth wondered. *It's time for John and Desire to get married, and I don't want to see it happen. Lord, Lord, I've tried so many times to give these feelings to you, and yet they still keep coming back.* Her prayer was silent. She turned on her side away from Desire.

Maybe I'm going to have to find someone to marry, or else.... the unthinkable thought came to her....*maybe I should leave.* John's very presence always seemed to awaken feelings in her over which she had no control. Would it always be that way? For a little while her concern over Richard had taken the edge off these feelings, but after his death they had returned stronger than ever.

"I don't want to leave. I've got to get this under control. Please, dear Lord, help me." A prayer formed on her lips. She determined then to try to avoid contact with John as much as possible. She should ask Governor Bradford to find another home for her, but how could she explain her wish to move until John and Desire actually married? She would have to handle it while still living here.

For the next week she stayed at the cottage and took over Desire's duties while her foot mended. Desire continued to be very quiet and John persisted in telling Elizabeth about each day's work in great detail. Always, before she knew it, she was caught up in his enthusiasm and was sharing in his plans for the next day. Fishing and hunting were keeping the men busy, and Elizabeth thrilled to John's details of shooting a wild turkey. She was annoyed at Desire for wrinkling up her nose in distaste at the prospect of cleaning the big bird.

Before they knew it, harvest season had arrived, and Desire was well enough that Elizabeth could return to the fields. She hung back as they started across the hill, but it was no use. John was soon lagging with her.

"We're going to pull the ears off the stalks today, and take them to the Common House for storage," he explained. "We'll husk later. You can pick, and I'll carry the ears down for you."

"Thank you, John Howland, I'll carry my own like everyone else," Elizabeth said, glancing down at the bag slung from her shoulder and resting on her hip.

John laughed. "I should have known better than suggest such a thing."

That evening as Elizabeth paused by the door splashing cool water over her face to remove the dust of the day's work, John came up with a twinkle in his eye.

"We're going to have a harvest festival, just like we used to have in the village at home. It looks like the crop is pretty good, and we certainly have much to rejoice over. I suggested it to Governor Bradford, and he liked the idea," he announced, sounding very pleased with himself.

"What fun!" Elizabeth said, wiping her face with an old towel that hung outside. Their eyes met as Elizabeth lowered the towel. A quiver went through her almost as if he had kissed her. This was happening much too often lately.

She lowered her eyes quickly and said, "You must tell Desire right away." He nodded and went into the house.

Elizabeth hung the ragged cloth back on its peg and walked away from the house toward the beach. For the first time she noticed a few red leaves of a brilliance that she had never before seen, and for a moment her attention was diverted from her own thoughts. In England only ivy changed to a dark reddish brown before it fell. She wondered briefly if the whole tree would be that color or if this was some kind of aberration, a little like her feelings for John— entirely out of place. She could see fog rising outside their harbor and stood watching as it gradually rolled in on a damp breeze. She shivered. Autumn was near with winter close behind. A great wave of sadness swept over her. Would she be here to see another harvest?

The thoughts of returning to England as the way to solve her problem had continued to plague her since the day Desire fell. John's eyes, when they met hers, seemed to carry her into a secret place all their own. Did he feel it too? She feared he did.

Her head and her will told her he must marry Desire. He had promised. Her heart said he never would as long as she was here. John needed a wife, and children— especially children. The thought nagged at her as she remembered Desire's reaction to childbirth. But then, she supposed, lots of women were afraid and had children anyway. John needed to be a father, and the colony needed to be bringing the next generation into the world.

A lone gull swooped low, mewing mournfully, and lighted near where she stood statue still. How much she had come to love this land already, and how strongly she believed in its future, but was her future here? Perhaps her greatest contribution would be to leave.

If she returned to England and eventually found someone she could love properly she could come again, and still make this land of promise her home. It was a wisp of an idea, and she had trouble holding it. Even as she made up her mind that she must go, she knew she would never come back.

The quiet bay blurred before her eyes more rapidly than the rolling mists could cover it. A tear spilled over and ran down her cheek. She wouldn't let herself look behind at the tiny village that had become home. She set her face stoically toward England. She would tell John and Desire of her plan tonight. The first ship that came would carry her away, leaving them free to begin their own home and family.

How long she stood on the pebbly beach she never knew, except that it was deep twilight before she made her way back to the cottage. She paused outside the open door and saw John talking animatedly to Desire whose cheeks by the firelight seemed to be brighter than Elizabeth had seen them for weeks.

Her decision was confirmed. Desire and John would soon marry, when she was out of the picture. Perhaps they had just been waiting all along for her to be settled. She was misinterpreting the way John looked at her. Elizabeth drew a long breath and let it escape in a sigh so deep that John heard her and jumped to his feet.

"Elizabeth, is that you?" he called and hurried to the door.

Elizabeth lifted her chin high and stepped inside.

"I was just telling Desire that I ought to go to look for you, but she assured me that you were all right. But there is something wrong. What is it?" John asked.

"I've decided to go back to England on the first ship that arrives," she said and caught her lower lip between her teeth.

John stared at her in disbelief.

Desire rose abruptly from the stool by the hearth. "You, go back to England! There's no woman here who likes this place the way you do," she said.

Elizabeth suddenly realized that she hadn't really thought of a good explanation for her decision. She lifted her hands to her temples that had begun to throb. Her eyes were stinging. She turned abruptly and ran heedlessly out into the night.

Chapter 21

Elizabeth heard John's feet pounding behind her. Overtaking her, he grabbed her by the arm.

"What's this all about?" John demanded when he had dragged her back into the house.

"Let me alone," she said. Jerking away from him, she ran behind the partition and threw herself on the bed.

She heard Desire mumble something and the door bang. Then she felt a gentle hand on her shoulder.

"There's got to be a reason for this sudden change." It was Desire speaking softly. "I'm your best friend. Surely, you can tell me."

Elizabeth was trapped and knew nothing but the truth would do.

"I'm going so you and John will get married," she blubbered into the bolster. "I feel like I keep coming between you, and it isn't right. Besides I'm afraid I love John, and that isn't right either."

Desire was silent for so long that at last Elizabeth rolled over and sat up, more concerned for her friend than for herself. *What have I done to her*, she wondered.

"Desire," she said, groping for her hand in the darkness. "It's all right. Sometimes things happen this way. I'm sure God knows what's best for us. I just want to do the right thing, and too often I haven't. I'm afraid deep down inside I have been trying to show John that I was better than you. Or maybe it was myself I was trying to prove it to. Can you forgive me?"

Desire began to cry, and Elizabeth waited quietly for her friend to accept her confession.

"But you're right," Desire choked out her words. "You are better for John than I am."

"No! We're just different," Elizabeth protested. "And you'll make him a good wife. You like all the things wives are supposed to do, and I'm afraid I really don't."

"None of that matters. What does matter to both of us is what will make John happy." Desire spoke calmly, but her foot was tapping against the bed frame. "It's you John loves. You are the one who is right for this new land. I'm really not. It frightens me terribly, and I'm the one who is going back to England on the first boat that comes."

"Desire, I'm so sorry. It's all my fault. I should have moved in with the Hopkins' when Mistress Carver died," Elizabeth said.

"Don't blame yourself." Desire's foot was still now, and her words came slowly. "I came because Carvers picked John out for me. I realized that it was risky business to cross an ocean to marry a man someone else chose. I knew there was the possibility he might have other ideas. There didn't seem to be anyone else in Holland, and so I ventured forth hoping it might be God's plan for me. It turns out it wasn't."

Elizabeth's cheeks were wet with tears for her friend. What should she do? Was Desire right? Had she read his eyes correctly? Was that why John so often aroused in her a funny quivery feeling? She thought of how often John asked her opinion, and how much in accord they always were. More tears flowed, but these were for the joy that arose with the recognition that what Desire had said was true.

When Desire shared the switch of plans with John the next morning, he looked in bewilderment from one young woman to the other. These two girls that formed the hub of his life, what was going on with them?

All had been quiet behind the partition when he had returned and climbed into the loft last night. The men had been outlining plans for the Harvest Festival at a meeting in the Common House, but he had lost his enthusiasm for it. If Elizabeth left, nothing would have the same luster any longer.

He had wandered to the beach after the meeting and heaved stone after stone into the mist-shrouded water. Each splash echoed dully in his head.

Finally he acknowledged to himself that if Elizabeth didn't leave he might never bring himself to marry Desire. Carvers had expected it, and while they were gone, his obligation to them still existed. John Carver had made him his heir and Desire went with the inheritance. In all fairness to Desire it was time to marry. Perhaps if they went ahead with their plans Elizabeth would stay.

He had determined to set their wedding date to coincide with the Harvest Festival, but before he had a chance to tell Desire he was greeted with the news his bride-to-be was leaving. To make matters worse, the women refused to discuss it. Both quickly turned away from him, busying themselves with household chores. He shrugged, and reaching for his musket, stomped out of the cottage.

As he tramped though the woods toward the pond that attracted the waterfowl, he stopped short, staring at the black-veined sandy path. He had been struck by an unthinkable thought.

Am I obligated to return to England with Desire? I couldn't face the prospect of Elizabeth's leaving. To have to go back myself would be worse than death. But my Christian duty comes first, he sighed, feeling as if a falling tree had pinned his chest to the ground.

John continued to wrestle with the idea for several days hoping to learn the Lord's will for him. Men were needed so badly to make the colony work. Surely the Lord didn't want him to leave. Or was he only reading his own wishes into the situation? It occurred to him that if Desire left Elizabeth might consent to marry him. He felt guilty about the emotions that flooded over him at the thought. Finally he decided to ask Elder Brewster's opinion.

He overtook the elder as they were carrying a load of corn down to the Common House, and explained the situation to him briefly.

"Give me time to consult the Scriptures and pray about this," Elder Brewster answered as they neared the village.

"I've been trying to find God's will," John said. "I've prayed and searched the Scriptures, and the only answer I have gotten comes from I Corinthians where Paul talks about behaving uncomely toward one's virgin. If she's passed the flower of her age...let them marry, he says. I'm afraid I haven't done right by Desire by not going ahead with the wedding."

"I'll study the passage and ask the Holy Spirit to lead me to other Scriptures that might have a bearing on your situation," Elder Brewster said.

But before the elder gave him his answer, John was called on by Governor Bradford to travel with Squanto and several others up the coast to try to find Indians with whom they could open a fur trade. *If I have to leave the New World I'd like to see as much of it as I can,* John told himself as he accepted the assignment.

The zest of exploring came over him as the shallop set sail on a bright morning in late September. *Women! What a relief to get away from them for a awhile,* he thought.

Elizabeth and Desire had both come to the beach to see him off, but it seemed as though they had shut him out of their lives ever since the contest had developed over who was leaving. Sometimes he feared they might both go, though he couldn't believe that Elizabeth really wanted to go back. If it came to that he would certainly have to marry Desire and return to England for Elizabeth's sake. But he determined not to think about it while he was gone.

A favorable breeze bore them uneventfully up the amazingly beautiful coast. Patches of red and gold shone against the evergreens, and Squanto told them this remarkable display happened every year. To the northeast they discovered a large protected harbor that John could see was a much better site than their own for a settlement. Reluctantly everyone agreed that their little colony was too well established to move.

About the time they were ready to pull away from the shore they encountered their first Indians. Several brown-skinned women came trailing out of the forest dressed in what they were looking for, beaver pelts.

John turned immediately to Squanto. "Ask them if they have any more beaver skins cached nearby, and tell them we'd like to trade with them."

"They bad people. They threaten you. Take their coats.

"No matter how bad they are, we can't do that. It would only give them an excuse to attack us, and we don't want to fight with anyone if we can help it." John spoke for all of them.

Squanto shrugged. "They like beads," he suggested.

Prepared for such an opportunity, John opened his treasures and invited the women to look at beads. One brave soul came close enough to look in his box. John lifted up a string of red glass beads that sparkled in the sunlight. Her eyes widened and she smiled broadly.

"Tell her this is hers in trade for a beaver skin," John told Squanto.

When he did, she turned to the rest of the women who chattered together for a few minutes and then disappeared into the wood.

"That's funny," John said, "I thought she was really interested."

"She be back," Squanto predicted. "We wait."

Squanto proved to be right. John felt his face grow hot at the sight of bare brown women holding scratchy branches of juniper in front of them with one hand, and holding out their clothes with the other.

Looking quickly away from them John saw that, with the exception of Squanto, there wasn't a man in the boat whose face hadn't turned scarlet.

"Tell them we can't take their clothing," John said.

"Must take, you promise," Squanto grunted with displeasure.

"You give them what's fair." John turned the dealing over to Squanto while he studiously examined the chain of islands that surrounded the spacious harbor. *The Brewsters might be a good name for them*, he thought, *in honor of the whole Brewster family*.

John knew the trading was over, when he heard the happy chatter of the women, and looked in time to see them backing into the woods. "Tell them if they can collect more furs we'll come again to trade," John instructed Squanto.

John suggested going further north, but Squanto discouraged them. "Bad Indians up there come steal corn from Massachusetts soon. We go back Plymouth now."

Squanto was right. John realized that he hadn't been

Squanto was right. John realized that he hadn't been anxious to return to Plymouth, because he feared Elder Brewster's answer to his question. But it had to be faced. The Indian women had agreed that they would try to round up more pelts for them, and they would come again.

But would he? The next boat John boarded might be heading back to England. He had determined to accept Elder Brewster's answer because he respected him as the Lord's servant, and his spiritual mentor. Dark shadows cast on the water by gathering clouds seemed to engulf John.

He was disappointed in the reception he received on his return. It seemed as if the women were almost sorry to see him.

Leaving them to husk the corn the next day, John shouldered an axe and set out to cut lumber. The men were working to have a shipload ready to send to England on the first the vessel that came. Surely one would arrive before long.

On the way to the woods, Elder Brewster drew John aside. John's heart beat faster as he realized that the elder must have his answer.

"John," he began, "I have studied carefully the whole passage in I Corinthians that you quoted. In your reading you must have missed an earlier verse that says, 'let not the wife depart from her husband.' In the Old Testament when God told Abraham to go from his country Sarah went too, and I'm sure he wouldn't have turned back for her. It's the wife's place to follow her husband. If Desire is really set on going back to England, let her go. Unless you feel the Lord wants you to return, you shouldn't. First though, you must make it perfectly plain to her that you are ready to be married. She may be doing this just to get things moving. You never know about women."

John nodded solemnly, "You're right. I must tell her I want us to be married on the day of the Harvest Festival. If she refuses, I've cast my lot with the plantation. I can't turn back. I feel God called me just as he called Abraham."

Returning from the woods at dusk, John spotted the two girls on their way back to the cottage. He knew he would have to take the initiative. Catching up with them, he came to the point.

"Desire, I must talk to you a few minutes alone," he said.

A look of fear came into her eyes, but she stopped and Elizabeth hurried on to the house followed by the children.

"I had just about decided that you and I should be married during the Harvest Festival," he said. "I can't marry you if you go back to England, but if you will stay I expect you to become my wife soon."

Desire had her answer ready. "John, I wouldn't make you a good wife. Everything about this wilderness frightens me." She glanced over his shoulder toward the deep woods that were already shrouded in darkness. The shortening days seemed to make this blackness even more pervasive. "It was a mistake for me to come." She shuddered.

John felt no compunction to argue with her. But he still didn't have an explanation for Elizabeth's announcement that she was going back, and the sudden switch.

"You're going, and Elizabeth is staying? Tell me, what happened."

Desire shook her head, "You'll have to ask Elizabeth that question. I can only say that her decision made me realize that I should leave."

Chapter 22

The bright days of early October scurried past as John went back to working from dawn until dark felling trees and working them into clapboard. Life in the Carver household continued as it had all summer, except that John never ceased to delight in Elizabeth's exclamations of wonder as the leaves changed to red and gold in startling contrast to the evergreens. He marveled, too, when Squanto said this happened every year.

John couldn't seem to find an opportunity to talk with Elizabeth alone. She still wouldn't look at him. Finally, he realized that such a talk would have to wait until Desire had actually gone, even though no one knew when that would be. Perhaps then she would also explain why she had become engaged to Richard when she didn't love him? That question had been nagging at him since the night of the duel.

Soon the days set apart for the Harvest Festival arrived. The men took a break from cutting lumber to hunt and fish. Wild duck and geese were easy to shoot as hundreds of flocks flew quacking and honking overhead. John returned with his birds to find that Elizabeth and Desire had cooked up wild plums, and squash from the kitchen garden. The house smelled of fresh-baked corn bread and the last of the salad greens.

Governor Bradford had sent Squanto off with an invitation to Massasoit to join in their time of feasting and thanksgiving. As the households gathered to meet their guests, John caught the look of consternation on Elizabeth's face and heard her counting under her breath the seemingly endless parade of Indians marching into the village. Fifty, fifty-one, and on they came, sixty, seventy, eighty, "Ninety men!" she whispered to Desire.

Desire's face was pale. "What if they decided to turn against us? They outnumber us almost five to one."

"That's not the problem. We've lived in peace with them all summer. No reason to think they would turn on us now." John was pleased with Elizabeth's courageous answer. "I'm just wondering how long our food supply will hold out." John could understand her concern.

In one way the harvest was a disappointment. The peas and wheat brought from England hadn't done well, but the twenty acres of corn planted under Squanto's tutelage had produced satisfactorily, and everyone's food ration had been increased. But if the Indians ate too much they might have less than ever.

At the end of Massasoit's band marched two sets of braves each carrying a deer between them. John heard Elizabeth's sigh of relief as they marched straight to the governor and laid their offering down in front of him. Governor Bradford thanked them with dignity, and at a signal from Massasoit the Indians fell to dressing the deer.

John couldn't help but admire the skill of the young Indians as they deftly skinned the two animals and cut up the venison. When Elizabeth and Desire left to roast some of the meat in the oven behind their cottage, John joined the militia to put on a drill for Massasoit's men.

"It doesn't hurt to keep reminding the Indians what our weapons can do," Capt. Standish had told them as he had planned the review. "After all, it's the only advantage we have over their numbers," he added.

John could not help thinking that they had another important advantage. The Lord was on their side.

His chest almost bursting with pride, John marched in line to the parade ground behind the drum and bugle "corps". How well they responded now to the captain's crisp orders! He smiled to himself as he remembered the disorganized group that fell against each other on the deck of the Mayflower. Back and forth they marched, turning sharply at each command. Glancing at the Indians, he felt sure they were impressed, especially when, for a grand finale, they discharged their muskets to honor their guests.

After the review John discarded his gun for a stick as two three-legged stools were produced and Edward Dotey and Edward Leister chose teams for a game of stool ball. Better this kind of a contest than a duel, John thought as each of the Edwards plunked his stool down at opposite ends of the drill field.

When John stood up opposite Edward Leister who was his teammate, the score was tied.

"Come on John, protect your stool," he heard Elizabeth call. *She does know I'm still around,* he thought. Every muscle tensed to do her bidding.

He slammed the ball with all his pent-up anger over the way the girls had been treating him, and it flew far out to the side of the field. A great scramble was on as the other team tried to get it and touch the second stool before John did. Clutching his batting stick, he got there first, scoring the winning point. When John looked for Elizabeth to share the victory, she was going off with the other women. Time to eat, his stomach told him.

The Indians, anxious to join in the games, suggested races. Both individual and relay races were run with the Indians victorious every time. Finally, just before dinner was announced, someone produced a rope and the Indians mingled with the settlers in a tug of war that left everyone laughing as John's winning team collapsed in the dust.

Wooden horses holding boards laden with crisp golden fowl and mouth-watering brown roasts of venison along with other dishes the women had prepared were waiting for them in the Common House. John was relieved to see that no one would go hungry that day. He was especially anxious to try the chestnut stuffing that Elizabeth had made. He had heard her exclaiming over the chestnut tree she had found at the edge of the woods. But he was even more anxious to share his victories with her. He would surely catch her eye when he came close to where she stood behind the serving table.

All day Elizabeth had been especially aware of John's fine figure. Marching down the street, whacking the ball across the field, racing the Indians and almost winning, then straining at the rope with strong muscles bulging under his shirt, she had watched his every move. But when he came through the food line, his face flushed from all the exercise, her glance was covert. She wanted so badly to let him know how proud she was of him, but she looked down when he came opposite where she stood. In fairness to Desire she didn't dare meet his eyes for fear she might reveal too much.

It was time now for the women to fill their plates, and Elizabeth was hungry. She soon realized as she moved along the board that she wouldn't be able to eat as much as she wished because her stomach had shrunk from the limited rations they had become accustomed to. But she noticed the men, especially Massasoit's, had had no such problem.

When everyone had eaten their fill there was food left over, and Massasoit announced, "We come tomorrow." More than one day's celebration would make a real harvest festival, Elizabeth thought, and was glad.

John was waiting for her when the women finished cleaning up from the feast. "How did you like the way I hit the ball today?" he asked, falling in beside Desire and Elizabeth on the way back to the cottage.

"We had to leave about then to get the food ready," she said, moving closer to Desire and taking her arm. It seemed safer just now to keep John at a distance.

The Indians came the next day and the next as well, but the supply of foul and venison held out. The climax of the festival came after their guests had marched away. Their usual Thursday evening teaching service became a time of joyful prayers of thanksgiving to God for his gracious provision for them. Elizabeth felt that everyone went back to their daily tasks much refreshed in body and spirit.

The pile of lumber at the edge of the woods grew larger every day, and it seemed to Elizabeth that John's shirts were tighter across his chest and shoulders when he would shed his jacket by the fire in the evening. How handsome he looked, she couldn't help thinking, so strong and healthy. In fact, she realized gratefully, they were all much better. No one had died since early summer.

The discussion in the evenings centered on how to winterize their cottage. "Perhaps we could shovel some dirt up around the outside walls," John suggested one evening.

"And we could use some of the deer skins to cover the windows. It will be dark inside, but that's better than being cold. Would you mind too much, Desire?" Elizabeth said, trying to draw her friend into the conversation.

But Desire had nothing to say. She seemed to Elizabeth to have removed herself mentally from Plymouth already even though there was little expectation now of a ship arriving before spring. A heaviness settled in Elizabeth's chest every time she thought of Desire leaving. It would be like another death, for she felt sure she would never see her again on this earth.

It was with mixed emotions that Elizabeth, who was working in the yard rubbing oak bark into a dried deer skin one day in early November, heard a shout ring out. "A ship, A ship's coming."

Joining the excited villagers on the beach, Elizabeth watched Elder Brewster embrace the first young man to step ashore. Tears sprang to her eyes as Mistress Brewster exclaimed, "Jonathan!" It was their beloved eldest son.

Then came a ragtag band of coatless men. She counted thirty-five. The Lord knew they could use more workers, but the Merchant Adventurers had sent no supplies and later John reported on a letter from Thomas Weston. "It denounced us for sending the Mayflower back empty and accused us of more 'weakness of judgment than weakness of hand.' Then he demanded that we sign the revised agreement that we had turned down before. At least he promised that he will never desert us even if everyone else does." Then John added solemnly, "Maybe Master Weston is justified in his charges."

"But we had to be sure our village site was suitable," Elizabeth tried to reassure him. "And Master Weston has no idea how sick we all were."

"I'll tell him when I get back," Desire spoke up. "He can't possibly imagine what it's like to face a wilderness full of savages and try to build some semblance of civilization, the emotional as well as physical drain, and to stand by and watch friends and relatives die. How dare he condemn us for not sending a cargo on the returning Mayflower? It's only by the grace of God that any of us even survived."

"They didn't even send us any supplies for the men who

arrived," John said. "Just this morning we were assessing our
supplies and discovered that we overestimated our harvest.
Besides taking them into our homes we'll have to share our
rations with them."

"We can take in several here. With God's help, we'll make
do," Elizabeth said, even as she began to wonder if the coming
winter might be as hungry a time as the preceding one.

"At any rate," Desire said, "there'll be one less mouth to feed.
Master Barton plans to return to England immediately and I
talked to him about going."

On a grey December morning a few weeks later Elizabeth
again stood on the beach waving off another vessel. This one
carried the one woman who had come to mean more to her than
any other.

The returning ship carried a signed agreement putting off
the division of land into individual plots until all their debts had
been paid. However, John was optimistic that one more ship
loaded with lumber and pelts, as was the returning Fortune,
would clear their accounts and leave them a free people.

The night before everyone had sat very quietly by the fire for
a long time, lost in thought. Elizabeth knew it was the last time
Desire would ever sit with John and her here.

"Don't worry about me," Desire had said earlier. "I have a
cousin in London who will take me in."

Finally John had cleared his throat and made one more
attempt to persuade Desire to marry him. "I think the hardest
times are behind us," he said. "If you'll marry me and stay, I'm
sure this place will soon be so civilized we'll be looking for more
room somewhere else." He tried to laugh. "Already we have all
these new settlers, and more will come every year, and you'll get
over your fears."

Elizabeth's stomach churned. This should have been a
private conversation, but he had spoken in front of her and the
children. *What a sorry time this is, and it's all my fault,* she told
herself. *I'm the one who should be leaving,* and she added her
plea to John's for Desire to stay. Desire was not to be dissuaded.

Finally John lighted a candle and picked up the Carvers'
Bible as he had done every night since the governor had died.
Choosing the 43rd chapter of Isaiah, he read words of reassur-
ance for Desire. "Fear not: for I have redeemed thee...thou art

mine. When thou passest through the waters, I will be with thee...they shall not overflow thee...I will even make a way in the wilderness."

The tears ran freely down Elizabeth's cheeks, but Desire sat calmly drinking in every word. After prayers, when she and Elizabeth crawled under their ticking, she whispered to Elizabeth, "Please, no matter what happens, I don't want you ever to blame yourself. Remember what John read. The Lord has promised to make a way in the sea for me and a way in the wilderness for you!"

Elizabeth was silent as she gulped back great sobs. Desire caught her hand under the covers. "Promise. No blame," she whispered again.

"I'll try." She could scarcely hear herself, but Desire must have heard for she seemed satisfied.

As the two girls clung together before the ship sailed, Desire whispered to Elizabeth, "I love you very much. I wish you every happiness with John. Perhaps I never really loved him at all. It was more an ideal that I fell for. Never forget, Elizabeth, that you're right for him. God bless you both."

Elizabeth's eyes were so blurred that she could scarcely see the ship sail away. All the sobs she had choked back the night before were about to burst out. She turned and ran up the deserted street with dry leaves swirling about her feet. Dashing into the empty house, she threw herself on the bed she would no longer share with her friend and cried until she could cry no more. At length, lifting her head from the pillow, she reached for her father's Bible which had become her constant source of comfort.

It was then she became aware of John standing at the edge of the partition. His face was a study of sympathy, questions and, above all, Elizabeth felt, love.

She got to her feet and began to look in her chest for a clean handkerchief. For a long time neither of them spoke. Then John posed the questions he had waited several months to ask. "Elizabeth, why did you decide to go back to England?"

Her answer was simple and direct. "Because I didn't want to be here when you and Desire were married."

"Why not?"

"Because I loved you too much to see you married to

someone else."

"Any other reason?" There was almost a twinkle in his eye.

"Yes, I was afraid you wouldn't marry her as long as I was around."

"I guess you were right," he said, coming very close to her. "All the time I wanted Elizabeth Tilley to become Mistress Howland. Desire knew that, didn't she?"

Filled with wonder of his love Elizabeth looked up into his hazel eyes. "Yes," she said.

"Will you?"

Before she could answer, his arms were around her. Their lips met. Behind closed eyelids she looked into light almost as dazzling as the sun.

When Elizabeth opened her eyes again the sun had broken through the clouds and was streaming in the small window by the bed, enfolding them in its warmth.

John had one more question. "Why did you become engaged to Richard if you didn't love him?"

Elizabeth felt the blood rush into her face as she was honest with both of them for the first time. "Because I wanted to come to the New World on the Mayflower so I could always be near you."

"And so you shall be so long as the Lord lets us live," John said and drew her close again.

"Oh Elizabeth! My life, my light, my joy! I love you so," he whispered.

The End

EPILOGUE

The author explored many sources of information about the Pilgrim experience, but the orignal source is William Bradford's own account, *Of Plymouth Plantation 1620-1647*. The main events in *Daughter of the Dawn* actually happened, including John Howland's falling overboard, and the Edwards' duel. However, no one can know for sure *why* such incidents occurred, and here the author felt free to use her imagination as Longfellow did with the story of Priscilla and John Alden. The Howland's fictionalized romance grew out of the fact that Desire did come with the Carvers and also returned to England where she died a few years later.

John and Elizabeth had nine children, one of which they named Desire, leading the author to believe they must have thought highly of her. There are now thousands of descendants all over the United States, and a John Howland Society is based in Plymouth, Massachusetts where the members hold an annual meeting each September. The Jabez Howland House at Plymouth, where Elizabeth died in her eighties, is open to the public during the summer season.

Making a whole chicken pie